A NECESSARY ACT

A Novel

By Tony Wirt

Sarah —
Don't let this keep you
up *too* late!!

Tony Wirt

Printed in the United States of America.

ISBN 978-0-9972010-0-0

Broken Bricks Publishing
Cover by Design for Writers

www.TonyWirt.com
tony@tonywirt.com

To my wife Erin —
No way this happens without you.

1996

1

THE SOUND OF EXPOSED SKIN screeching across the hardwood cut Matt and David's conversation off mid-sentence. The boys snapped their heads to see Lake Mills High School's only special education student gingerly pick himself up off the floor.

"Jesus," David muttered from their daily perch in the bleachers. The gymnasium served as a holding area for the students after lunch, and the odor of that day's tuna casserole wafted in whenever somebody came through the doors.

As Noah Cooke attempted to corral the football he'd sacrificed his skin for, a voice boomed over the clamor of a couple hundred students.

"NICE CATCH, *ED*!"

David wasn't surprised to see Carl and Russ Blake across the gym, chortling with delight, considering they were the only ones in school who still called Noah "Special Ed".

For the most part, the other students accepted Noah and did what they could to make him feel like he belonged there. But a two-time freshman who spends his afternoons down in the elementary building alongside a dyslexic third grader and an 11-year-old with Down's syndrome was an easy target. His puppy-like combination of boundless energy, poor judgment and a longing for acceptance made him easily manipulated—especially for cousins who'd been in a two-man race to be the biggest prick since birth.

Noah trotted the ball back across the gym. Carl snatched it from his hands, not bothering to hide the sick amusement he found in the red bursting forth from the kid's legs.

"HUT!" Carl shouted.

Noah took off across the gym with wild abandon. David and Matt watched as Carl heaved the ball in a massive arc over the heads of half the student body.

"What is he..." was all David got out before Noah went crashing to the floor again, sending another squeal of flesh through the gym in an effort to catch a ball obviously thrown well out of his reach.

David shot bolt upright. His gaze was locked on Noah, who got up much slower this time. Even from the bleachers he could see the angry red rash extending along his entire leg.

The second crash was enough to turn a few more heads, but more seemed to purposely ignore whatever scene was unfolding. Not surprising, considering the Blake Boys' reputation, nobody wanted to get them involved in their day.

The ball bounded into a group of girls sitting in the far corner, where one swatted it away.

Noah limped towards the ball and scooped it up.

"LET'S GO, ED!" Russ shouted, getting his considerable weight behind it. His face was a grimace of mean-spirited glee, while his cousin Carl now openly cackled.

Noah responded by breaking into a jog, which with the condition of his legs appeared more like an awkward skip.

David watched in disbelief as Noah returned the ball to Carl Blake. It was too much, and David stood up.

Before he could take a step down the bleachers, Matt's hand snagged his elbow. "Where are you going?"

"Somebody's got to do something," David glanced back at Matt, but made no move towards the gym floor. Part of him was relieved his friend stopped him, because it wasn't like the Blake Boys were going to accept someone telling them how to have fun without violence.

"Hold on." Matt nodded towards the floor.

Scott Alston had walked up and joined Carl and Russ. One hand was on Noah's shoulder as he spoke softly in his ear.

A river of ice ran down David's spine at the sight of Scott, and seeing a beaming smile cross Noah's face did nothing to stem the tide. He remained frozen in the bleachers when Noah handed the ball to Scott and sprinted off once again. The kid's floor-burned legs pumped as fast as they could go, all trace of a limp gone. Scott waited until he'd covered two-thirds of the gym before letting the ball fly. Seeing the ball's trajectory, it didn't take a trigonometry genius to know exactly where this was headed.

David opened his mouth, but nothing came out.

Noah never took his eyes off the ball as he rocketed across the gym. He blasted through a group of kids sitting under the basketball hoop and went flying into the concrete wall. The football slapped the wall at the same time as Noah's face.

He slid down like a cartoon character and landed in a crumpled heap on the floor.

The entire gym went eerily silent. David stood rooted in his spot, watching a pool of blood spread out from under Noah's head. A crowd formed near the wall, blocking David's view. He could feel the panic bloom in the gymnasium as the whispered murmurs from below steadily grew.

Somebody must have run off to alert the teachers, because seemingly the entire staff flooded in through the doors and shoved their way through the mass of students. Commands of "Give him room" floated up from the crowd.

The principal, Mr. Donald, walked into the gym and made his way over to a trio of teachers kneeling over their student. He exchanged a few quick words with Mr. Roderick, who turned to the crowd with his hands up.

"*OK, EVERYBODY BACK IN THE CAFETERIA,*" He bellowed. "*ALL STUDENTS RETURN TO THE CAFETERIA. NOW PEOPLE, LET'S GO.*"

The request had little effect. Like David, most kids were riveted where they stood. Eventually, enough teachers were on hand to herd the students through the two sets of doors and back into the lunchroom.

"I can't believe that sick fuck," David muttered. He stared at the far side of the gym, where Carl and Russ Blake were nowhere to be found. Scott still stood there, staring at where Noah was just starting to regain consciousness. "He ran him right into the fucking wall."

Matt's voice filtered up towards him. "You think?"

David turned away from the scene below. By this point, the school nurse had arrived and was holding a gym towel to Noah's face.

"That ball was halfway up the wall," David said. "No way he misses a throw that bad. He ran him right into the wall."

If Matt responded, David didn't hear it as memories cascaded through his head and poured over the dam he'd built years ago to keep them at bay. He turned back towards the floor, where Scott was turning to leave. His eyes caught sight of David and he paused, a half-cocked smile crossing his face as he continued towards the far door.

The look lit a fire of fear in David's gut.

"Somebody has to do something," David said as Matt made his way down the bleachers. "He can't keep getting away with this shit."

ROW AFTER ROW OF GIANT, razor-sharp teeth. The kind that pierced, held, and devoured whatever found its way into their path. Apex-level predator teeth.

Scott wanted to look away, but couldn't. The teeth had a hold of him, almost as if they picked up the sunlight from the lone window in a way that washed out the rest of the office. Not that there was anything else worth looking at. Principal James Donald had collected a decisively small number of personal effects for someone who had inhabited the same workspace for 16 years. The shelves behind his desk contained books, procedural binders and a tacky gold frame with a few family pictures. There was a group shot of the Donald clan, flanked by woefully out-of-date pictures of his two children.

But mounted to the wall beside the desk, a 51-inch muskie dominated the room. Its maw was perpetually agape, with dagger-like teeth greeting anyone who walked through the door. The neon green jerkbait used to land it dangled from its bottom jaw, treble hooks and all.

Scott knew he needed to pay attention—to play his part—but he kept stealing glances at the great muskie's teeth as he sat in one of the two chairs across from Principal Donald's desk.

The teeth fascinated him. They reminded him of his own trophies back in the fort.

"Scott, are you listening to me?" Principal Donald snapped.

"Yes, sir. Sorry," he replied, pulled back from his thoughts and into another boring conversation. But he was ready. "Just thinking about what happened with Noah. I mean, I know he just tripped, but I can't help but think that it was my fault."

Principal Donald eyed him suspiciously. Probably expected more defiance on this one; more *you don't want me to call my dad*.

Scott had used that tactic before, certainly, but that was when he was younger. His impulses had landed him in the principal's office plenty during elementary school—before he learned control. Now he didn't need his Holy Roller of a stepfather bringing his righteous indignation raining down on the principal's desk. He could talk his way out of this with half his brain tied behind his back.

"How so?"

Scott gave his principal a look that betrayed nothing of what was going on behind it.

"I mean, you know how he is. Running around like crazy all the time. We were playing catch and Noah kept trying to intercept the ball, you know, trying to get in the game."

"Uh-huh…"

"Well, he kept knocking it away and Russ was starting to get pretty pissed–I mean mad. Sorry." Scott said. "So he chucks it all across the gym and makes Noah run after it. Just to get him away from us, I guess. Well, he picks it up and brings it to me. And I figure if I throw him one maybe he'll leave us alone.

"I tell him to go out for a pass and he takes off like a wildman. Before I can even say anything he is already halfway across the gym, so I just try and throw it as far as I can. Noah kept running and goes right through this group of people sitting kinda by the basket. First I thought he dove, but I think he tripped up on somebody's leg or something because he went flying into the wall. I just stood there waiting for him to get up, but he just laid there.

"When I realized he was really hurt, not just lying there, I went to go get somebody, but by then I saw the teachers. People were all crowded around him and stuff. Kinda freaking out. I mean, I didn't know what to do."

It wasn't what happened, but Scott knew he'd buy it. Noah Cooke *was* completely hyperactive and always going at 100 mph. Nobody would be surprised when he had an accident, which is what made him a perfect plaything.

He could still see the blood pooling on the floor and the excitement welled up inside him. His eyes drifted back to the muskie. The teeth.

"So you were just playing catch and he went tearing off," Principal Donald said, much more a statement than a question.

"Well, yeah. I mean, like I said, we weren't really playing catch with him," Scott replied. "I just wanted to get him away from us. It's my fault. I should have just told Russ to let him be. Is he OK? I mean, is he going to be all right? I tried to ask Mr. Roderick after it happened, but he just kept pushing us all towards the cafeteria."

"I don't know," Mr. Donald said. The tone of his voice told Scott he'd already won. "The paramedics took him down to the clinic, but they thought they might have to take him down to Mason City to get some tests because he was out when he hit the ground."

6

"Man, that's scary," Scott said. "Hope he's OK."

"Yeah, me too," Principal Donald said. He gave Scott one last stern look before dismissing him, probably to assure him he hadn't pulled one over on him.

It was all Scott could do not to laugh.

2

DAVID JERKED AWAKE, his bed damp with sweat. He sat up, gasping with the panicked breath of a drowning victim. It took a few moments before he felt the relief of cool air in his lungs. He glanced over at his bedside clock, which shone a red *3:48* into his otherwise black bedroom. He wiped his brow with his sheet and gently lay back on his pillow. It was still moist, so he turned it over.

He lay on his back, staring at the ceiling. It had been years since he'd had a nightmare like that, and he hoped this wasn't the start of another round.

When he was younger, he'd routinely wake up screaming in the middle of the night. His mother would run in and hold him while he cried himself back to sleep. At first, she would ask him about the dreams, even begging him to tell her so she could understand what terrified him so badly.

But he couldn't. How can a kid explain howls of torture, the smell of burning—some sensations so intense they followed him out of his dreams and into his bedroom?

It got bad enough that Cathy Rowe eventually took her son to their doctor, who promised her that the nightmares weren't anything to worry about. The doctor assured her many children suffer from nightmares, especially when dealing with the loss of a parent. He recommended grief counseling, but with money tight it wasn't an option. Besides, David knew that wasn't it.

Eventually, David learned to hide his fear. He knew it worried his mother, and as he got older he didn't mention anything when the dreams returned every now and then—usually during periods of high stress.

David did his best to forget the dream as he attempted to get back to sleep. Unfortunately, the only other topic in his head was what had probably prompted it: Noah's 'accident'.

By 5 a.m., it was clear that David wouldn't get any more sleep that night. He got out of bed and shuffled over to his desk. He had a page of algebra problems due the following day, but had planned on knocking them out in study hall. David cracked open his notebook and grabbed a pencil from the Minnesota Twins coffee mug on his desk, willing to think about anything other than the smell of burning and that god-awful yowling.

MATT CARLTON DROPPED HIS BOOKS at his usual spot in the LMHS cafeteria. With actual classroom space limited in a small-town high school, the lunchroom was used for study halls six periods a day. Between his two study hall periods and lunch, Matt spent almost three hours a day in the same spot, holding down a bench in the southeast corner.

He pulled his algebra notebook out. He and David had Algebra III together, so they often worked on their problems during second-hour study hall. He glanced up and saw his best friend—his only friend, if he was being honest—walking over to their regular spot.

When Matt moved to Lake Mills during eighth grade, he felt like an extra, kind of like one of those background kids in a high school drama where all the teens are played by 25-year-olds. Not that it was surprising. By that point of their lives, most teenagers in a small-town school had already settled in with a group of friends and weren't taking any more applications, thank you for asking.

It also didn't help that the only thing Matt was exceptional at was being average. Team sports didn't hold much interest for him, and he didn't have much aptitude for music or the arts. On the other side of the spectrum, he wasn't smart enough to be a nerd, not awkward enough to be a dork and too normal to be an outcast. Not that he wanted to be any of those, but at least it would have put him on the radar. Small town circles are hard to crack, but nerds can at least hang out with other nerds.

Luckily, Matt found a kindred spirit in David Rowe. Like Matt, David was fairly unremarkable and had no real circle of friends he clung to. However, by virtue of spending his entire life in Lake Mills, David was a known commodity, enabling him to intermingle with the various cliques and students in town.

By the start of freshman year, Matt and David had become close friends, forming their own two-man group. David gave Matt just enough local cred that he could go from actively ignored to simply unnoticed, which was a much more important step than it sounded. By the time the two were sophomores, nobody thought of Matt as the "new kid" anymore.

Matt had just opened his notebook when David plopped down in his customary spot across from him.

"What's up man?" David said, more as a greeting than an actual question.

"Not much. Just getting ready to plow through some hard-core math. I've started on the first couple, so if you want to take five through ten we can switch."

"Already got 'em." David rubbed his eyes.

"Seriously?"

"Yeah, I did 'em last night. Here." David flipped his spiral bound notebook open to the page he filled out at his desk early that morning and tossed it across the table.

"Nice." Matt started copying down the answers. "What got into you?"

"Couldn't sleep so I figured I would be productive," David replied.

"Works for me."

Matt was halfway through transcribing the sixth set of x's, y's and z's when he noticed David blankly following his scribbling. He looked like a zombie.

"You all right?" Matt asked.

David snapped back out of the fog. "Yeah, just tired."

"Bummer." Matt went back to copying David's last four algebra problems.

The two kept silent as Matt finished up his forgery. Just as he was putting the final touches on his paper (mostly erasing a few things and writing them again to make it look like he had worked them out on his own), David spoke.

"I think we should talk to Mr. Donald."

Matt wanted to be confused, but he knew what his friend was talking about.

"You mean about the thing with Noah?"

"Yeah."

"Why?" Matt asked. "I mean, what's to tell, really?"

"That he smashed him right into the wall."

"Maybe, but how are you going to get Mr. Donald to believe that? Scott will just say it was an accident."

David didn't say anything to that. The two sat in silence as Matt finished writing.

"You know he's a psycho, right?" David finally said.

"What?"

"The guy is a psycho, and he keeps getting away with all this shit."

"Yeah, he can be a real dick," Matt said, closing up his notebook and wishing this conversation over. "But whattya gonna do, eh?"

David had no response.

NOAH COOKE ENDED UP with a broken nose, two missing teeth, and a concussion, which kept him in the hospital overnight. He then spent another week at home recuperating.

Without any real friends to miss him, life at school quickly moved on. The incident that dominated that Tuesday afternoon was replaced by the more pressing news of a lowly freshman asking out (and being abruptly shot down by) a senior football cheerleader. Then Mr. Holdan went an entire class with his fly down. By the time Ryan and Chelsea broke up after school on Friday, Noah and his injuries had been pretty much forgotten.

David sat alone in the school's spacious library, a stack of old magazines in front of him, and tabbed through a dog-eared copy of the *Newsweek*. The tiny type blurred together. David rubbed his eyes and put his face in his hands. He couldn't continue like this much longer. He needed sleep. It was starting to affect his schoolwork, and he was already way behind on this social studies paper.

As he flipped through the magazine scanning for an article about some central Asian republic, a different headline jumped out at him.

A REAL-LIFE HANNIBAL THE CANNIBAL?

David paused. He had seen the movie *Silence of the Lambs* a few years back and had been fascinated with Anthony Hopkins' creepy portrayal of the serial killer Hannibal Lecter. Walking home from Matt's house after seeing it on video had been one of the most terrifying walks of his life. He was sure a psychotic killer was waiting in every bush to jump out and eat his liver with some fava beans and a nice Chianti.

The article had been published just after the arrest of Milwaukee serial killer Jeffery Dahmer, which had come right in the middle of *Silence of the Lambs'* theater run.

David knew the basics of Dahmer's story, mostly because he had recently been killed in prison and the news re-hashed all its old coverage of him. He killed 17 people, although at the time this article was written he had only confessed to 11. What tied him in with Hannibal Lecter was their shared propensity to eat their victims.

He continued reading the lurid descriptions of what went on in Dahmer's apartment, partially fascinated that such a movie-esque bad guy could exist anywhere but the silver screen. As he turned the page, a sidebar in a faded red box caught his eye.

What Makes a Serial Killer?

He immediately abandoned the Dahmer story to read the small supplement. His jaw dropped as he read through the list of characteristics serial killers share. He read through the small box repeatedly, recognizing more and more of the traits each time.

It was everything he knew about Scott Alston.

The bell rang to end the period, jerking David out of his thoughts. He abandoned the stack of magazines he'd fished out of the back room and ran up to the counter with the *Newsweek* in hand.

The librarian stared at him with thinly veiled disapproval as she checked out the magazine. The perm in her short, grey, hair made the tiny curls look perpetually wet, and she had a trio of frown lines etched on each side of her mouth.

"You're going to be late," she said.

"Yeah, I know," David replied. When she found the stack of magazines he'd left out on the table she'd throw a fit. He would definitely hear about it next time.

She stamped and filed the card away, handing the magazine back to David. He snatched it from her hands and darted towards the door.

"No running!" she called after him, but he was already out into the hallway.

David was late to his next class, but it wasn't the tardy slip that bothered him. That *Newsweek* article had been a lightning bolt to the brain, and he couldn't concentrate on anything else. He just kept going down the list, mentally checking off every box.

AS SOON AS THE BELL RANG in his last class, Matt swung by his locker to get his bag and headed down the hall to find David. His friend had already grabbed his backpack and was walking over to meet him.

"What's up?" Matt called out.

"Not much. Ready to roll?"

The herd of students gradually grew as more grey lockers shut and kids flocked down the hallway. Matt and David joined the flow and headed down the steps towards the front doors. Since they both lived on the south end of town, they always walked home together.

The sun shone brightly overhead, a last gasp of summer before the days shortened. The trees lining the street were still green, although that would change in a few weeks. A steady stream of cars passed by, and Matt could see some younger kids walking about a block ahead of them.

"So I found this article..." David said as they walked away from the afterschool exodus.

"Um, OK?" Matt responded. "What about?"

"Well, it was about Jeffery Dahmer,"

"You mean the dude that ate people?" Matt said. "What about him?"

"Well, the article had a thing in it about the signs of a serial killer, you know, like before they start killing."

"Yeah?" Matt had no idea where he was going with this.

"They fit Scott Alston to a freaking 'T'."

Matt stopped. Ever since that thing with Noah Cooke happened, David had been on a weird jag about Scott Alston. Not that Matt liked him or anything. He'd heard some crazy stories about how he was in elementary school. That sometimes he'd refuse to talk for entire days. He'd follow people around, just staring at them. He'd carry dead bugs in his pocket.

Creepy stuff, but he'd never seen Scott do anything like that anymore. Kids can be weird, but they grow out of it.

"You think Scott's a serial killer?"

"Read this," David said, digging a magazine out of his backpack. He folded it open to a page in the middle and thrust it into Matt's chest. "The red box."

Matt took the magazine. In the middle of a story about Jeffery Dahmer was a sidebar box that listed 14 personality traits that serial killers supposedly share.

What Makes a Serial Killer?

1. Over 90 percent of serial killers are male.
2. They tend to be intelligent, with IQ's in the "bright normal" range.
3. They do poorly in school, have trouble holding down jobs, and often work as unskilled laborers.
4. They tend to come from markedly unstable families.
5. As children, they are abandoned by their fathers and raised by domineering mothers.
6. Their families often have criminal, psychiatric and alcoholic histories.
7. They hate their fathers and mothers.
8. They are commonly abused as children – psychologically, physically and sexually. Often the abuse is by a family member
9. Many serial killers spend time in institutions as children and have records of early psychiatric problems.
10. They have high rates of suicide attempts.
11. From an early age, many are intensely interested in voyeurism, fetishism, and sadomasochistic pornography.
12. More than 60 percent of serial killers wet their beds beyond the age of 12.
13. Many serial killers are fascinated with fire starting.
14. They are involved with sadistic activity or tormenting small creatures.

"OK," Matt said after he finished reading the list. By this time, the boys had reached the park a few blocks south of the school. It was a square block of towering oak trees, interspersed with a merry-go-round, slide, a pair of large picnic shelters and a large playset surrounded by sand in the center. The boys meandered toward a bank of swings on the east end.

"You think Scott has some of these?"

"Some?" David said, sounding somewhat incredulous. "He's got ALL of them."

Matt could see Scott Alston matching a few spots on the list. Aside from the obvious demographics of being a white male, Matt had heard a few rumors about Scott's biological father, and after hearing a few fire and brimstone sermons on Sunday morning, it was no stretch whatsoever to imagine his stepdad, Pastor Alston, as a strict disciplinarian.

15

"Look at this," David sat down on a weatherbeaten metal bench. "He's male – obviously. He doesn't do well in school, but he gets through because he knows how to work the teachers and they are afraid of his stepdad, right?"

Matt had to admit David had a point there. Scott always seemed about to fail, but he would somehow get through in the end. Even so, anyone would be hard pressed to call him dumb. David was right—Scott was definitely smart enough to work the system.

"OK"

"You've heard about his parents, right?" David asked. "His real dad was a hard-core druggie and supposedly his mom was one too before they moved out here. Then his dad died in jail when Scott was just a baby, so that is 4-5-6 on there. And you KNOW what Pastor Alston is like. That guy is insane, and I guarantee he knocked both Scott and his mom around when he was young."

Matt just listened as David continued to rattle off his theory. Made some sense, but there were still some holes. Matt leaned back and scanned the park. A fair number of kids walked along Lake Street on the far side, but other than a pair of kids playing on top of the picnic tables in one of the shelters, they were alone.

"OK, but what about the rest of it?" Matt asked. "Suicide, porno, bedwetting?"

"Dude, he wet his bed until he was like thirteen."

Matt raised an eyebrow. He'd admit that there were a few coincidences on the list, but now it seemed like his friend was just making stuff up.

"What are you talking about?" Matt asked.

"When I was a kid I had to go out to his place a couple times to get babysat," David said. "He had to wear these diapers to bed then."

"What?" Matt asked.

"Yeah," David exclaimed, beginning to get worked up. "His closet was full of them. Diapers for older kids. They were called Underjams or something. There were boxes of those things in his closet. Like a ton."

Matt's brow knitted in disbelief.

"Seriously?"

"Hand to God," David swore. "And his mom treated him like a baby. She would cut his food all up and give him whatever he wanted so he wouldn't throw a fit. And his room was all clowns and stuff. Seriously. Even then it was like she thought he was four or something. It was insane."

As Matt listened to David describe it, he had to admit some of it fit, but it was hard not to pass his friend's ideas off as paranoid ramblings.

Serial killer? That was movie stuff.

"All right," Matt said. "But what about the last stuff? Killing animals, fires."

David's eyes shifted to whatever was beyond his shoulder, staring into the trees. It took a minute for him to respond.

"Yeah," David said quietly.

"What do you mean, 'yeah'?"

The question hung for what seemed an eternity. Matt could tell David was thinking long and hard about something, but didn't know what to say about it. He let the silence hang for a minute.

"What?" Matt asked.

"He did it," David responded in a small voice. Quiet. Almost inaudible.

"What?" Matt asked again, watching his friend sit there, his gaze shifting to the ground.

Before Matt could ask again, David told him the story he hadn't told anyone in the seven years since it happened.

3

"SCOTTY HONEY, HE'S HERE!" Karen Alston called into the backyard with a shrill, sing-song voice that grated David in a way he could almost taste.

"He's out behind the shed, Davey," Scott's mom said.

He hated being called Davey.

"You two have fun now."

David drifted out into the backyard, in no hurry to locate Scott Alston. The only reason he was here was because his mom had a stupid job interview, and this was going to suck.

Even early on, the students of Lake Mills Elementary could tell there was something off about Scott. He had no friends, and David Rowe wasn't looking to be the first.

Scott was a freak.

Sometimes in the middle of class, he would just get up from his desk and go do something. It didn't matter what they were supposed to be doing, or even if the teacher was in the middle of a sentence, he'd just wander over to the window. Maybe look through the books. Some teachers stopped to steer him back to his seat, some just let him go.

Sometimes he wouldn't talk.

To anybody.

For hours.

One time, Miss Sorenson asked Scott a question and he went into one of his silent spells. She repeated it and got nothing. Scott just looked up at her with this tiny little smirk. Usually when he pulled this she just ignored him, moved on to somebody else, but something must have gotten to her that time because she lost it.

The rest of the class sat in silence as she started yelling at him, fingers clenched white around the front of his desk. David, his spot just two rows away, had been terrified at the sight of his teacher, red-faced and screaming. Shortly after it started, the classroom door flew open and another teacher ran in to pull Miss Sorenson away.

Throughout the whole ordeal, Scott's expression never changed. Just blank eyes and the tiniest smile, which he kept as he was led from the room.

Never said a word.

On the playground, sometimes Scott would just follow people around, watching from a short distance. Naturally, this sort of odd behavior couldn't be tolerated by some of the older kids.

One time, David saw a group of sixth graders hold Scott down and take turns punching him in the shoulder. He never fought back. The next day at recess, Scott went right back to the same group of older kids and asked them to hit him again. Surprising everyone (including the guys that had beat him the day before) he was denied. As they walked away, Scott followed, begging them to hit him some more. Whether they were afraid it was some sort of entrapment or just creeped out by the request, all Scott got was a half-hearted shove and a mumbled "freak". They wanted nothing to do with Scott Alston. Nobody did.

Sometimes kids just knew.

David hoped if he walked slow enough maybe Scott would be gone by the time he got there.

No such luck. Scott emerged from behind the shed, and David froze.

In contrast to all the memories swirling through David's head, Scott broke the silence first.

"Hey. Come here, will ya?"

It sounded so normal, not freakish at all. Just a kid with a friend over. David had no idea how to react, so he just stared.

19

Who was the freak now?

"I gotta go get some more wood, come on," Scott said.

"Huh?"

"There's a bunch of wood over on the side of the garage. Let's go."

He followed Scott over towards the family's newly built two-car garage alongside the house. A stack of old plywood leaned up against it on the far side. Scott counted out three pieces and motioned for David to take the opposite side. Clueless as to what he was getting into, David grabbed the other end and walked backwards as Scott guided the way.

David carried in silence as they crossed the lawn and maneuvered behind the shed. The treeline started less than ten feet from the back end of the old, white storage building, and a small opening in the foliage indicated the start of a path into the woods.

"We're gonna have to hold them up-and-down on the path," Scott said. "It's way too narrow."

They tilted the wood upright as David backed onto the dirt trail and into the trees. Scott went a little fast as he guided them back, but David kept up without falling on his backside. About 50 yards in, Scott stopped and set his end down.

"Put it down here for now," he said.

David set his end down and turned around for the first time. The beginnings of a primitive lean-to stood in a small clearing along the path. A ten-foot long rectangle of plywood had already been nailed to a pair of trees to make the back wall, and branches had been laid out to show the footprint of the foundation.

David finally found his voice.

"What are you building?"

"A fort," Scott said. "We've got all this extra wood from the garage and my dad said I could have it. I figure these can be the side walls, but I'm going to have to get another big one for the roof. I'm gonna cover the roof with a tarp, then put a bunch of branches and leaves on top of it so the rain doesn't get in."

Like any ten-year-old boy, David was intrigued. Maybe

this wouldn't be so bad after all.

The two hauled wood and worked on Scott's design the rest of the morning. David remained wary of his co-builder, but with every piece they carried back his trepidation lessened. They managed to get most of the wood back to the fort—including the piece for the roof, which was both awkward and heavy—before they heard Scott's mother calling them to lunch.

Scott carried on about his plans over peanut butter and jelly sandwiches with the crusts cut off—David couldn't remember the last time someone had done that for him, but whatever—and chocolate milk. Mrs. Alston had originally brought white milk, but Scott demanded chocolate before the cups were even on the table.

"I know, honey, I'm going back to get the Qwik mix," she said with a smile. Scott's rather abrupt order didn't seem to faze his mom, which set David back. Had he taken that tone with his mother, the odds of him getting a scoop of cocoa in his milk would be nil. Maybe Scott's mom was more laid back.

Mrs. Alston popped in a few times with offers of more food, milk or maybe cookies for desert. After they had wolfed through everything she put in front of them, they headed straight back to the build.

The afternoon was a blur. Scott had a vision of what he wanted, and David did what he could to make it happen. He had always loved building things, so he didn't really mind Scott taking the foreman role. It was like playing with life-sized Legos.

They had erected both side walls and cleared the brush between them by the time David's mom arrived to pick him up.

"DAVEY... YOUR MOMMY'S HERE HONEY!!" Mrs. Alston's piercing voice echoed down the path.

To his surprise, he was not ready to leave. Scott had been friendly, talkative and, well, normal—nothing like he was at school. David couldn't help but think that if he acted like this with his classmates, maybe people wouldn't think he was such a freak.

"Are you coming back?" Scott asked.

"I dunno," David replied. "Maybe if my mom has another job interview."

"But I gotta get this finished up." Scott's voice suddenly had a note of panic in it. "Does she have an interview tomorrow?"

David glanced back down the path, then back at Scott. He could see Scott's facial expression changing. His eyes grew wide, boring into him. For a second David thought he was going to have some sort of tantrum.

The ground he'd been on had shifted again, and the unease he'd felt upon his arrival crept back.

"Come on kiddo, let's roll!" This time it was David's mom, and he used it as an ejection seat before things got awkward. He'd liked this Scott, and didn't want to see him disappear.

"All right, well, gotta go," David said, turning back down the path before Scott could say any more. "See you later."

Scott didn't respond. He just stared at David as he trotted down the path towards the backyard. The second he was out of sight, Scott whipped the hammer he'd been holding into the front wall of the fort, leaving a dent the size of a quarter in the plywood.

WHEN DAVID EMERGED from behind the shed, both moms were waiting for him.

"Hey buddy," Cathy Rowe said.

"Hey." David still had the sweat from a hard day's work on his brow and he was a little out of breath. He turned towards Mrs. Alston. "Scott's still back there."

"You boys really put in a big day, huh?" she replied.

"Yeah," David said. "It's pretty good."

"What's that?" Cathy asked.

"The fort," He answered with the enthusiasm of a ten-year-old explaining something to an adult. "We've got like two walls up and the base is mostly around. But the roof isn't up, but we can't do that til the walls are ready. We're probably going to need to saw off the big branch by the second wall to get them up though. It's really big."

"Wow, sounds like you guys had a good time," Cathy said.

"Yeah, it was cool,"

"Well, it's time to get moving. Dinner's in the car."

"OK," said David, taking off towards the driveway.

"Hey," Cathy called out after her son. "You forget to say something?"

"Thank you," David said to the general area Scott's mom was standing in.

"You're very welcome, Davey," Karen sang. "Come back anytime."

"Seriously, thank you," Cathy said, turning back towards Mrs. Alston. "This was a life-saver."

"Well I'm glad it worked out. And I hope the interview went well."

"It did," Cathy said. "I actually have a pretty good feeling about this one. It's down to me and one other guy they are going to interview tomorrow then they are going to make a decision by Thursday."

"Well good luck, I'll be praying for you."

Cathy Rowe nodded politely. "Thank you. And thanks again for watching David."

"No problem at all. It's so nice for Scotty to have someone to play with. And they got along so well. Just like peas in a pod. I could just see them being best friends."

AGAINST WHAT AT ONE TIME seemed the collective will of the Universe, Cathy got the job. For the first time since Paul's death, there was a breath of optimism in the house. More importantly, there would be a living wage deposited into the bank each month.

With a full-time job a good forty minutes away, Cathy had to find someone to watch David on a more permanent basis. Luckily, school would be starting soon and the neighbors had a son in middle school that was willing to entertain David until she got home just before dinner. Karen Alston had offered to let David stay out at their place with Scott, but you can't beat the convenience of a neighbor.

But Cathy was scheduled to start the week before school started and the neighbors were going to squeeze in one more camping trip, so she had to find a place for David those last few days of summer.

"Oh we'd be de-LIGHT-ed to have Davey come back," Karen Alston said. She hit the second syllable of 'delighted' so hard that Cathy actually had to pull the phone away from her ear.

"Are you sure?" she asked. "It would only be until school starts, but I don't want to impose if you guys have any end-of-summer plans or anything."

"Absolutely not. It would be great to have Davey over. Scotty had so much fun with him the last time. You know, he's been out back in that little house they built every day. It's like he wants to live out there."

Cathy was relieved. She hadn't thought Karen Alston would turn her down, but she still felt guilty about asking. It wasn't like she knew the Alstons very well at all, and she didn't want to take advantage of their hospitality.

"Well thank you very much. You are very kind to do this," Cathy said.

"It's no problem," Karen gushed. "No problem at all. We're so excited!!"

There was a small pause, and when her voice came back, much of the over-the-top enthusiasm had left.

"Although I will have to ask my husband if this is something he wants me to do," she said.

"Of course," Cathy said.

"But I'm sure he will say yes," Karen said, eagerness back in full force. "It'll be so great to have Davey out here. Scotty loved him so much."

"OK, well.... great. Just let me know if anything comes up when you talk to Pastor Alston. If not, I guess we'll just see you Monday morning?"

"Perfect. Perfect!!" Karen said. "We're so ex-CITE-ed."

A Necessary Act

DAVID HAD BEEN FIDGETING in the passenger seat the entire ride out to the Alston's, head brimming with ideas and improvements for the fort. He bounded out onto the driveway the second the car rolled to a stop and was halfway to the backyard when Mrs. Alston's sing-song voice cut through his excitement.

"He's in his room, sweetie."

David turned to see Scott's mom on the steps leading to the house's side door, smiling rainbows. He resisted the urge to continue back into the woods and forced a smile back as he turned back toward the house.

Mrs. Alston patted him on the head when he passed, then stepped down to go over the details of the day with his mom.

Inside the house, David made his way back down the hallway looking for Scott. A door was closed at the far end. He knocked but got no reply, so he opened it and poked his head inside. Scott was nowhere to be found.

David looked around the room and was stunned by the decor. The carpet was an old, red, shag, while the wallpaper extended up from it with red, blue and yellow stripes on a graying white background. Farther up was a border that encircled the room with tumbling clowns and balloons.

It was toddler stuff.

Curiosity firmly in the driver's seat, he stepped farther in. Plenty of toys lay strewn across the floor—trucks, tanks and a full brigade of GI Joe guys. Near the half-open closet he saw the Cobra H.I.S.S., an awesome black tank with a dual laser turret on top. It was easily the GI Joe vehicle he'd wanted the most, so the temptation was too much to deny.

He jumped on the floor and grabbed the H.I.S.S. to take it for a test run. He'd aimed the turret towards a line of soldiers near the closet when he noticed a stack of odd boxes hiding behind some clothes. He crawled over, the tank mowing through the short red jungle.

A happy looking kid with smiling eyes was peeking out from behind a sheet he'd pulled up to his nose.

Underjams Absorbent Nighttime Pants. Wake up to a drier morning!

25

David stared at the boxes, dumbfounded. Apparently Scott still wet the bed. Unbelievable. He thought about that for a moment. Having repeated kindergarten, Scott was almost a full two years older than David, which put him at 12.

What 12-year-old still wets the bed?

As he moved in closer to get a better look, he heard a shuffling in the doorway. David shot away from the closet, terrified he'd been caught snooping.

"Is he not in here honey?"

It was Scott's mother, and she seemed oblivious to what he'd discovered.

"He must have gone out back," she said. "Want me to walk out with you?"

David tried to keep his eyes from looking back in the closet, but it was hard.

"Come on, I can take you back there."

As the adrenaline seeped from his bloodstream, he finally found his voice.

"Um, no, that's OK," he said as he rose to his feet. "I know where he is. I'll go back."

"Have fun," Scott's mom said.

David stumbled as he crossed the room, tripping over the same Cobra H.I.S.S. that had lured him into Scott's room. He heard the snap as one of the laser cannons broke off under his foot. A fresh wave of fear flooded though him, but Karen Alston didn't seem to notice. She just stood there with that same Pollyanna smile she always wore. All he wanted was to get out of the room as fast as possible, so he darted past Scott's mom and tore down the hallway towards the door.

David ran across the Alston's yard and into the trees. He slowed down once he hit the path and ambled back towards the fort. He was still trying to process what had happened in Scott's room when he reached the clearing.

The fort stood in front of him in all its juvenile glory. Since he'd left, Scott had gotten all four walls up. Three of the plywood sheets they had hauled back had been nailed to the two trees on the far end of the clearing. The fourth wall stood on the opposite side, but left about a two-foot gap in the near corner, which served as a de-facto door. Random pieces of scrap wood had been nailed to random spots on the walls, which David assumed were each vital in terms of keeping the fort standing. The roof was covered in a thicket ranging from full, four-inch branches to twigs with the leaves still attached, and David could see the blue tarp that lay underneath hanging down over the edge.

As rickety as it may have looked to an outside observer, for a ten-year-old it was an impregnable garrison that could be used for secret meetings, mission headquarters or a legendary standoff.

As David stood admiring the primitive structure, Scott emerged from inside.

"What are you doing here?"

For the second time since he had arrived at the Alston house, David was jolted back out of his thoughts. "I dunno," David replied. "This is awesome. How did you get all this done?"

"I had to get my fucking mother to help with the wood."

David had heard what he referred to as the 'f-word' plenty of times in his life. He had even said it on occasion. It was a way for kids to feel like badasses. But something about the way it shot from Scott's mouth was disconcerting. There was an unexpected edge there.

"But whatever," he continued, turning his gaze back towards the fort. "It's done now, and it's mine. She can't come back here anymore. This is *my* place."

The silence hung in the air for a minute.

"Well it's awesome," David ventured.

"Yeah, I know."

David stood there, waiting for Scott to continue, but nothing came. Maybe Scott had meant that it wasn't just his mother who wasn't welcome back here, but everybody else. That would make for an awkward day.

"So... wanna go in?" David asked, and for a second he thought Scott was going to tell him to get back to the house.

"Sure," Scott said, and disappeared back into the fort. David dislodged from the spot he'd been camping in and headed towards the fort. As he got to the door, David looked up at the roof and admired the effort Scott had obviously put in over the last week. The blue tarp he'd procured from somewhere was actually covering more plywood, which served as a ceiling. The only problem was while it assumedly kept out the rain, it also blocked out most of the light. It took almost a full minute before he could make out any more than dark shapes towards the back. When his eyes finally adjusted, he saw Scott standing towards the back corner.

"Wow, it's dark in here."

David looked around the fort. The inside of the walls were covered with dozens of 2x4s in various lengths. He couldn't tell if they actually supported the plywood wall or if they had just been randomly nailed to the inside. Some reached all the way to the ceiling while others were only a foot or so off the ground.

As he approached Scott, his nose picked up a strange smell. It reminded him a bit of those nasty salty pickles his mom liked—or maybe what they would smell like if they'd been left on the counter for a few days. He didn't say anything, just kept looking around.

Along the back wall, David saw a five-gallon bucket with a piece of plywood over the top. As he approached it, the smell got stronger. Scott sidled up beside him.

"What's that?" David asked.

Scott didn't say anything, just reached down and pulled the plywood back.

The smell slapped David across the face like a wet towel and forced him to take a step back. He closed his eyes and wrinkled his face up, as if that would keep the odor at bay. He blinked the water out of his eyes, torn between his initial instinct to retreat and the morbid curiosity of knowing what could possibly make such a stench. He leaned forward again, Scott seemingly oblivious to the rancid smell.

At the bottom of the bucket was the small carcass of a squirrel. It was well into its decomposition, but the matted fur along its long tail gave it away.

"Ugh," David suddenly had to choke back a throat full

of puke. He took two full steps back and held the back of his hand across his mouth. Scott laid the cover across the bucket.

"What is that?" David asked, despite knowing exactly what it was.

"Have you ever seen anything dead before?" Scott asked. "It's pretty cool, because you can check them out any way you want. When they're alive you can't get anywhere near them. They always run away. But when they're dead, you can do whatever you want."

"What are you doing with it?" The words were out of David's mouth before he knew he'd said them. He didn't think he wanted to know what Scott was doing with a dead squirrel.

"I'm getting the skeleton," he said. "Then I can hang it on the wall. Won't that be cool?"

David looked at the wall. He'd seen dead things mounted before. His mom had taken him to that restaurant up in Rochester that had all those heads on the wall. Deer, elk, moose. That was OK. Cool even. He'd loved it.

But a stuffed deer head was fine. The thought of a bare skeleton mounted up on the inside of a kid's fort was creepy.

"Yeah, I guess," David said, looking towards the oasis of fresh air that the door provided. Mounting stuff on the wall was one thing, but being in the same space as a rotting animal was a step David wasn't willing to take. He felt shivers running up his spine, trying to branch out towards his arms. Had he been older, David would have probably come up with a smooth way to get out of the fort. Instead, he just turned and walked out.

The cool air in the clearing bathed his face in cleanliness as he sucked in lungfuls, then blew out the contaminated, dead squirrel air.

As the budding panic left him, David turned back to the fort and realized Scott was still in there. He watched the door for a second, then took a half-step towards it to say something. He wasn't going back in, just wanted to see if he could coax Scott out.

Just as he opened his mouth, a massive ball of fire shot

towards his face from the entrance of the fort. Instinct took hold of David's body and dropped him on the seat of his pants. As the smell of ozone filled his nostrils, he could hear Scott cackling in the background.

"Woohhoooo!!" Scott shrieked through the laughs. "Almost gotcha!"

David sat on the ground thunderstruck. As his brain was trying to process the fact that an enormous fireball had seemingly come within inches of his face, he saw Scott step out of the doorway. With a lighter in his left hand and a can of hairspray in his right, he sent another plume of fire into the air.

Awe replaced the fear as he watched Scott produce fireballs from his hands. It was amazing.

"Holy crap," he said, still on the ground where the first round of fire had put him.

"I know," Scott said. "Have you ever tried this before? I saw it in a movie once. It's freaking awesome."

David figured this was probably dangerous, and he knew his mom would flip if she found out, but the lure was way too much to resist.

"Can I try?" David asked.

"Grab a can."

Scott reached back into the doorway and snatched up a can of his mom's hairspray. As David rose to his feet, Scott handed him the can and a blue plastic cigarette lighter.

"OK, just hold it a few inches in front of the can and let 'er rip," Scott said, demonstrating the distance with his own can.

David fumbled with the lighter, having never used one before. He repeatedly flicked his thumb, getting nothing but a spark before Scott showed him how to hold in the safety button. After getting the hang of the lighter, David positioned the can and hit the spray.

Fire erupted from the can like it was coming from the hands of some dark magician. David had never felt more powerful.

"Awesome, right?" Scott said. "Just make sure you don't hit the fort or the trees."

They spent the next ten minutes shooting fireballs all over the clearing. Scott had some of his old G.I. Joe guys back in the fort, and they strung them up on a branch with some yarn. The two took turns blasting them as they hung from their makeshift nooses.

"Watch their faces melt," Scott said as he kept a steady flame on one of his Cobra Crimson Guard figures. "It's like that guy in Indiana Jones."

Most of the time David would have had trouble destroying perfectly good G.I. Joe guys, many of whom had been on his birthday list just a few months before, but the lure of the flame proved too much. Soon what had once been a squadron of elite fighting toys was reduced to a pile of mutilated plastic, which in itself was pretty cool. By the time they were done, David's fear of the dead squirrel had melted away as well.

"BUT THIS IS TOP SECRET, OK? You can never tell anyone about any of this."

They hadn't been back at the fort the last two days, which was OK with David. He had no desire to be around that dead squirrel. That said, he really wanted to shoot some fireballs again. By the time Friday afternoon came around, David knew it would be his last chance. Dead rodent or not, he had to ask.

As casually as a 10-year-old can, David broached the subject after lunch. Unfortunately, every GI Joe guy Scott owned had been reduced to a molten pile during their first flame throwing session.

But Scott said he might have something else—something better—so they made their way down the path behind the shed and towards the fort.

"Seriously," Scott said. "You say a word about this and I'll kill you."

It was a threat David took seriously, as any fourth grader would. He'd seen a classmate get killed before, and it wasn't pretty. Tripped, repeatedly pushed down, hit, even kicked a few times in the leg before left crying. And if you told the teacher, they'd kill you again.

Without waiting for a response, Scott turned back towards the path. When they hit the clearing where the fort stood, Scott continued past. David hadn't been any farther into the woods than the fort, but he dutifully followed Scott. The path narrowed the farther they got away from the fort, and they eventually came upon a downed log that had fallen across the path. Instead of hopping over it, Scott stepped up on it and walked along it into the trees.

"C'mon," He said without looking back. "Back this way."

David left the path and stepped down the log like a balance beam. Up ahead, Scott hopped from one log to another. There was a good amount of foliage on the ground, growing up and around trees that had dropped to the forest floor over the years.

"You gotta stay on the logs," he said. "There's lots of poison ivy around on the ground. It's like a lava moat and you gotta stay above it."

Scott kept going from log to log, leading David farther and farther into the woods. Finally, David saw Scott jump down off his log and head out from under the trees. They had reached the southern edge of the woods, which emptied out into a swath of tall prairie grass. A large portion of the grasses had been trampled down, leading up to the cornfield that stretched for acres. The stalks were at least six feet high, giving the little clearing a tall back wall.

David looked back towards the woods as he stepped out, trying to figure how far they were from Scott's house. It would still be a while before his mom came to pick him up, but if they were still here when she showed up, there would be no way they'd hear Scott's mom call to them. He didn't have a watch on, so he'd have to make sure they weren't back here too long.

As David turned back towards the clearing, he saw a silver cage in the grass on the far side. It was roughly five feet long and a foot high, with two poles on one end that held up a trap door towards the cornfield. Or had. The door had come down into place and was currently keeping something from getting out. Scott was already on his way over.

"What is that?" David asked.

"It's an old fox trap we had in the shed," Scott replied. "Len got it a few years ago when my mom insisted she saw a fox in the backyard and was terrified it was going to attack me or something."

"Did he ever get it?" David asked, suddenly concerned about man-eating foxes hurtling out of the underbrush.

"Nah, he just bought it to shut her up. It had been sitting in the shed forever until I found it. Works great though."

"You caught the fox?"

"Never seen a fox," Scott said. "But I got a few rabbits. I've been looking for..." He trailed off as he crossed the clearing towards the cage.

"YES!!" he exclaimed.

"What is it?" David asked.

"Finally got ya, you little shit," Scott said towards the cage.

As David approached he saw a small, skinny cat curled in the back corner of the cage. It was a dark calico, with short black and orange fur covering most of its body. When it raised its head from the ground, David could see the left side of its face was covered in white fur from the eye down, where it extended to a small patch on its chest. The left paw was the only other spot of white on it. It was these small patches of white that betrayed the cat's condition. The dirt that would have just blended in on the rest of its body was in full view against the stark white fur. David could also see a bunch of small cockleburs matted together near the cat's shoulder. It had been out here for a while.

"You weren't going to outsmart me, no way," Scott said. "I KNEW I would get ya."

"Is he yours?" asked David. "Did he get away from your house or something?"

"No, but he's mine now. I've seen him sneaking around here for a while," Scott replied, never taking his eyes off the cage. "I knew I'd get him."

The cat remained huddled in the far corner, but kept its

33

head up with a sharp eye on the two kids who loomed just outside the cage. David knelt and pressed his fingers up against the silver mesh. The cat remained still, but had the look of a semi-domesticated animal that was torn between fear and a desire to be petted again. Probably a barn cat from one of the farms around here.

"Hey buddy," David said in his most reassuring voice. "Come here."

As David's attention was on trying to coerce the skinny calico out of its corner, Scott slipped away. The cat lifted its nose towards David's outstretched fingers and took as good a whiff as it could from the distance. It cautiously rose and slinked over towards him. After giving David's fingers another good sniff, the cat rubbed its face against them with great abandon. David did what he could to scratch its chin and behind its ears, but the cage walls and the cat's excitement it made that a difficult task.

As the cat purred away, Scott returned with a small squeeze bottle in his hand.

"Good. Keep him there, will ya."

Before David could ask what he was talking about, Scott squirted the cat's tail and backside with a good amount of water. The cat jumped away from David's hand, and landed with its back arched and eyes locked on Scott. He continued to soak the grass inside the cage.

"What are you doing?" asked David. Up until then he hadn't thought of why Scott had made it his mission to trap a stray cat out in the woods, but squirting it with water while it was stuck in a cage just seemed mean.

"Watch this," Scott said.

As he looked up at Scott, David noticed two things. First was the creepy look in Scott's eyes as he talked. He didn't make any eye contact, just stared at the cat like there was nothing else in the world. Almost trancelike. Second was the fact that the squeeze bottle Scott had just dropped at his feet wasn't a water bottle.

It was lighter fluid.

Scott dug into the pocket of his jeans and came up with a tattered book of matches. Before David could process what was going on, Scott drug the scarlet head across the rough strip and tossed the lit match into the cage. It missed the cat, but landed on a spot of lighter fluid just under its feet. As the grass ignited, the cat immediately jumped back. Unfortunately, its tail passed too close to the light blue flame and was immediately ablaze.

The cat let out a yowl unlike anything David had ever heard. Its high pitch bored its way into his brain, where it set up a little fire of its own behind his eyes. He watched in shock as the cat rolled from side to side, bouncing off the walls, slamming into the ceiling in an attempt to get away from the fire rapidly flying up its tail. The acrid smell of burnt fur filled his nostrils as he watched in horror. The wailing filled the clearing as David looked up at Scott for some kind of explanation, only to see a face devoid of emotion. The reflection of the fire that was rapidly engulfing the cat danced in Scott's glassy eyes, while a wry but serene smile spread across his lips.

David had no idea what to do. The yowling of the cat not only didn't fade, but intensified. The cage shook as the cat repeatedly slammed against its side. Panic flooded him, and he didn't have the ability to process something so terrifying. He just knew he had to get away from that sound.

At some point, he turned and ran.

The cat's yowling followed him as he stumbled over and off the logs, into and through the poison ivy, down the path past the fort. It stayed with him well past the point where he was out of earshot and would be unable to hear anything. The yowling just repeatedly bounced around the walls of his head, growing louder and louder.

4

MATT SAT IN STUNNED SILENCE as David finished his story. There were so many questions he wanted to ask, but offered none, as he couldn't even decide what he wanted to know first. The story was fantastically unbelievable, but there was little doubt in Matt's mind that every word of it was true.

How had I not heard this before?

He stared at his friend. David, in turn, hadn't taken his eyes off the faded blue swing in front of him since he started speaking. A slight breeze pushed it back and forth ever so slightly.

"Holy shit."

David finally looked up at Matt.

"Yeah."

Another minute passed before either one spoke. The kids in the shelter house were still hopping from table to table, yelling back and forth.

"So you think he's like... messed up," Matt said. "I mean, like, for real messed up. Psycho."

"Yeah," David replied.

Matt reached down and picked up the magazine. It was still folded to the sidebar David had him read earlier, and he scanned down the list again. As much as he didn't want to believe it, everything David had said made sense.

"So what does this mean?" Matt asked. "This doesn't mean that he's for sure going to be a serial killer, does it?"

"I don't know," David said as he took the magazine from Matt's hands. "It says this is what the FBI looks for in a serial killer. This is what they are. These are the signs."

"Right, but you don't really think Scott is going to start killing people." Matt said.

"I don't know, but he fits everything on this list," David shot back.

"I know, I know," Matt said. "But, you know... holy shit."

"Yeah, I don't know what to do," David said.

"I mean, what can we do?" Matt asked.

"We can stay the fuck away from Scott Alston, that's what."

"No kidding." Matt nodded. He took the magazine back from David, looking it over for a third time. "Does he know?"

"Know what?"

"That you know all this?" Matt said. "I mean, has he ever said anything to you?"

"No."

"Did you ever tell anybody?"

"I couldn't," David replied. "I was way too scared. And he knows it too. I think that's what he likes. That I am still so scared of it."

The kids in the shelter house had hopped down off the tables and made their way out of the park, leaving Matt and David alone. The flow of students walking past on the street had slowed to a trickle, so the only sound was the faint rustling of the fall leaves.

"I dreamed about that for months afterward. Still do... sometimes."

"What about that day?" Matt asked. "What did you do right after? What did you tell your mom?"

"I don't remember running away," David said. "But I must have just tore through the woods because I ended up with scratches and poison ivy all over my legs. I was just in the front yard, sitting out by the mailbox near the road. I remember Mrs. Alston tried to take me in the house, but I wouldn't go. There was no way I was going back in that house. I just kept kicking and pulling away. Eventually, my mom showed up and I just grabbed her and wouldn't let go. All I wanted was to go home. I assume she just thought I was freaked out because of my legs. Eventually we got in the car and left.

"I have no idea where Scott was. Probably still back there. I remember Mrs. Alston sent a bottle of calamine lotion with us though. Mom made me sit in the tub and rub it on that night when my legs started to itch."

"Jeez," Matt said. It was all he could offer.

"When school started, he never said a word to me. But he would stare. I'd be out on the playground and turn around and there he was. Watching. In the hallway, in the lunchroom, it was always the same. And he would give me that fucking smile. He KNEW I wasn't going to say anything, and it was like he got off on it.

"Then one day there was a bunch of black shit in my backpack. Ashes."

Matt recoiled.

"Ugh," he said. "Like… cat ashes?"

"I don't know what they were, but they freaked me out," David said. "He must have put them in. I didn't dare tell anybody. Every time I saw dirt in the hallway I was afraid it was more ashes.

"About a month later was the thing with Eric Henderson."

Matt looked across the bench in confusion.

"Huh?"

"The locker?"

"I have no idea what you are talking about," Matt replied. "I wasn't here, remember?"

David leaned back on the bench and looked up toward the trees.

"Jeez, I forgot," He let out a big breath. "I can't believe you never heard about that."

David put his elbows on his knees, his hands clasped together in front of him.

38

"When we were in fourth grade this first grader just goes missing one day. Eric Henderson. So they start tearing the place apart. They're checking all the classrooms, the gym, library, down in the boiler room—everywhere. Then the police show up. They're searching all around outside, down the block, the park. Nobody can find him. We had to stay in our classrooms all day, no recess, no gym, nothing.

"So the day ends and they still haven't found him. By this time, there are police all over the place. And there are parents everywhere because they weren't letting anybody go home alone, so your mom or dad had to come pick you up.

Matt shifts to try and find a comfortable spot on the bench.

"What happened?"

"Some fifth grader goes to open up his locker and there he is. He's been inside the whole day."

Matt's eyes ballooned.

"Ends up Scott stuffed him in this kid's locker during morning recess."

Something wasn't quite right. Even though he'd never used them, Matt knew the fifth grade lockers were lined up along the main hallway of the elementary section of the school. People would have walked right past the kid about a hundred times.

"How did nobody find him earlier? Couldn't they hear kicking or something?"

"He didn't make a peep," David said. "He just stood in there."

"Why?"

"Who knows? Maybe he was too scared. Maybe Scott said if he made a sound he kill him."

Matt shook his head in bewilderment.

"When the kid finally told what happened, Scott was out of school for a week. They never said anything, but everybody said he was going to be sent away. It was the best week of school I ever had. I wasn't scared anymore. And it wasn't just me, everybody seemed happy. It was like a weight had been lifted off the whole damn place.

"Then, he was back. No explanation. He was just back. Everyone figured his stepdad threw a fit about it and he was back."

"What about the kid?"

David took a deep breath. "He never came back. They open enrolled him to Forest City after that, then ended up moving. I guess the dad was really pissed that nothing happened to Scott.

"Join the fucking club."

5

THE PAST MONTH HAD BEEN A REVELATION for Scott Alston. Making that Cooke kid crumple to the ground—seeing that pool of blood—had awakened something inside of him, and it had been growing ever since.

As a child, Scott had been a compulsive masturbator, or whatever you call it when kids that age pleasure themselves. He seemed to get excited constantly, and would use whatever methods he could to gratify himself. That ended one afternoon when his mother walked in on him with his pants off, humping one of her velvet throw pillows. Her reaction was a mix of shock and embarrassment, and she quickly backed out of the room without saying anything. Scott hadn't been embarrassed, just upset that his mother had dared interrupt him. By then he knew there would be no repercussions from Karen Alston.

His stepfather was another story.

About 30 minutes later, Scott heard the tires of Pastor Len Alston's Cadillac Seville turn into their driveway and come to a halt in front of the garage.

Pastor Alston's reaction was swift. He walked into Scott's room with his well-worn Bible and the jar of Icy Hot he used on his arthritic back. He then forced Scott to masturbate using the menthol rub while he read passages from the Bible. Pastor Alston kept preaching about "spilling your seed on the ground" while making Scott continually rub his increasingly burning genitals. After 45 minutes, Len closed his holy book and left the room without a word. The fire between Scott's legs remained, however. He held his tears back as his mother gave him his nightly bath, as the water did nothing to wash away the pain.

Sometime during that sleepless night the burning faded, but it never truly went away. That fire sparked the kindling of hatred Scott had stored away in his mind. From then on, a smoldering pile of rage replaced his constant arousal.

But the Cooke kid stoked that fire into something new. Something bigger.

After that, Scott embarked on two weeks of relentless re-acquaintance with self-gratification. Eventually, he realized he needed a better outlet, and he found it at one of the North Shore beer parties his classmates loved so much.

Scott sat at the bonfire, nursing a can of Busch Light and watching Amy Martin through the flames. He'd never paid any real attention to any of his classmates—Scott found them all unbearably boring—but she had enough of a small-town cuteness to draw his eye that night. Amy had sandy blonde hair, dark eyes and a set of legs that looked fantastic in her cheerleading skirt. Unfortunately for her, she also had a bad combination of low intelligence and even lower self-esteem.

She'd be a perfect plaything.

It happened quickly, because he'd wanted it to. Scott slid over towards her and turned on the charm he'd been practicing the past few years. He listened to whatever inane drivel poured from Amy's mouth and made sure she always had a fresh beer. The alcohol probably worked more than the sweet talk, and soon enough Scott had her in the back of his Mustang with the front seats folded up as far as they would go.

He wasted no time going after his goal, and was soon on top of Amy, violently thrusting into her. He raced towards the finish line, oblivious to her sighs of pain as the seatbelt buckle dug into the base of her spine. After he finished, Scott untangled himself from her legs and leaned his head back against the window. He looked down at Amy, who was searching for her underwear. Her face was flushed and he thought he saw a glint of water in her eye. As she reached behind her to scoop up her jeans, her center of gravity shifted and she had to brace herself on the back of the passenger seat to keep from sliding off into the footwell. Scott couldn't help but chuckle. Amy looked up at him and let out a nervous laugh.

"Heh," she said. "Clumsy eh?"

He didn't respond, stretching his legs out across the backseat as he basked in the aftermath. Amy fought to untangle her underwear from her jeans, then leaned back over Scott's legs in an attempt to get them back on. Scott quickly raised his feet, lifting her off the seat until she took the hint and sat back up. She managed to turn around inside the cramped backseat and park her naked backside on the folded up passenger seat. With the back of her head pressed against the car's roof, Amy was able to straighten her legs enough to pull both her underwear and jeans on.

"Wanna head back out?" she asked.

Scott didn't reply, just lay across the backseat with his jeans and old-fashioned tighty whities bunched up around his right ankle.

Amy sat on the back of the passenger seat. Maybe she wanted to move back onto the seat, to sit with him the way they had beside the fire, but that wasn't going to happen. Scott wanted her gone. Gone now. But she wasn't moving.

Why wasn't she moving?

He stared at her, willing her to leave, but she just looked back with a forced smile on her face.

How fucking stupid are you?

Eventually she took the hint.

"Well, I think I am going to head back out, OK?" She asked.

Amy hesitated for another moment, probably waiting for a response. When it didn't come, she reached past the headrest behind her and opened the door. A puff of cool air swept in as she stepped out, but instead of closing the door and leaving him alone, she leaned back in.

"See you in a bit," she said.

The next time Scott saw her was Monday at school.

AMY MARTIN HAD DONE EVERYTHING she could to figure out what she did wrong that night. She was convinced Scott had liked her — their time in the backseat proved that — so she knew she must have done something wrong that caused his mood shift. All she needed was another chance and she could make it right.

Amy approached Scott at his locker before first period, her stomach a tangle of butterflies as she tapped him on the shoulder. Scott turned around and looked at her. She had no idea what to say as his eyes met hers, but then suddenly... a smile.

"Hey," Scott said. "How are you?"

"Great," she said, all the doubts and anxieties she had dealt with melted away with that one grin. "How... um. How was your weekend?"

"Good," Scott replied. "What are you doing tonight?"

6

THE SCHOOL'S CAFETERIA WAS PACKED as Matt scanned the room for his friend. You could almost feel a haze of maple syrup in the air, and the sizzle of the griddle was audible over the dozens of conversations going on. He was shocked at the number of people, but Matt realized he should have expected it.

Who wouldn't want to help out a four-year-old girl with cancer?

Leah Peterson was sitting with her mom at a table displaying a bunch of items lined up for a silent auction. She was a cute little thing, her smile beaming out from under a pink stocking cap.

He didn't know the Petersons personally, but everybody in town knew their story by now. Leah's mom, Kim, took her to the doctor because of nosebleeds and they left with a diagnosis of leukemia. They didn't have any family around with Kim's parents dead and Leah's dad long gone, but small towns can be great at picking up the slack. As news got out, people went over and cleaned, mowed their lawn, and stocked the freezer with enough casseroles to survive a nuclear winter.

Matt scooted out of the way as two members of the girl's volleyball team rushed past with massive trays of pancakes. The team was volunteering as servers that night.

"Hey," came a voice from behind.

Matt turned around and nodded at David, who was approaching from the kitchen area.

"Dude, this is nuts," Matt said.

"Yeah, it's been this way since five. They're gonna make a ton of money."

Matt looked back towards the silent auction table.

"Anything cool over there?" he asked.

"I dunno," David replied. "I've been helping my mom in the kitchen since we got here. Wanna go scope it out?"

The table stretched the entire length of the back wall and was crammed with donated items. Matt was amazed at what the organizers had pulled together as he made his way through the line. Not only was there the requisite local stuff—gift certificates for free movies, pizzas, haircuts—but they'd gotten an autographed helmet from the Minnesota Vikings, a baseball from the Twins and two sets of Hawkeye basketball tickets. The bids were already well out of Matt's price range, which was probably a good sign. It was a fundraiser, after all.

Matt was checking out a putter donated by the Country Club when he felt David lean in.

"What the hell is he doing?"

Matt used all the subtlety of a teenaged boy as he followed David's gaze behind the table.

Scott Alston was perched next to Leah Peterson, his arm on the back of her chair. Before Matt could say anything, David cut through the line to the spot across the table from them. Matt was hit with a wave of panic, terrified his friend was about to do something publicly stupid.

And potentially dangerous.

"Hey Scott, Amy is looking for you," David said.

Scott looked up from Leah with a lopsided smirk.

"Well she can wait," he replied. "I'm talking with my new girl Leah here."

The four-year-old giggled and hugged her stuffed bear. She wore one of the "Team Leah" shirts that the servers had on, and somebody had put a knot in the bottom so it didn't reach her knees. Matt saw Leah's mom a few feet away, talking with Scott's mom and Pastor Alston.

"She was just telling me about her cat," he said, eyes locked on David.

Matt's panic jumped a notch.

Did he just say cat?

Matt saw David was riveted and didn't even look down as the girl described the new kitty she'd gotten last week.

"I told her I used to have a cat too," Scott said. "But he got lost out in the woods behind our house."

"But you could find him," Leah said with a four-year-old's optimism.

Scott broke his stare into David to look down at Leah.

"Maybe I could, but I would need some help."

His voice was unnervingly natural, like any guy telling a little girl about his pet.

Just not mentioning the part about burning it alive.

"What do you think? Want to come back to the woods and help me find my cat, Davey?"

This was insane. Matt grabbed David's arm and pulled him away before he could say anything. Luckily, Kim Peterson had finished her conversation and came back to rejoin her daughter.

Matt led his friend through the crowd and away from any potential confrontation.

"What the hell was that?" He asked after they had crossed the room. "Was he talking about cats? Like, *that* cat?"

David looked ashen. His eyes kept darting around the room, not focusing on anything.

"You all right?" Matt asked.

"Yeah, fine." David looked back towards Leah. She was digging into the stack of pancakes her mom had plopped in front of her. The Alstons had left. "He shouldn't be around her."

Matt had no idea how to respond, so he didn't. He saw his family sitting at a table just off the kitchen, and the two joined them. Matt's little brother was putting on a pancake-eating clinic, which helped lighten the mood.

"Not hungry David?" Matt's mom asked.

"I had some earlier."

As they were finishing up, one of the volleyball players came over to bus the table, a giant blob of syrup smeared across the 'M' on her Team Leah shirt.

"Any chance you guys have seen a teddy bear around?" she asked as she stacked the plates.

"Um, no," Judy Carlton said. "Why?"

"Oh, Leah can't seem to find her Chemo Bear."

Matt looked across the room and saw Kim Peterson holding her daughter, whose face was red with tears.

"Oh no," Matt's mom said, anxiously looking around and under the table. "I don't see anything. Poor thing... if we find it we'll get it right over to her."

Judy looked towards Matt and David.

"Would you boys go look around for a bit?"

Matt got an angry, knowing look from David as they got up.

7

THINGS REMAINED RELATIVELY UNEVENTFUL at school through the fall. The football team finished a surprising 8-2 on the year, but were upset in the first round of the playoffs by North Central High. A major factor in the loss was playing without star running back Carl Blake, who was suspended for violation of the Student Conduct Code after hosting a keg party at his parents' farm the previous weekend.

Amy Martin was there every game, cheering alongside her squad and taking the coveted spot at the top of the pyramid. She even convinced Scott to attend a game and watch. That was probably the highlight of the season for Amy, regardless of how much Scott actually paid attention. It was, to put it mildly, an up-and-down relationship. Scott had a hearty appetite for her, and she learned early on that he did not like to be denied. He never got overtly violent, although the sex could be awfully rough. She was there when he needed it.

Often multiple times a week.

When her parents started asking questions about her weeknight absences, she developed a lengthy and reliable list of excuses that eased their suspicions – studying Spanish with Shawna, group projects, working on a new cheerleading routine. Being the youngest of four kids didn't hurt, as her parents had become much more permissive over the years.

In her stronger moments Amy was able to stand up for herself, but those moments were infrequent and often fleeting. The couple did officially break up once during the fall, but it lasted all of three hours. While Scott was emotionally cold most of the time, he figured out how to come through with just enough whenever Amy approached her breaking point, bringing her back into the fold.

As the days got shorter, David often showed up to school with bags under his eyes and completed homework. Not knowing what else to do, Matt took it upon himself to keep his friend pre-occupied as the fall crept away. Weekends consisted of movies and video games, with the occasional sojourn uptown. The weather was relatively mild for that time of year, so the two spent a decent amount of time wandering the streets and hanging out on the front steps at Salem Lutheran Church, talking about anything except Scott Alston.

Shortly after Christmas Break, winter decided to stake its claim with a wicked cold snap. The mercury didn't get much above zero the whole first week back to school, and that Friday night saw nasty winds take the wind chill to the -20 range.

That would leave downtown relatively quiet. A perfect night to get David out and about.

After a bit of explanation and a touch more convincing, Matt convinced his friend to borrow his mom's car and drive them uptown.

For most high school kids in Lake Mills, the weekend hangout was the Wreck, an old townie bar that lost its liquor license (for serving alcohol to minors, ironically) but decided to stay open as a place for teenagers to hang out. In the same way some kids used high school to prepare them for college, others used the Wreck to prepare them for the day they would spend their weekends across the street at Frank's Place. A training bar, if you will. It remained the dark, seedy hole it always was, but now stocked only pop. With no more liquor bottles to stand in front of it, the old mirror that hung behind the bar shone through and almost doubled the perceived size of the room, which was in reality a very cramped space. Two pool tables stood perpendicular to the bar, close enough to each other that players often had to wait for their adjacent compatriots to complete a shot before addressing their own.

With the smoking age just 18, cigarettes were much easier to acquire than beer and the Wreck kept the hazy atmosphere it always had. There were always rumors that the cops were going to bust the place for allowing underage smoking "this weekend for sure", even though it never actually happened.

Whether it was ridiculous rumors or the cold, Matt's forecast was right. The Wreck was dead for a Friday night. Woody, the dive's owner, was on a stool at the far end of the bar, watching a basketball game on TV while a group of sophomores clustered around the front corner of the bar. They were taking advantage of the lack of upperclassmen to get some time on the Mega Touch video game. Both pool tables were vacant, so Matt lined up some quarters on the rail and grabbed a cue while David racked up the balls for their first game.

David seemed to relax a bit as the night went on— winning the first two games probably helped—and the two friends slid into a familiar banter that had been increasingly absent. Matt chuckled as Woody eyeballed the sophomores pumping quarters into his bar-top video game. They didn't know it yet, but they were getting perilously close to getting booted into the cold for giving Woody "a goddam headache". Not that they were making more noise than anyone else, they just didn't know how to handle the temperamental owner yet. Woody was the type of guy who would toss a kid out just to show the rest he could, and you had to earn your points with him. The fresher the face, the shorter the leash.

As Matt and David got into their fourth game, the Wreck started to fill up, and they could feel a blast of bitter cold every time somebody walked in. Every time it was left open for more than a few seconds, a gruff call of "Close the goddam door!" would erupt from Woody's end of the bar.

"You want to keep playing?" Matt asked. With the sudden influx of people, they would have to add a few quarters to the rail if they wanted to keep the table.

"Yeah, sure," David replied.

"I'll go get some change." Matt headed up to the bar, happy. David was as normal as he'd been in months.

Matt caught Woody's eye and asked for a Coke and some change for his dollar. Woody handed him the quarters and planted the can of soda on a coaster that had probably been sitting in that spot since the night before.

"Thanks a lot." Matt pretended not to notice the whiskey on his breath. Everybody knew Woody kept a fifth stashed under the bar, and Matt suspected there was a lot less than a fifth remaining.

Matt always made a point to be polite with Woody, as a little respect went a long way in terms of his attitude. His deference obviously worked, because he had never been yelled at, much less kicked out of the Wreck. There weren't many kids from Lake Mills that could say that.

He turned back to the table and lined up two more quarters along the rail while David racked the balls up on the near side. He carefully lifted the plastic triangle off the table, trying to keep the balls as tight as possible as Carl and Russ Blake entered the Wreck through the back entrance. Matt shot his friend a quick glance, but David was trying to subtly look down the back hallway behind them.

Probably to see if Scott was following.

Carl stopped by the jukebox to play as much county music as his dollar would allow, while Russ headed over to the bar and bought a bag of Doritos. Chips in hand, he met up with his cousin at the corner booth, where he settled his considerable girth down on a chair and propped his feet up on the bench. His shoes covered the vinyl seat with the gray mixture of slush and parking lot salt everyone tracked around this time of year.

Russ's spot in the Wreck was in no danger, however. Both his and Carl's fathers had been regulars during the Wreck's days as an actual bar, so the goodwill earned from years of Busch Light purchases had been passed down by Woody like an Ivy League legacy.

David stayed at the far end of the table, keeping a wary eye on the Blake boys and the back hall as Matt prepared his opening break. Aside from the occasional bathroom patron, nobody emerged. Matt caught a roll and drained four consecutive striped balls to take a quick lead.

"I told you this one is for money, right?" Matt joked.

"Yeah, talk now," David said, his attention slowly coming back to the game. "You'll still choke it away."

David responded by sinking two of his own. As he lined up his next shot, Scott popped open the back door and came strolling past the bathrooms. He headed over to where Russ and Carl were sitting, kicked past Russ's feet and slid into the booth alongside Carl.

"Your shot man," Matt said. David stood with his face down towards the table, but his eyes were locked on the corner booth where the Blake boys were listening intently to whatever Scott was telling them.

"Hey," Matt said. "You still in?"

"Yeah, I'm just... you know..." he said as he gestured towards the pool table.

"Well miss and get on with it," Matt said.

"Uh huh," David said, bending down to line up his shot again. He pulled the cue back and fired, his 3-ball careening off the far rail and racing back towards the corner pocket. The solid red ball struck just to the left of the hole, rattled back and forth at the mouth, and fell in. David looked over to Matt with a satisfied, albeit surprised, look on his face.

Matt gave a bewildered smile. "Jesus, nice shot."

Just as chuckle escaped David's mouth, a howl of laughter erupted from Scott's booth.

David and Matt both looked over, convinced the burst involved them. Paranoia was hard to shake.

"No fucking way," Carl brayed over the sound of the music and general din of the Wreck. Russ had leaned back

53

with his eyes closed and face pointed toward the ceiling, contorted like he was passing a kidney stone. Scott just sat there with a satisfied look on his face, continuing with whatever story was so entertaining his lackeys.

David looked over to Matt, who gave the slightest eyebrow raise and tilt of the head. Matt had no idea what was so incredibly hilarious, but was silently happy it wasn't about them. As they continued the game, he moved over to the corner nearest the booth in an effort to eavesdrop and figure out what was so interesting. He pretended to be watching the television as David looked for his next shot.

"...still?" Russ asked.

"Fuck it," Carl said. "I'm checking this out." He slid out of the booth and headed down the hallway towards the backdoor. Russ pushed his chair back and followed.

The area out back of the Wreck was ready-made for privacy. Since the building was much smaller than its neighbors, there was a deceptively large space formed by the outer walls of Bruchman's TV and Stereo on the left, Northwest Insurance on the right and the back end of the old theatre that sat just around the corner on Main Street. You could get into the spot from either of a pair of alleys, one coming in from Mill Street and one from First Ave., but since the Wreck was so much shorter than the buildings adjacent, the two alleys opened into an area that couldn't be seen from the street. Years ago, Woody attempted to turn it into an outdoor beer garden, but now it was used as a parking lot that could accommodate about five vehicles. A good amount of people, including some Wreck patrons, didn't realize how much space was back there. Most just came and went through the front.

Matt looked over at his friend with questioning eyes, who took another look down the back hall. Carl was holding the door open, leaning outside with his cousin fighting to peer over his shoulder. David looked back to Matt and shrugged. Suddenly Carl elbowed Russ aside and ducked past, howling with laugher. He leaned back against the wall, eyes pressed shut and a cackling grimace plastered on his face. Russ leaned out farther, then backtracked and let the

54

door swing shut. He rubbed his hands together as he returned to the bar, chuckling to himself. Carl released himself from the wall and followed. They were both still laughing when they returned to Scott's table and started peppering him with questions. His only response was a triumphantly smug smile and a spread of his hands over the table.

Not wanting to be caught staring, Matt quickly lined up his next shot and missed badly.

"You're up dude," he called across to David. "Let's do it, eh?"

As David lined up his shot, Matt leaned down towards him.

"What was that?" he asked in a hushed voice.

"No idea," David replied. "Something out back. They just poked their heads out the door and kept laughing."

"They mess with somebody's car?"

David gave Matt a clueless look and bent down to take his shot.

It took a bit for the two to finish up their game, but fittingly the rubber match came down to a battle for the eight ball. Each had a shot at ending things before Matt left an easy make on the table for David, who buried it to take the win and the five-game series.

"Done?" Matt asked after David finally cleared the table.

"Yeah, I'm good."

Matt picked up their remaining quarter off the rail and handed his cue across the felt to the next players.

David was already at the bar with can of Mountain Dew in front of him and his eyes seemingly locked on the television. Matt took the stool next to him. Before he could flag down Woody for another soda, David nudged him.

"What the hell is up back there?"

Matt turned and saw Carl re-emerge from the back hall, giggling like a kindergartener who just heard a poop joke.

Before he could say anything, David was off his stool.

"Screw it, I'm gonna go check."

Matt grabbed his arm. "Whoa, hold on."

David shrugged his grip off and leaned down towards the bar. "Keep an eye on them through the mirror. If one of them gets up, just gimmie a wave."

Matt's protests went unsaid as David strolled back to the hallway. He glanced back as he passed the bathrooms on the right, and continued towards the door. David reached out to open it, but the handle disappeared from his grasp as the back door flew open and Amy Martin blew past him. David wheeled around, staring at the girl retreating towards the bathroom. Her face was stained with tears, and she was topless with her arms folded across her chest. The shoulder she used to push open the bathroom door was an angry red, as if somebody had spent the last half hour slapping it.

Matt craned his neck back for a better view, only to see David rooted by the door. He looked around the Wreck, but everyone else was engrossed in his or her own Friday night uptown.

David made his way back to the bar, where Matt greeted him with a lost look.

"What the hell was that?"

"No clue," David said.

Matt leaned closer and lowered his voice.

"Was she naked?"

"Yeah," David said. "I mean, she didn't have a shirt on."

"What the hell?"

David looked back down the hallway. There was no movement from the bathrooms.

"I dunno," David answered. "Did you see her arms?"

"No."

"They were freaking red," David said. "I don't know if it was frostbite or something, but man, it was nasty."

As they were talking, Jessica McTell walked past them towards the hallway. David and Matt watched as she stepped into the women's bathroom. Neither said anything as they waited for some sort of reaction. After a few long minutes, Jessica emerged with a pale look on her face. She came to the entrance of the hallway and quickly scanned the crowd at the Wreck. She momentarily looked over towards

Scott, but then made her way to the front, approaching a group of kids clustered near the front door. Jessica pulled aside Megan Larson and Shawna Miller, who were both on the cheerleading squad with Amy and two of her best friends. They had just arrived and hadn't taken their coats off before Jessica led them back towards the bathroom, where they vanished behind the door.

Jessica appeared after a minute and rejoined her friends at the front booth opposite of where Scott sat with Russ and Carl, oblivious to the drama unfolding with his girlfriend just around the corner. Even from across the room Matt could tell Jessica was recounting the story to her friends.

"Seriously, what is happening here?"

THIRTY MINUTES AFTER Jessica McTell summoned them to the women's bathroom, Shawna and Megan emerged with Amy between them. She was wearing Shawna's winter coat and her face was still flushed and red. Amy obviously spent her entire time in the bathroom crying, as her eyes were glassy and bloodshot.

Carl once again dislodged himself from the booth and headed for the back door. When he saw the three girls standing outside the bathroom, he immediately doubled back. He leaned in to say something to Scott, who stood up and headed towards the hallway.

David and Matt watched as he stepped past Amy's friends and led her out the back door without a hint of protest. Shawna and Megan stood talking quietly, but apparently angrily, to each other, and both wore looks of barely contained indignation when they came back to the bar area.

It didn't take long for the story to circulate through the crowd. Apparently when he and Amy arrived earlier that night, Scott decided the seclusion behind the Wreck was a perfect opportunity for another quick twirl in the backseat of his Mustang. Midway through, after he had worked Amy's shirt off, Scott told her he had to run inside quick but thought it would be hot if she waited for him "just as she was". As he opened the door, Scott grabbed the ball of clothes containing Amy's shirt and bra, surreptitiously dropped them to the ground and kicked them under the car. He then reached back for his coat, which was conveniently on top of Amy's, allowing him to grab them both without her noticing. After five minutes, the heat they had built up had escaped out the front window Scott had cracked to keep the car from getting steamed up. As the bitter cold outside began to take hold and Scott refused to return, Amy began to search the car for her shirt. When both it and her coat were nowhere to be found, she started looking for anything to put around her to keep the biting chill off her shoulders, but found nothing. She tried the rubber floormats, but they were just as cold as the air and offered no comfort. All told, she spent 40 minutes in the cold before she finally ran into the Wreck, where her friends reported it took at least 15 minutes for her shivering to stop.

The story wasted no time making its way through LMCHS on Monday, picking up some charming details along the way. By the end of the day, half the student body was convinced that Amy Martin had lost her left nipple to frostbite.

8

THE ANGRY RAP OF A HARD SPRING RAIN on the window pulled Matt out of his sleep. He rolled over and saw his clock flashing a red 12:00 at him. The storm that rolled through must have been stronger than expected, but Matt had slept right through it. As his mother often noted, a train could rumble through his room and not disturb her oldest boy. He sat up and swung his legs over the side of his bed, then reached down to grab a pair of shorts off the floor. He stepped over the black duffle bag he used for school and opened his door.

The house was quiet. His younger brother Ryan, who was usually up watching cartoons on Saturday morning, was nowhere to be found. Matt shuffled out towards the kitchen, where his Dad was sipping a cup of freshly brewed coffee at the kitchen table.

"You're up early," Jon Carlton said.

"Huh?" Matt responded, cutting the word short with a yawn.

His father motioned up towards the clock above the kitchen sink, which was battery operated and kept time through the storm.

7:10

"Whoa," Matt said. That explained why his brother had yet to make an appearance.

"Yeah," his dad said with a chuckle. "Didn't expect to see you for a while."

Matt grabbed a bowl and pulled a box of cereal down from the pantry. He crossed the faded linoleum squares to the refrigerator, where he fished out some milk.

"Yeah, I dunno," Matt said, pouring the milk onto his Raisin Bran. "Just woke up and figured it was later."

His dad put his coffee cup down on the same small, round kitchen table they'd had for years.

"Any plans for today?"

Matt's eyes went towards the window. Streaks of water turned the giant tree in their front lawn into a green blur.

"David and I had talked about going golfing this morning, but it doesn't look like that's going to happen."

Jon Carlton leaned forward and pushed against his knees as he got up.

"Well," he said, knees popping like gunfire as he stood. "I think it's supposed to stop pretty quick here. It's already slowed down quite a bit since I've been up. You guys should be OK. Might be a little soggy, but you should be fine."

"Cool," Matt said, setting his bowl on the table across from the spot his father just vacated.

"If you use the cart, make sure you plug it back in before you leave. I'm going to try to get out there tomorrow," Matt's dad said. The Carlton's rented a shed out at Rice Lake Community Golf Course where they kept their golf cart and clubs. Matt let David keep his clubs out there as well, that way they could just ride their bikes out when they wanted to play.

"Tell your mother I ran out to Brackey's to get the mower serviced. Assuming we get it back quick, you're going to have to mow this week. It's already getting long, and this rain will really get it going."

"No problem," Matt said. His dad usually had some work for him to do, but was pretty good about letting him get around to it on his schedule. Matt tried to peer through the sheet of rain drizzling down the window, but couldn't tell if it was letting up or not. He turned back to his bowl and dug in.

JON CARLTON WAS RIGHT. By 9 am, the rain had slowed to a drizzle. An hour later, the sun was starting to poke its way through the clouds.

"You know, it might actually be a nice day," David said as he and Matt were pedaling out of town towards Rice Lake Golf Course. Like many rural roads in the area, the route out to the course hadn't been re-done in years and never drained properly, leaving huge puddles on the road for the boys to weave around.

The spring rain had turned the Iowa countryside a striking green, from the grasses lining the road to the trees just getting their leaves. The sun even warmed the air enough Matt didn't regret his choice to wear shorts.

"Wanna try the trail?" David asked. About a mile outside Lake Mills, an old horse trail came off the road and bisected a cornfield before disappearing into the woods. It led out towards Rice Lake, eventually emptying out just behind the tee box on hole No. 3. It cut the distance to the golf course in half, although the rough terrain made for slower going. The trail could still cut a good five minutes off the trip, assuming you didn't get ejected from your bike by a random fallen branch or exposed root. Last summer, the boys took the trail pretty regularly, except on Wednesday's, which was Senior League Day. The course was reserved all morning for the old guys, but they always tended to forget the public was welcome after noon. A foursome of 70-year-olds could get especially prickly when a pair of teenagers emerged from the woods behind them while they were getting ready to tee off.

"I don't know," Matt answered. "It's probably pretty muddy. Let's take the long way."

The guys rode past the mouth of the trail and continued south. David's mother never liked them riding their bikes out to Rice Lake, always afraid they were going to get run over by some driver fiddling with his radio. In reality, the route out to the course was fairly safe. County Road 225, which led out the south side of Lake Mills, was a quiet stretch of road used mostly by farmers and golfers. When they did come upon a car, Matt and David always made sure to move into the gravel shoulder, while the driver usually gave them a wide berth.

The only spot where it could get dicey was when they turned East onto County Road 34, which led up to and past Rice Lake Golf Course, then on to weave between the fields of Winnebago County. It was a long, flat, straight stretch of road that ran perpendicular to 225. The residents of Lake Mills referred to it as the Quarter Mile, despite the fact that it was just over a mile in length from the entrance to Rice Lake to where it ended in a "T" intersection with 225. It got its nickname back in the 1960s when the high school kids would regularly take their muscle cars out to the flattest section for drag races.

While the drag racing tradition had ended years ago, the open stretch of flat road will always be a temptation for someone to open the throttle.

As the guys approached the turnoff onto the Quarter Mile, Matt glanced behind them to make sure no cars were coming from behind.

"We're good," he said, nodding towards David to head across the road. Matt fell in behind his friend, then noticed David's left shoelace dangling towards the pavement.

"Dude... shoelace," Matt said, nodding towards his feet.

David looked down and saw his Nike had indeed become untied. He straightened his leg and held it out, away from the gears.

"Thanks," he said, coasting towards the shoulder on the south side of the Quarter Mile. David plopped his foot down and hopped off his bike. "Hold up a sec."

He knelt down and quickly began to tie his shoe as Matt pulled up behind him and walked his bike to the far edge of the gravel, just above the grassy ditch. The shoulder was still soft from the rain, and the light colored mud was sticking to the toes of his shoes as he steadied himself with his feet.

"Aw man..." David said. Matt looked up and saw his friend had instinctively knelt down to tie his shoe, only to come away with a wet, gritty spot soaking though the knee of his jeans. Matt chuckled to himself, then looked up to see a car approaching them on the Quarter Mile.

"Car," he said to David, who was bent at the waist, trying to tie his increasingly soggy shoelaces. David peeked up, and saw the car barreling down on them.

A bright red Mustang.

Both boys recognized Scott's car immediately. The Alston house was just across from the golf course, and their gravel driveway emptied out onto the Quarter Mile about a hundred yards west.

Matt watched as the car sped towards them.

"You might wanna get over here."

David stood up, shoe half tied, and shuffled over towards the ditch. He grabbed the handlebars of his bike and led it away from the road without taking his eyes of the car rapidly approaching.

It was obvious Scott was doing well over the posted limit of 55, and he seemed to be picking up speed the closer he got. Matt shot a questioning look over towards David, but his friend hadn't taken his eyes off the black grill tearing towards them.

Just as Scott came roaring past, his car hit a huge puddle in the road and started hydroplaning. It became a red blur as it went flying towards the intersection. Matt immediately jumped back, his bike crashing to the ground as he stumbled getting his feet disengaged from it.

The mustang's tires reconnected with the pavement as it went careening past, leaving deep black skids in the asphalt as Scott clamped down on the breaks. The back end of the car swung forward as it shot past the stop sign and through County Road 225. Scott's car came to a shuddering stop in the gravel on the far side of the road, its front end pointed toward Lake Mills.

David and Matt stood with their mouths agape. They could see Scott in the driver's seat, with a look of frightened bewilderment on his face. He quickly shook his head as if to clear it, then hit the gas, crossed back into the correct lane and tore off towards town.

"Holy shit," Matt finally said.

David stood silent.

"Seriously," Matt said. "What if somebody had been coming the other way?"

He looked over at David, whose eyes were still on Scott's disappearing taillights.

9

THE NICE WEATHER CONTINUED into the night and brought the high school kids out in droves. By 9 p.m., Main Street was full of cars cruising around town and there was even a group of kids standing around the parking lot of the Qwik Stop. Unsurprisingly, the Wreck was packed. Teenagers lined the barstools and filled every table. Bon Jovi blared from the jukebox, competing with the din of high schoolers shaking off a long, cold winter. This created a cacophony of noise, which was being uncharacteristically tolerated by a relatively sober Woody.

David and Matt sat against the wall opposite the bar, watching the games going on at both pool tables. There was already a line of quarters on both rails that would take most of the night to use up, so the pair had to be content hanging on the sidelines. Matt had managed to procure a stool along the wall, but David was forced to stand. He continually shifted from foot to foot, and Matt noticed his eyes darting around the crowded room.

The wall of noise reverberating around the small bar made conversation difficult without yelling across the table, and both guys were frequently forced to move out of the way as a player lined up his shot.

"Wanna head down to the Quik Stop?" David finally asked.

They weaved their way through the mass of teenagers and headed out the front door. The cool air outside felt good after the amped up heat of the Wreck. It was probably still jacket weather, but it always felt warmer at the beginning of spring. Come fall, the same temperature would see everyone breaking out their heavy coats.

The pair walked down Main Street to the Qwik Stop, where each grabbed a slice of pepperoni and a drink. They ate in the parking lot, checking in with the gang outside. There was something going on out at North Shore, and Beth Duncan's parents supposedly weren't home, so some kids were over there. Of course, with so many kids out tonight, the consensus was the cops would be out in full-force, so proceed with caution.

Matt and David finished up their slices, chucked the cardboard in the garbage and started back up Main Street.

"So can you freaking believe that today? On the way to the course?" Matt asked.

David kept walking, but Matt could tell he knew exactly what he was talking about.

"I mean, he's lucky he stayed in the road. Almost went flying into the ditch. All those trees down there would have banged up his precious Mustang pretty good."

A snort came out of David's mouth, and he just kept walking.

They continued with silence hanging between them. Matt kept waiting for David to say something, but instead broke the quiet himself.

"But seriously, what if there had been like a semi or something? Shit. He would have been a greasy smear on the road. No way he survives."

That brought David into the conversation.

"Like that would be some tragedy?"

Matt was taken aback by the aggressive tone. The two continued their walk in silence.

They rounded the corner and turned back towards the Wreck. From the street, the place looked even more packed than when they had left. There wasn't an open parking spot on the street, and a small group of underclassmen had even

66

spilled out onto the sidewalk outside the door. They could hear Garth Brooks blaring from the jukebox every time somebody opened the door.

"Jeez," Matt said glancing over at David as they crossed the street towards the Wreck. "Place is packed."

"Yeah."

Matt could tell David was uneasy with the prospect of fighting the Saturday night crowd.

"Wanna just head back to my place?" Matt asked. "Watch SNL or something?"

David readily agreed. They walked past the front door, where Matt nodded a hello to the group of underclassmen, getting a half-wave in return. The pair continued down the street and turned east at the end of the block. The two-building buffer from the Wreck cut the volume instantly, and the stars immediately burst from the black cloth of night. There was no streetlight on the block, so the quarter moon would have to do until they made their way back to Main Street.

"Actually pretty nice out, eh?" Matt said.

"Yup, and if it..."

A muffled cry sprung from the alley to their right.

"You hear that?" David asked, peering down into the darkness that led to the back of the Wreck.

Matt raised his eyebrows and shrugged, while David stepped towards the mouth of the alley. Matt reached out to stop him when they heard more voices from the far end.

Followed by crying.

David turned down the alleyway and slowly crept along the backside of the shops that neighbored the Wreck. Matt quietly followed.

"I'm sorry... so sorry..."

The boys snuck behind a Dumpster and peeked around the side.

Amy Martin was backed into the far corner, haloed by the lamp above the Wreck's backdoor. Tears caught the light as they streaked down her face. Scott was in front of her, frantically pacing and pushing his hands through his hair, squeezing the back of his neck. He reminded Matt of the jaguar at the zoo when he was a kid — three steps right, turn, three steps left. The pacing was manic. Creepy.

And there was no glass barrier this time.

Scott's Mustang was one of three cars parked behind the Wreck, a good twenty feet from where Matt and David hid, and it partially blocked what was going on. Amy continued her stream of apologies, which were as fast as they were non-specific.

"Shut the fuck up," Scott said without breaking stride.

Amy sniffed her nose and wiped her tears on the back of her hand. As Scott stalked past her, she reached out to place her hand on the back of his shoulder.

"Listen, I'll do whatever you want. Nobody has to know anything... I promise, Scotty."

Scott wheeled around with a vicious backhand. Amy's head bounced off the brick wall with the sound of someone kicking a watermelon. Scott's face was contorted with fury.

"DON'T YOU EVER FUCKING CALL ME THAT. I TOLD YOU TO SHUT THE FUCK UP, AND I GODDAM FUCKING MEAN IT."

The outburst quashed any bit of control Amy had. She slowly slid down into a fetal position along the wall, where Scott's car hid her from view.

"I'm sorry... sorry..." She babbled, her voice barely floating down the alley. "I swear to God I'll take care of..."

Her words were cut off as Scott pulled her up by a fistful of hair and buried a fist deep into her midsection. Every molecule of air in her lungs was expelled in a raspy gasp. Her crying didn't stop despite the lack of oxygen, but was reduced to an odd retching cough.

Scott took her throat in his right hand and pinned her up against the wall.

"Shut the fuck up, OK?" Scott said. The fury in his voice was completely gone, replaced by an eerie calm.

Amy's eyes bulged to the size of silver dollars and her face rapidly turned crimson. Her mouth opened, but all it let out was something that sounded like a small burp.

"Now I told you to shut the fuck up, and I fucking mean it, OK?" Scott said, adding his other hand to her throat. He was steely cold.

David and Matt crouched behind the dumpster in stunned silence. It took a second to realize what they were seeing.

Matt quickly turned and bolted back towards the street.

DAVID REMAINED FROZEN behind the dumpster. Out of the corner of his eye he saw an old beer bottle standing up against the wall. Instinctively, he reached out and grabbed it. Bottle in hand, he peaked around the dumpster and saw Scott continuing to choke the life out of his girlfriend. David didn't know how long she could hold out, but her face was changing from a dark red to purple and Scott showed no signs of letting up.

Somebody has to do something.

Before he knew what was happening, he stepped out from behind the Dumpster and chucked the empty Busch Light as hard as he could. David stood transfixed, watching the dark brown projectile arc over the cars. Whether it was haste or a lack of aim, the bottle missed its target by at least ten feet, smashing into the side of the building well to the left of Scott. The sound of the glass breaking seemingly snapped Scott back into the moment. He released Amy and whipped his head towards the sound.

It wasn't until then David realized he was standing in the middle of the dark alley. His brain was screaming at him to run, hide—*anything*—but he remained rooted.

Somebody has to do something.

Scott turned and stared towards David. The light above illuminated Scott, throwing shadows across his face that made his smirk look positively evil.

"What the fuck was that?" Scott said.

David never knew a calm voice could sound so menacing. But, shockingly, he wasn't scared. Something had put the clamps on the terror in his brain.

Somebody has to do something.

Scott hadn't moved, still staring from the far side of his Mustang. A series of coughs came from the far corner, but both ignored them. David saw another bottle lying across the alley.

Somebody has to do something.

He lurched towards it from behind the dumpster just as the back door of the Wreck exploded open and a tidal wave of teenagers spilled out.

10

MATT EXPLODED ONTO THE STREET, frantically looking for someone—anyone—who could help. But it was deserted. He looked up and down the street, searching for anybody he could pass this responsibility off to. Panic was building.

To his right, Mill Street would surely be abandoned. Its main tenants were a bank and a hardware store, both closed for the night. He quickly turned back towards the front of the Wreck, which was still lit up and bustling with activity. It would be all kids, but there had to be somebody there that could help.

Just go. Find somebody.

As he ran towards the corner it clicked.

Hopefully they were still there.

He rounded back onto Washington and saw Bobby Fjellstead and his friends still camped out in front of the Wreck. He was entertaining the crew with an elaborate story that apparently required some intricate re-enacting.

"Dude… cops!!" Matt called out.

All four sophomores snapped their heads around and looked towards Matt. He could see them all processing the information, momentarily frozen.

"COPS!!" Matt repeated, out of breath more from the stress than the actual physical exertion.

It was Todd Sheff who finally took the bait. He slapped Bobby across the chest with a backhand and bolted through the front door of the Wreck. It took a second for the other three to catch on, but they eventually followed Todd inside. All were eager to cash in on the social rewards sure to come to whoever warned the patrons inside of the long-rumored tobacco bust.

After seeing the four sophomores depart, Matt bent over with his hands on his knees and attempted to catch his breath. He sucked lungfuls of air, then stood up and looked back towards the alley. Thank God underclassmen were always eager to prove themselves useful.

His mind was still racing, trying to comprehend what he'd seen. Scott was literally in the process of killing Amy Martin. He saw it with his own eyes — watched as Scott stood there and choked the life out of his girlfriend.

David was right.

11

IT WAS AS IF THE ENTIRE WRECK suddenly flocked out the back door, filling up the back alley instantly. He desperately scanned the crowd for Scott, but found no sign of him. It was like he'd been swallowed by the masses. Amy was nowhere to be found either, but she could easily be cowering behind the door of the Wreck.

Two kids jogged up to David.

"You see 'em?"

David stared back with total confusion, his brain fighting its way out of combat mode. The pair kept on towards the mouth of the alley, where they peeked out and carefully looked up and down the street.

A hand clamped onto David's shoulder, sending a fresh jolt of terror through him. He wheeled around, ready to throw the bottle he was no longer holding, only to see Matt. As the adrenaline seeped from his veins, he began to feel unsteady.

"What the hell's going on?" David asked.

"Let's just go," Matt replied, heading towards the street. "Come on."

David trotted a few steps to catch up, then looked back—convinced he'd see Scott striding towards him—but he was gone.

They blended in with the exodus of kids before breaking off towards Matt's house. Plenty of cars cruised up and down Main Street, and David kept a sharp eye out for a red Mustang.

"So what happened back there?" David asked.

"I told Felly and those guys the cops were coming," Matt said.

"Really?" David asked. "Wow... OK. Well they must have went in and told everybody in the Wreck, because they all came flying out back."

"Yeah, but what happened with Scott and Amy?" Matt asked.

David searched for the words. Just five minutes had passed since he watched a classmate try to kill his girlfriend. The same kid he'd seen burn a cat alive as an eight-year-old. The same kid who matched all 14 signs of a future serial killer.

"Nothing... I mean he let go when everybody came out back and then he was gone."

"So... do we call the police?" Matt asked.

"What are they going to do?" David asked.

"I don't know, arrest him or something?"

"You wanna go in there and tell the cops about Scott?" David asked. "Because if you do, he's going to know who did it."

"We could just, like, call in an anonymous tip," Matt suggested.

The image of Scott staring him down from across the alley filled David's mind.

"What are they going to do with that?" David replied. "Jesus, he'll probably be in school Monday."

"Well... I don't know," Matt said. "I mean... *somebody's* got to do something, right?"

David took a deep breath and looked off to the side. There was a pair of bicycles laying in the yard next to them. Dirt bikes. One black and gold with mag wheels, one white and red with pegs in back. It was the Stanley's house, he thought. They had young kids.

"I don't know," David said, staring into the yard. He felt like Scott's eyes were boring into him from every spot of darkness. "But we can't call the cops. He'll know."

Matt turned and walked towards his house. The streetlight on the corner blinked out, leaving the two with just the light from the moon.

"Is this for real?" Matt muttered. "I mean, do you really — *honestly* — think he is some kind of killer?"

"He's a psycho," David said. "A fucking psycho, and I don't need a list to tell me that. I've known it my whole life. Did you hear his voice? When he was choking her? Not freaking out, just as calm as can be. He was going to kill her tonight. No doubt.

"And if we hadn't walked by she'd be fucking dead."

12

SCOTT ALSTON COULDN'T GET HIS LEG to stop moving.

He was sitting in a patio chair, in the dark. There were no lights on, not in the house or the backyard he was in. There were lots of trees, giant pines on one side, and a huge weeping willow in the center of the yard. They did a good job of blocking out any light the moon or stars could provide, along with anything the streetlight may throw back. So it was dark. About as dark as you could get in town.

Scott had no idea whose yard he was in, nor did he care. He just sat there, on somebody's outdoor patio, with his knee bouncing up and down. The adrenaline was still coursing through his body. It was the most amazing feeling he had ever experienced.

Right there, in his hands. He'd had her.

He'd fantasized about it his whole life. Not her, specifically, although he definitely had dreamed of killing Amy. Taking her throat. Squeezing. Watching her eyes as the terror filled them beyond capacity, then seeing the light drain right in front of him. By his hand.

His chest felt tight. On fire. His breath was rapid. And then there was his leg. He looked down.

Still going.

He leaned back and closed his eyes. Just felt the glow inside of him. It was *so* good. The greatest feeling he'd ever had. Every second he'd held her neck was ecstasy.

But it had stopped. Why? Why had he stopped?

The bottle.

What the hell was that? He remembered a loud crash to his left. He'd wanted to ignore it. Keep going. But something told him to stop. He looked over and saw a broken beer bottle.

What's a bottle, anyway, right? He wasn't afraid of bottles.

Fuck bottles.

But there was someone. Someone out in the dark. And before he could find out who, they had all come.

So he had to stop. Run off. Leave his moment behind.

Why? Why would they all come out at that moment?

Maybe the guy sent them. Same guy that sent the bottle.

Somebody wanted to spoil his fun.

Fuck him.

That's right. Nobody was going to spoil his fun. Not anymore. Scott had a taste, and he liked it. A lot. It was amazing. The greatest thing ever. What was that stupid book his mom used to read to him?

Look at me!

Look at me!

Look at me NOW!

It is fun to have fun but you have to know how!

Now he knew how. But he couldn't have fun, no, not right now.

HA!

That's OK. He could wait. Waiting was another form of control, and he'd always had control.

He looked down again. His knee was still — *see, control* — but now there was a hard bulge in his pants. Had been there all along? Had he just not noticed it? He felt the ache of anticipation, so it must have been around a while. Maybe since he'd held her against the wall. He couldn't have all his fun now, but a little was OK. He undid his jeans and slid them down as he leaned back on the plastic chair. Scott closed his eyes and let his mind drift back 30 minutes. He could feel Amy's throat in his hand.

And he squeezed.

13

DAVID CROUCHED ON THE SIDE OF THE ROAD. *His shoelace had come undone and was completely entangled in his bike. It was wrapped around his pedal, but also stretched over and interwoven in the gears. His right knee was hurting where the gravel dug into it, but he couldn't stand up until his shoelace was free. Every time he tried to get it out of the gears, they would snap down on his fingers. Matt was there somewhere, but he was no help. David couldn't see him, but he was there. Not helping.*

In the distance he heard it. Approaching fast. He looked up from his bike and saw Scott's car flying towards him. Only it didn't sound like a car.

It sounded like a cat on fire.

The awful yowling that had been in his head for ten years grew louder as Scott approached. David frantically tried to get his shoelace free, but the gears took a small chunk off his right index finger when he reached in. The blood flowed, covering the chain, pedal and shoelace, making them too slick to hold onto. His fingers kept slipping down his shoelace as he tried to pull it free.

The caterwauling grew louder to the point it was all David could hear. It had entered his brain, clouding his thinking. He looked up and saw Matt across the road. He saw his mouth moving, screaming something, but David couldn't hear a word. Matt was frantically waving his arms towards the side of the road, so David stood up and tried to pull his bike towards the ditch. He looked down and saw the gravel had shredded his knee and a large blood spot formed on his jeans.

His mom was going to be pissed.

David saw Matt continuing to motion towards the side of the road, so he reached for the handlebars to walk his bike to the side. The grips were red hot and immediately charred his palms. He whipped his hands away and screamed, but he couldn't hear his own voice. The cat must be upon him by now. Its sound surrounded them.

David ran towards the ditch, dragging his bike along the gravel by his shoelace, which was still tightly attached to his foot. As he dove for the grass ravine, he looked back in time to see Scott's Mustang go shooting past. The color was different. It was still red, but not fire engine red. It was a glowing red like the burners on his mother's stove. Atop the car, a giant cage was strapped to the roof. Inside was the cat, fur scorched off and blisters weeping pus in waves. Noah Cooke sat next to Amy Martin, both of whom seemed oblivious to their situation.

From behind the wheel, Scott gave David that little smirk as he flew by.

When the wheels hit the puddles on the road, steam filled the air and a giant hissing sound drowned out the cat's yowling. The car continued down the road, through the stop sign and across the intersection. They flew across 225 and vaulted into the air.

The Mustang left a vapor trail behind, then crashed spectacularly into the huge pine trees that lined the cornfield that ran along the far side of county road 225.

As the burning wreckage fell to the ground, David noticed his shoelace had come undone from his bike.

And the yowling had stopped.

IT WASN'T A BAD PLAN, as night terrors go.

When he'd first bolted up from the dream, it was the same as every other time during the last ten years—drenched in sweat, frantically assessing his surroundings, faint scent of burning in his nose.

But as he sat in his bed, clock radio beaming a red 4:27 into the blackness of his room, something was different. It took a few moments before he put it together.

Every other time he'd dreamt about Scott, he'd wake with his ears ringing that horrific sound of the burnt cat's wailing. This time, it was gone.

When Scott hit those trees, it silenced the cat.

As David lay back on his bed, he couldn't help but think that maybe those trees could silence the cat for real. He and Matt had seen Scott nearly go flying across the road the day before, maybe it could happen again? *Had* it happened? Is that why he'd had the dream? Some sort of psychic premonition?

His brief glimmer of hope blinked out when logic caught up with him. He didn't believe in that psychic crap, and he'd seen enough to know that karma certainly didn't exist. Besides, the odds of Scott hitting another puddle, in the same spot, and flying into the intersection were pretty low.

Maybe I could help adjust those odds.

He knew that was crazy. There was no way around the fact that if he did anything—no matter how small—that caused Scott to crash, he would be responsible for his death. Murder, as it was called in court and in movies. David couldn't be responsible for somebody's death. He couldn't kill. He couldn't be a murderer.

He should go to the police, like Matt had said. If he told them what he saw, they'd have to listen. Scott was killing Amy right in front of them. He hit her, choked her blue.

It's not like it would be just his word, there would surely be marks.

They would have to listen.

Just like in elementary school?

It wouldn't be like that this time. It couldn't. This was much worse than stuffing a kid in a locker. They'd have to do something. If they didn't, they'd be sorry later. Scott was a ticking time bomb.

David thought back to the list he found, mentally checking off every box. He wasn't being paranoid or overly dramatic. Scott fit every characteristic of a serial killer, and just tonight was choking his girlfriend to death behind the Wreck.

Until you stopped him.

Yes, he had stopped him. There was no doubt in his mind that had he and Matt not walked by at that particular time, Amy Martin would be dead. David thought back to the sound of Scott's voice as he squeezed his fingers around her throat. Steely cold. There was no panic there, no anger. He hadn't been pushed into an uncontrollable rage. Scott had been in perfect control, and if that article was right, it was only a matter of time before he tried again. If it wasn't Amy, it would be somebody else.

Holy shit... he saw me.

THAT MONDAY IN SCHOOL, David felt Scott's stare on him all the way from Saturday night. The anxiety set up camp in the front of his brain and squeezed anything else out—Algebra and Econ be damned.

Sitting in class was bad, but the hallways were torture. Scott jumped out from every corner, stared out from every classroom and followed David everywhere, only to disappear whenever he turned around.

David shuffled between classes, his classmates a blur, until a face caught his eye on the stairs. Amy Martin was heading down to the first floor wearing a clunky peach turtleneck, despite most sweaters having been packed away in cedar chests weeks ago. He turned down the steps after her, unconsciously following even though his next class was the other direction. David watched as Amy continued into the lunchroom where students were beginning to fill the tables for study hall. She carried her books toward the tables in the far right corner, where the teacher's eat their lunch, and plopped her books down.

Right across from Scott.

David stood in the doorway for another beat, then spun around and quickly headed for the door to the auditorium. He could cut across the stage and make it to class in time. He didn't need the time to think anymore.

I have to do something.

14

THE LMCHS LIBRARY was more or less deserted as David sat leafing through back issues of *Popular Mechanics*. He'd bolted the minute study hall started, probably disappointing Matt, who was certainly hoping to collaborate on their algebra. With the amount of completed work he'd contributed over the past few months, David didn't feel bad taking a day off. Besides, his mind was too preoccupied to deal with pointless x's and y's right now.

He'd decided the police were not an option. As he debated another way to reach his objective, he kept coming back to his dream. The trees that lined 225 were probably as good as he would get. They could be untraceable, believable and final. Scott was well known for tearing around town in his car, so an accident would spawn a lot of "Unfortunately, it doesn't surprise me..." conversations.

Now he just had to find a way to make that accident happen.

When they had seen him fly across the intersection, the wet pavement provided the spark. But there was no way to count on Mother Nature doing that again, and doing something to the pavement himself was completely impractical. You'd never know who would come through there at any given time, and he'd be just as likely to kill an innocent driver as a budding serial killer.

That left Scott's car, which made much more sense since he could be sure it would affect Scott and *only* Scott. People cut the brakes all the time in movies, but it couldn't be that simple, could it? Well, apparently it could. A quick check of the *Readers' Guide to Periodical Literature* sent him to a box full of *Popular Mechanics* magazines. Articles on brake repair came with very handy diagrams of just where the brake lines were located, and a segment on "What to Do if Your Brakes Go Out" explained the mechanics of it nicely.

When you press on the brake pedal in almost all cars today, you're pushing on a piston. That piston pushes on brake fluid in the master cylinder, pressurizing the brake fluid. It flows through thin pipes, called **brake lines**, to pistons at each wheel. Those pistons apply pressure to the brake pads, and they squeeze against a disk or a drum to stop the car. If you were to have a catastrophic loss of brake fluid or if someone were to cut your brake lines, nothing would happen when you hit the brake pedal.

Sounds good.

If you had developed a small hole in your brake line, your car would have some stopping ability until most/all of the brake fluid had been forced out of the hole. When this happens, often people will notice their brakes feeling "mushy" the first time they apply them, but continue on only to find their brakes completely out when they try to stop farther down the road.

That was it. David could make a small hole in the line, then Scott would be able to back out of his garage, turn around and head up the driveway onto the Quarter Mile. He'd probably have to apply the brakes once when he turned around, then again at the end of the drive. That should be enough to force all the brake fluid out and leave him unable to stop once he revved it up on the road.

Perfect.

As he was admiring how well his plan was coming together, David had a chilling realization that he previously

84

hadn't thought about Scott's need to brake when coming out of the garage. He was just lucky he'd stumbled across this particular article. Had he just cut the brakes completely, Scott would have eased out of his garage in reverse, found himself unable to stop and probably rolled across the yard at 10 miles per hour until he either coasted to a stop or bumped up against a tree in the yard.

A fender-bender was not going to help.

Then Scott would probably look to see why his brakes hadn't worked.

He'd see the lines were cut.

Maybe he calls the police.

What if they check for fingerprints? Find mine? Holy shit.

The thought hit David hard. This wasn't a game. He'd have to be more careful than he had imagined. Think of every conceivable outcome, or there could be severe consequences.

He kept reading.

"WHAT DO YOU MEAN?" Matt asked as he looked away from his friend and down at his ball. They were putting out on the third green when David brought up the events from the previous weekend. The day they'd seen Scott skid through the intersection. The night they'd seen him try to kill his girlfriend.

Matt pulled back his putter and followed through. His ball rolled towards the hole, passed on the high side and continued a good four feet beyond the cup.

"Goddammit" he said, following the path his ball had taken past the hole.

"I mean do you think it's OK to kill someone to save somebody else's life?"

"Are you serious?" Matt asked. He stood behind his ball, looking across the green where David held the flag in his hands. He'd debated talking to Matt at all, but in the end his desire for support won out. Someone to bounce ideas off of would be useful, and subconsciously he wanted someone to help shoulder the burden. If somebody else went along with it, then he wasn't crazy.

David had planned this conversation for days, and while it wasn't going how he'd hoped, it was going as expected. After what they had seen that night, he knew Matt agreed something needed to be done about Scott Alston. But what should be done remained open to interpretation, and the further they'd gotten away from the incident behind the Wreck, the more Matt seemed to be rationalizing things.

"I don't know, I'm just asking."

"Wouldn't that make you just as bad?" Matt asked, looking down at the path his ball would have to take to the hole.

"What about Hitler," David asked. "It you could go back in time and kill Hitler, that wouldn't be a bad thing, right? Think of all the people you'd save."

Matt addressed his ball and sent it rolling four feet back and into the hole.

"Well, yeah," Matt said, bending down to pull his ball out of the hole. "I mean, if you can kill Hitler I guess you gotta do it."

David planted the flag back in the hole.

"OK, then what about somebody like Jeffery Dahmer?"

Matt looked over at David with a curious look. He could tell Matt suspected where he was going with this, and realized he was on his own. Matt was not only a fundamentally good person, he was somebody who *needed* to be a good person. It was the way he was brought up. A Midwest thing, really. Always be nice. Always be polite. Always think the right things, even when you don't. It's why so many people who have no true faith went to church every Sunday, because they were good people and that's what good people do.

David was sure that deep down Matt agreed with him on Scott. He would want to help him. He would know what David was planning was the right thing, but he wouldn't be able to make himself go along with it. Even if David was able to convince him initially, Matt would back out at the last minute. Then who knew what would happen—the conscience was a strange thing.

"Let's say you could completely get away with it."

"I don't know," Matt responded. "That's... I don't know."

The two boys walked off the green towards the fourth tee, where they had parked Matt's dad's golf cart. There wasn't a cloud in the sky and the leaves were finally filling out the trees around the course.

Matt stopped to put his putter and wedge back in the bag hanging off the back of the cart. He pulled out his three-wood and looked over at David.

"What about you? Would you do it?"

"Yup," David said, without hesitation. "In a heartbeat." He didn't know why he said it, because if he was trying to deflect any future suspicions, it was the wrong answer. Maybe he felt he needed to play a part. Maybe, deep down, he wanted Matt to know that when all this went down, he had done it.

Or maybe he just didn't want to lie to his friend.

15

ONCE DAVID REALIZED this would be a solo project, his planning began in earnest. After reading all the library could offer about brake lines, David crawled under his mom's car and located them. He then waited until dark one night and snuck under a few of the other cars on the block, just to make sure the line placement was pretty standard.

David tried to check out Scott's house every time he biked past on the way to the golf course that spring. He took note of the trees in the yard, the location of the garage, and anything else that may have changed since he had last been there as a child. But there was only so much he could take in during the 15 seconds it took them to cruise by, especially if he didn't want Matt to catch him looking.

One Sunday Matt was out of town for the weekend with his family, so David decided to take a ride out to the course on his own. He told his mom he was biking out to the driving range to hit some balls, which was true, but his main objective was to get a decent look at the Alston house. He figured on a Sunday morning, the place should be deserted until well past noon, as Pastor Alston always had his family with him at the post-worship coffee in the fellowship hall. That left only passing cars on the road, and he'd see them coming in plenty of time.

David pedaled out of the driveway just as the 10 o'clock service started and headed out of town. He met a few cars on the way, but by the time he was to the Alston house, the Quarter Mile was empty in both directions. He coasted to a stop and put his feet down.

The Alston's driveway was short by rural standards, roughly 30 yards, and covered in asphalt from the garage to the road. The detached garage remained where it had been, and Scott's parents occupied both stalls. Now on the west side, where all the wood used for the fort had been stored years ago, was a well-worn spot where Scott always parked his Mustang.

Perfect. He wouldn't have to get into the garage.

A sidewalk led from the garage to the house, where Scott's mom obviously spent a lot of time and effort keeping up her flowerbeds. They were already blooming, adding an explosion of color alongside the white siding. There were a few massive oak trees in the front yard, and a double line of evergreen trees along the west side, running parallel to the driveway between the house and the cornfield that ran along the Quarter Mile. The evergreens served as a windbreak for the house and should provide perfect cover as he approached. David could walk between them, unseen from either side, until he was alongside Scott's car, then cut across to the side of the garage.

David noticed a floodlight mounted above the garage. From here, he couldn't tell if it had a motion sensor on it. He looked at the house, which was obviously deserted, then glanced up and down the Quarter Mile.

No cars.

He checked his watch, and it was only 10:20. The Alston's wouldn't be home for at least another hour and a half. He looked down the road again, then glided his bike down the grassy decline on the far side of the driveway.

Just being in the Alston's yard threw his stomach into flips.

David hopped off his bike and quickly walked it into the trees on the west side of the property. It never hit him that if, in fact, nobody was home, he could have just gone down the paved drive and right up to the garage. Paranoia brought an abundance of caution.

Satisfied his bike was hidden from view for any passing cars, he walked down the inside of the treeline until he was even with the garage. He crept between the branches of two evergreens, but couldn't bring himself to step beyond them. David took a deep breath, reminding himself that nobody was home. After a minute, he stepped out past the trees.

The feeling of exposure was as intense as it was irrational. David was able to take two steps before the small element of panic blossoming in his brain asked him to jog, and the jog quickly morphed into a crouched run towards the side of the garage. It wasn't until his feet crunched on the gravel of Scott's parking spot that he let the breath out he never realized he was holding in. David took a second to compose himself before peering around the garage at the floodlight. A small black sensor peeked out from under the bulbs, ready to bathe the driveway in light whenever anything dared approach. That was fine, though. He looked down at Scott's parking spot. The gravel spread out into the yard beyond, and he could see packed dirt and grass intermingled with it. As long as he kept in the trees until he got behind the front of the garage, he should be able to easily avoid tripping the light.

While part of his brain was telling him to get his bike and get the hell out of there, another part began to find its voice, and it was curious. David studied the area behind the garage as he walked towards the treeline.

At the back of the yard, he saw the old shed.

He thought of the path he'd taken behind there years ago and what it led to. He felt the pull. It was unexplainable. The panic in his brain was screaming at him to get his bike and go.

David checked his watch again.

He looked back towards the road. Hidden amongst the trees, his bike was concealed from view. He stood between the garage and the trees, no longer caring if he was completely exposed. The panicked spot in his brain was throwing a tantrum, doing anything it could to get him back on the bike and pedaling away. Even the logical part of his brain nodded along with the panic, gently suggesting that maybe it would be best to get out of Dodge.

But the pull was too strong.

David turned back toward the shed and walked across the back lawn, treading the same route at the same pace he'd taken the first time his mother had dropped him off at the Alston house. The sun was spinning towards the top of the sky, taking up the dew that had covered the lawn that morning. David's shoes picked up some of the moisture that remained, but he didn't notice.

He poked his head around the back of the shed. Some of the underbrush had grown in the years since he had been there, but the path was still there.

The panicked screams in his brain had died back upon seeing the hard-packed dirt stretch back into the woods. By then, even that part was a little curious.

David stepped behind the shed and brushed aside a pair of branches as he ducked onto the path. The ribbon of dirt led back to his past. He could almost feel the rough edge of the plywood digging into his palms as he walked back.

How many trips did we make that day?

David was jerked from his thoughts when he hit the clearing. Had it been this close before? As a kid it had seemed like the fort was buried deep in the woods. In reality, it wasn't far back at all. If not for the leaves on the trees, you may even be able to see the shed from here.

The fort looked as impressive as it had when he'd been a ten-year-old builder. The wood had been greyed by the elements, but other than that it was the same. The corner of the blue tarp still dangled in the top of the doorway, hanging down from under the tangle of branches on the roof. A worn patch of brown extended out from the fort at the bottom of the entryway, the grass trampled into oblivion from years of footsteps.

But how recent? David looked around the clearing for any sign of ongoing activity back here, and found none.

The pull took him across to the fort, where he brushed aside the triangle of tarp and ducked through the doorway.

91

Built by a couple kids, the fort hadn't been designed for someone of David's height. He kept his head tilted down, still feeling the back of his head brush against the ceiling occasionally.

The air inside the fort was heavy and musty. The grass it had been built upon had died long ago, and the floor was now the hard-packed dirt of the path leading back here. The earthy smell probably came from the dirt kicked up by his footsteps.

Or was it something else? What else could be in here, dusting the air with whatever nasty particles it could slough off?

The squirrel. In the bucket. Giving off that God-awful smell of death.

A river of ice cascaded down David's spine, the curious parts of David's brain rapidly losing their nerve. The pull was the only thing that kept him there.

It took a good minute for his eyes to adjust, but even during the dark blur he could tell that there was much more inside the fort than the last time he'd been back here. He blinked the black out of his eyes and saw white shapes covering the back wall. David knew what they were, even from this distance, buried on the far end of the darkness. He knew.

Bones. Dozens of them. Maybe hundreds. Everything from the tiny toothpick bones of birds to a pair of skulls that had to be dogs. All hung up on the wall in a completely haphazard way.

Except for the center. As his pupils adjusted to soak in every bit of light available in the dank enclosure, he saw that there was one spot that Scott had actually spelled out a word.

MINE

David stared at the word written in the skeletal remains of countless animals and could hear Scott's voice echoing through the fort years ago.

"It's done now, and it's mine."

"When they're dead you can do whatever you want."

"You say a word about this and I'll kill you."

How many of those bones had he gotten by luring their owners into that silver trap of his? David wiped his hand across the back of his forehead, which was suddenly damp with sweat. He fought off a shudder of revulsion as he noticed how close to the bones he had come. As he shuffled his feet backwards, David looked down and saw an old, worn blanket that had been stretched across the floor. He quickly jumped off, then dropped to his knees to spread it out again, instantly paranoid of leaving any sign of his intrusion.

As he smoothed the tattered blanket out, he saw some magazines against the wall with a teddy bear perched on top. The bear wasn't old, but its matted brown fur had a lot of wear on it. The remains of what was once an old fashioned doctor's head mirror went around the top of its head.

Not surprising for a boy's fort, there were a couple old *Playboys* and a copy of *Penthouse*. There was also a copy of the Sears catalog that had to be at least seven years old. As he leaned forward for a closer look, he noticed a pile of *National Geographic* magazines. Along the yellow spine of each were stickers of the Lake Mills High School library.

Vietnam: The hidden war – Photos from behind the lines.

He reached out and lifted the magazine with two fingers as if it was diseased. It immediately fell open to a two-page, black and white picture. David dropped it before he could even register what it was. The magazine landed open on the blanket, the blank eyes of the stacked bodies staring at him. Two rows of them, stretching back along what looked like a street in the remains of a burned-out village. The bodies themselves looked charred, as if they had been arranged on a barbeque grill. In the foreground, a trio of American soldiers was dragging another into the frame, starting another row of death. The one holding the dead man's wrists was shirtless with a bandana holding back his red hair. For some reason, David assumed it was red, even though it was impossible to tell in a black and white picture. The two other GIs were in full fatigues, each carrying a foot.

He stared through the dark at the magazine. A crease in its spine laid it flat on the tattered blanket. The dead eyes stared up at him. He wanted to close it, to put it back and get out, but he couldn't bring himself to touch it.

So he stared.

Eventually he felt the plywood ceiling against the back of his head.

Apparently he was standing again. He reached out with the toe of his shoe and flipped the *National Geographic* closed. Now that the dead eyes couldn't see him, he could move. He bent down, grabbed the magazine by the corner and plopped it back on top of a newer issue about someplace called Rwanda. He nudged the corner back so it aligned with the rest—*it HAD been that way, right?*—and put his hand on a little stool as he pushed himself up.

Maybe it was the rush of blood back to his head as he stood, or maybe it was the realization that the stool he'd just touched was the old squirrel bucket, but either way David was good and lightheaded as he looked back down.

It may not have been the exact same bucket, he hadn't remembered the details of it, only remembered what was inside it.

What is inside it now?

He didn't want to look.

For the first time in a while, all of David's brain was in lock-step agreement. The panicked part, the logical part, the curious part and any other section he could divide up all said the same thing. The investigation was over.

It was time to get the hell out.

AFTER THE DARK OF THE FORT, the sunlight that filtered down from the trees seemed downright blinding as it streamed in David's dilated pupils. He squinted down to slits as he waited for the adjustment. Not that he was in any hurry to get his vision back. He'd seen enough.

David scanned the ground for any evidence of his presence as he crossed the clearing and started down the path. No footprints that he could see, and he hadn't dropped anything.

Go.

He walked up towards the Alston's backyard, breaking into a jog without knowing it. When he emerged behind the shed, he took a cautionary glance around the backyard before heading back towards the treeline he had come in behind.

David was about five steps beyond the shed when he could finally see around the side of the garage.

Where Scott's red mustang was now parked.

David realized he could double back behind the shed, head down the path and make his way back towards his bike through the woods without a chance of being seen by anyone in the house. Unfortunately, those thoughts came hours later when he was sitting at home, capable of thinking. In the moment, the panic he had so successfully kept at bay boiled over and seized control, giving the only command it ever does.

Run.

David tore across the back of the Alston's backyard, eyes locked on the space between the two evergreens he'd emerged from earlier. He didn't give so much as a cursory glance at the Alston house to see if someone was looking out the window. He didn't look back towards Scott's car to see if he had just parked and was getting out.

He ran. Completely exposed.

The sprint to the cover of the treeline was the fastest he had moved in his life. He blasted between the evergreens, barely putting his hands up to shield his face from the branches reaching out to claw at him.

Not stopping to look back, David turned right without breaking stride and tore down along the row of trees. As he passed Scott's car, he glanced over but was unable to see much of anything. That was good, because if he couldn't see them, they couldn't see him.

Not that logic mattered now. It was just *GO-GO-GO!!*

He skidded to a stop at the third evergreen from the end, which he had used to conceal his bike. He wrenched the handlebars away from the branches holding it up and dragged his bike through the trees to the far side of the windbreak. The cornstalks in the field next to the Alston's property were just starting to poke through, leaving him an unobstructed view of the Quarter Mile.

His lungs tried their best to catch up as he pushed his bike towards the road, bringing in huge gulps of air, but David was too panicked to be winded.

Not seeing any cars approaching from town — and not thinking clear enough to check for people coming from the other direction — David pushed his bike up the grassy ditch and hopped on. He pedaled hard down the entire stretch of road, his only thoughts were get away and get away fast.

At the junction with 225, David noticed his arms were shaking. With the vice-like grip he had on the handlebars, it was making the whole bike wobble. He had to slow down.

He coasted around the corner, taking his first look behind him as he sucked in lungfuls of air.

The road was empty.

16

SLEEP HAD BEEN SPOTTY BEFORE. After David's trip to the fort, it was non-existent.

Luckily, it appeared he had gotten out undetected. Unfortunately, any relief was trumped by what he'd seen.

MINE.

The one advantage of his insomnia was time. David lay in his bed every night that week, repeatedly going over his plan. Some nights he would nod off from exhaustion after 3 a.m. came and went. Sometimes he'd still be rolling around when the clock hit five. Maybe he'd drifted off for a bit in there. It was hard to tell what was thinking and what was dreaming.

Regular visits to the dead of night showed David that Lake Mills became a ghost town after midnight on a weekday. He spent a good amount of time peering out his bedroom window, checking the activity level after 1 a.m., but never saw so much as a neighborhood cat. If he left his house in the middle of the night, around 2 a.m. or so, the roads should be deserted and he could get out to the Alston house in 20 minutes. The only people awake would be the third shift workers at Larson Manufacturing, and they were all busy making storm doors.

While Cathy Rowe had never mentioned anything to her son, David knew his mother had been relying on sleeping pills for years. This meant that once she was down, she was out, and he should have no problems getting out of the house without waking her. David, who didn't have the advantage of pharmaceuticals, had been getting up in the middle of the night for years and couldn't remember a time when his mother so much as stirred.

Once he got out of his house, David's bike should get him back out to Alston's without a problem. He even went as far as checking his chain and the air pressure in his tires to eliminate any potential problem. Once out there, he would leave his bike along the trees and make his way between the lines of evergreens just as he had before. With Scott's car parked on the far side of the garage, he would be able to keep out of sight from anyone in the house the entire time. And if, somehow, somebody came out of the house, he now realized he could easily slip back into the trees, then into the woods behind the house.

The layout couldn't be more perfect for him.

For himself, David dug up an old pair of black jeans and a navy hooded sweatshirt. He originally thought the hood would be enough, then reconsidered and dug though the closet until he found his old knitted ski mask. It was a little small, but it was dark and would cover his face.

You can't be too careful.

David's mother had recently refinished an old trunk in the basement, so he grabbed a pair of the latex gloves she'd used when staining. That should keep any potential fingerprints from showing up anywhere. In the back of his closet, David found an old pair of Asics running shoes. They were a size and a half too small, extremely beat up and he hadn't worn them in over a year, but he had decided whatever shoes he wore that night would be thrown away immediately. That way, any footprints found couldn't be traced back to him.

For the cutting, David zeroed in on his trusty Swiss Army Knife. Either blade would make quick work of the standard rubber hose, while the hacksaw blade or even the leather punch would help if Scott had upgraded to some of the stronger aftermarket hoses David had read about during his research.

Within a week, it had all come together. All David needed to do was pick a night.

17

MRS. SHALES STOOD IN FRONT of a giant Periodic Table of the Elements, which she had pulled down over the chalkboard, and droned on about atoms. Or maybe it was protons. Even if David had been sleeping regularly, it would have been brutal. Their chemistry teacher had been giving the exact same lessons at Lake Mills High School for the past 30 years, and wasn't exactly known for her engaging teaching style. She could point her worn yardstick to an element on the table without even turning around, which would have been impressive if it hadn't been so mind-numbingly boring.

"Hydrogen atoms react with each other to form Hydrogen gas, or H2."

David leaned forward on his hands. Half the class had their heads down on the glossy black tables spaced around the room like little two-person islands. Each had a pair of stools and a sink facing the center aisle of the classroom. David's lab partner, John Bach, was leaning back and quietly drumming a pair of pencils against his knee. He was one of the lucky few whose stool had a back. There were only three in the class, and they were highly prized. It was an incentive to get to class early, so you could pull a quick switch if your lab partner wasn't there yet.

David wondered if John had switched today. He could have used a back. The lack of sleep had initially taken its toll on David, but he thought he was getting used to it.

The dark bags under his eyes disagreed, and Mrs. Shales's recycled lecture wasn't helping. It wasn't just the content, but the delivery. Flat. Monotonous. Utterly boring. It was impossible to keep the mind from wandering. For the hundredth time, he mentally went over his plan. It was foolproof. He had thought of everything. Every contingency he could come up with had an answer and a way out. It was going to work.

Tonight was the night.

Think about all the people he would save. Not just Amy Martin, but all the people Scott would hurt in the future.

He'd be a hero.

Well, not really, since nobody will ever know what you did.

That was true. He'd really wished Matt were in this with him. It would have been good to have a sounding board. Someone to collaborate and bounce ideas off of. But it wasn't to be. David knew Matt didn't have the will to do this, and that's OK. That's the reason he had to do it, because nobody else had the will. Was it an unpleasant job, yes, but that didn't mean it didn't need to be done.

Ask one of Jeffery Dahmer's victims if they wished somebody had taken care of him long ago.

Mrs. Shales finished up by assigning another chapter for her class to read. David didn't bother to write it down as he got up and headed for the door. He joined the logjam, waiting to squeeze out into the hallway, then joined another river of students trickling down the steps. David made a pit stop at his locker, where he tossed his Applied Chemistry book on the top shelf and shut the door. He didn't bother grabbing any other textbooks before heading down to the lunchroom for study hall. Matt would be there working on their algebra, and David figured it was his turn to get some answers.

Matt was already camped at their customary table, stuff spread out all over his side. David dropped his notebook down, but kept walking.

"Gotta whizz," he said as he passed by. Matt barely looked up from his work. David hadn't noticed much lately, but he did notice that.

Probably pissed he won't be getting any free answers today. Sorry, but I've got something a bit more important than math on my mind.

David pushed open the door and took a spot at the nearest urinal. As he positioned himself, he heard the door open. He was at full stream when Scott Alston took a spot two urinals down from him.

A tiny little wind-up monkey was doing flips in his stomach. It wasn't really fear, surprisingly. David had realized Scott probably hadn't recognized him that night behind the Wreck, mostly due to the fact he was still alive. But it was something. Anticipation? Reluctance? David thought about it as he emptied his bladder into the full-length porcelain urinal. He glanced over at Scott. Even the way he peed screamed arrogance. His legs were spread in an especially wide stance, almost as if he was trying to take up as much space as possible. His head was tilted back with his face towards the ceiling, eyes closed.

Before David had a chance to look away, Scott's eyes snapped open and found his. David whipped his head back towards the wall. He finished up, quickly shook off the last drips and zipped up. He bolted across the bathroom, past the line of sinks and towards the door.

"Hey!"

The word ricocheted between the painted brick walls, the tile floor and around the inside of David's head like a bullet. It stopped him in his tracks. Half his brain was screaming at him to get out of there, but his feet were in concrete.

"Were you watching me pee?" Scott asked, not loudly, but David could hear the aggressive undertones in his voice. He said nothing. His eyes were closed. Somehow, for the first time he wasn't scared. He hated Scott. Hated him for what he was. Hated him for what he did to Amy Martin, Noah Cooke and God knows who else. But most of all, David hated Scott for making him live with what he had seen in the woods so many years ago. He hated him for the cat. A stupid farm cat that nobody cared about. Except Scott. He cared enough to trap it, douse it with lighter fluid and light it on fire.

"You aren't a faggot, are you?" Scott asked. "Or maybe you just like watching me, huh?"

Just three feet shy of the door, David turned around.

"You're always watching me, aren't you? You think I'm not paying attention, but I notice. I always notice. I notice everything. You're a little obsessed. But that's OK. I'm goddam fascinating."

Had he seen me?

"So how come you don't come out to my house anymore, Davey? We could go hang out in the fort."

One thing David never figured out was why Scott had shared that experience with him. It obviously hadn't been the first time, and he hadn't needed any help. It wasn't fair. David hadn't wanted that burden. Had Scott truly thought David would enjoy it? Was it some sort of twisted hand of friendship being offered, and was Scott now upset David had rejected him? Had he been trying to intimidate him? Torment him the same way he had been tormenting animals. Start with toys, then move up to animals before going after people.

Maybe he was just tired of hiding what he was from the world and picked David to reveal himself to.

David thought he was incapable of words. He'd gone over a million things in his head he'd wanted to say, but those were all fantasy. Imaginary tough talk that people always think about but rarely have the guts to put out in the world. But as David stood there, knowing what he planned to do that night, his hatred of Scott drowned out his fear. He figured he may as well take the moment before he retreated out the door back into the safety of study hall.

It wasn't like he'd have tomorrow.

"That was me, you know, behind the Wreck. I know what you are."

18

WHEN HIS CLOCK FINALLY FLASHED 1:59, David reached over to his nightstand and shut off the alarm. It had been set to go off at 2:00, but that was just a precaution. There had been no illusion that sleep would be an option. David knew he had to keep to his normal schedule, so after his mom went to bed, he shut his door at 10:30 and turned on *The Late Show*. He lay in bed with the lights off, watching one of Letterman's stage managers chuck watermelons off the roof of the studio. Then back-to-back re-runs of *Cheers*, eventually followed by the bread-and-butter of late-night television – infomercials. None really registered for David. Mostly he watched the clock.

He swung his legs over the side of his bed and took a deep breath. This was a moment that would change his life forever. Once it was over, he would be a murderer. There would be no way around that fact, no matter how much he might try to bury it in justifications, no matter how deserving the victim was. But that thought never crossed his mind. David just reached down for the clothes he had specially selected and got dressed.

His door opened without a sound and he padded down the hallway. His shoes were along the side of the garage, next to his bike. David briefly paused next to his mother's room, and could hear her light snoring through the door. If something somehow went wrong, the burden on his mother would probably be too much to bear. The death of her husband all those years back was still something she hadn't gotten over, and to have her only child involved in this would have been brutal.

This was also something David didn't think of that night.

He slipped out the front door and peered down the street. As expected, Lake Mills was tucked in for the night. David threw on his shoes and glided down the driveway and into the street. He pedaled hard to get out of town quickly, figuring that was the best chance for him to be seen. David scanned the houses as he passed, looking for lights in windows. He sure didn't want to get spotted by some old guy that couldn't sleep two hours without taking a piss. He flew down Winnebago Street and headed out of town. It was always amazing how well you could see at night when you got into the country. The lines on the road practically glowed as the moonlight bounced off the asphalt. The stars were as brilliant as ever, and seemed to double the farther you got from the streetlights. They so mesmerized David that the trip out to the Quarter Mile went by in a blink. He didn't even notice the trees across from the intersection that were so crucial to his plan.

Shortly after making the final turn towards Scott's house, David's eyes were ripped from the skies by a pair of headlights heading towards him in the distance. It was something he had planned for, so while his heart started beating like a hummingbird, he didn't really panic. The ditches along the side of the Quarter Mile were at least 8-10 feet deep, and David knew if he had to, he'd be able to hide in them as any car passed. He immediately cut across the gravel on the side of the road, hopped off his bike and flattened out along the grassy slope as his bike slid down towards the bottom. David could feel his heart beating in his chest as he waited for the car to pass. As he hugged the grass, he glanced down at his bike and realized there was one thing he hadn't thought about—the reflectors. Little silver rectangles waiting to throw back the beam of a headlight and scream, "DOWN HERE!!! LOOK DOWN HERE!!"

David rolled down the ditch toward his bike and dove on top of it. He clasped his hand over his front reflector, while trying to block off the pedal and wheel reflectors with his body. David held his breath and felt his heart hammering all the way up in his ears. He was just waiting to hear the crunch of gravel as the car pulled to the side of the road.

I shouldn't have hit the ditch. I should have just kept riding like I had nothing to hide.

As far as headlights cut through the darkness, the oncoming car was much farther away than David had thought, giving him an agonizing amount of time to wait in the ditch. His mind was racing, trying to come up with an excuse he could use when the car got here.

He looked up and saw a pair of empty beer cans sitting in a puddle at the bottom of the ditch.

Beer. I'll tell him I ditched some leftover beer here the other night on the way back from a party at North Shore. Had to get out here when nobody would see me. Couldn't find it, though. Some asshole probably took it. He'll buy it. High school kids are always doing stupid things for a couple cans of beer. He'll definitely buy it. Just laugh and tell his friends about it later. 'Shoulda seen this kid...'. Then go into some story about when he was a high school drunk. He'll buy it. Definitely. He'll buy it.

It took the car almost two minutes to pass the spot where David went in the ditch, easily the longest two minutes of his life. He then waited another five to make sure the car was long gone. Each second he laid in the grass, he expected to hear a door slam and somebody yell down to him, but it never happened. Eventually, he crawled off his bike and up the side of the ditch. He looked up and down the road about five times before finally realizing he was in the clear. David quickly made his way back down the ditch and hauled his bike back up towards the road. He ignored the stars and pedaled hard for the last half mile.

As David came up on the driveway, he veered off to the shoulder and once again hopped off his bike. The ditch was

105

shallower here, so he quickly walked his bike down the hill and in-between the row of trees that lined the West side of the Alston's yard. His forehead was covered in a sheen of sweat that was rapidly evaporating in the cool night air. His palms were a swamp, and David rubbed them on his jeans. He wheeled his bike down the line and away from the road, then propped it up against one of the trees. Head on a swivel, he slunk down the dark line of evergreens til he was past the front of the garage. He scanned the yard, both front and back, while trying to morph into the biggest tree in the line. He saw no movement whatsoever and, before he could have second thoughts, bolted across the yard towards Scott's car.

David huddled down against the wheel and wasted no time getting down on the ground and under the car. Pen light in his mouth, he found the brake line right where *Popular Mechanics* had shown. There were no upgrades, so he used the small blade on his knife. A bit of brake fluid came out when he withdrew his knife and dripped down on his hand. It dripped a few times and stopped – not enough that it would leave a noticeable puddle. He wiggled his way out, and did the other lines. Within a few minutes, he was once again whisking across the yard towards the trees. The motion sensor never caught wind of him, remaining dormant the entire time. As he hit the treeline, David paused a second and glanced back at the Alston house. Dark and quiet. Nobody had randomly popped out of bed and decided to take a quick walk out in the yard.

It seemed like it had gone perfectly.

Now get the hell out of here.

The ride home was a blur. No cars, no ditches and no made-up, beer-finding cover stories. He didn't even notice the stars, although they were as brilliant as before. He just rode for home—hard. He'd gotten this far, and the thought of getting busted now was unconscionable. He pedaled as fast as his legs would allow the entire way, riding away from what he'd done. It was over now, and soon he could just leave it behind, where it belonged.

106

The streets of Lake Mills were still deserted when he hit town. He raced down Lake Street, flew into his driveway and ditched his bike by the garage. He peeled off his shoes and carried them in the house with him. His mom's snoring hadn't changed since he left, and he slipped into his room where he sat down on his bed and shed his clothes.

The clock on his nightstand glowed 3:18.

David flopped back onto his bed and took a deep breath. He lay on his back, looked up at the ceiling and closed his eyes. There was no tossing and turning, no watching TV, no struggling to find the most comfortable position. For the first time since he was 10 years old, the minute David's head hit the pillow he was out.

19

"BIG, BIG, BIG DAY GIRLIE!!" Kim Peterson sang. She was bouncing around the kitchen, looking for her purse. She couldn't remember how many trips to Mason City began with her telling Leah it was a 'Big Day', but this could be the biggest yet. A clean test today, and her little girl was cured. Well, maybe not 'officially' cured—you don't get that distinction until you've been cancer-free for 10 years—but the doctors had said if this one comes back good, they are 99.99% in the clear. That was good enough for Kim.

Could this really be the end? Or, at least, the beginning of the end? It seemed like forever ago that Kim took Leah to the doctor to check on those nosebleeds she kept getting. She hadn't thought anything of it. When the doctor asked her about the bruises on her legs, Kim figured he was checking for signs of abuse, which she vehemently denied. Sure Leah had a lot of bruises, but she was an active four-year-old. She was always running around crashing into things. Little kids always had bruises, didn't they?

Apparently not like that. Combined with the nosebleeds, the doctor wanted to do some more tests. Kim's mind had gone wild, terrified of some rare bleeding disorder. Cancer never invaded her thoughts, and it wasn't until all the blood was drawn and they had sat alone in the exam room for 30 minutes that the doctor had mentioned the word 'leukemia'.

Kim had been floored. Cancer? In her little girl? Impossible. There was no history of cancer in her family. Certainly some bruises and a few nosebleeds didn't mean cancer for her little girl. Leah was only four years old for God's sake.

The tests came back positive. Acute Lymphocytic Leukemia. The doctors talked about catching it early. They talked numbers like white cell count of less than 50,000 and 90% remission rate. They called it "low-risk", but all she heard was that her little girl had cancer. She remained in shock until 3 a.m. that morning, when a soft sobbing drifted into her room. As she walked down the dark hallway towards the room she had painted pink with rainbows at Leah's request, she realized how much her little girl needed her. From that point on, Kim Peterson was the epitome of positivity. She routinely talked about fighting this as a team, with Leah as the captain.

Team Leah started chemotherapy the next week.

It was so hard for Kim to watch Leah go through it, she couldn't imagine what it was like for a four-year-old. They would sing silly songs while thick needles were jabbed into Leah's spine, injecting poison that would hopefully kill all the cancer cells before killing too many of the healthy ones. Kim got books of knock-knock jokes so Leah could tell them to the nurses as they came in to place another I.V. Kim held Leah's hair as she threw up countless times into a bucket by her bed, and cleaned her sheets and blankets when she didn't make the bucket in time.

After the first month, the doctors said they'd killed 99.1% of the cancer cells. Unfortunately, that left 100 million still alive in her little girl. So they moved on to phase two, the consolidation treatment, which was even worse than the initial chemo. There were more spinal taps, more vomiting and extreme fatigue. It was by far the most grueling, but when Team Leah thought they were at their limit, the cavalry showed up.

To say the attention had been overwhelming was an understatement. As their story filtered through the barbershop and knitting circles, people Kim barely recognized began stopping her in the grocery store, asking what they could do to help. And Leah, well, she became a local celebrity. She was featured in the local newspaper, and two of the local television stations interviewed them about the benefit set up for them. Seeing herself on TV, sporting one of her Team Leah t-shirts, may have been the best medicine she received throughout her treatment. Kim had recorded the broadcast, and for weeks Leah was always asking to see "her tape".

Yes, Lake Mills had come through. If today's test came back clean, she and Leah wouldn't be the only ones celebrating. When Kim had told Leah's preschool teacher that she'd be absent today, she could hardly contain her excitement.

Team Leah was much bigger now.

"C'mon Team, let's do it!!"

20

*K*NOCK, KNOCK, KNOCK
      It was such a foreign sound, coming from far away — slowly dragging David up from a deep, deep hole of sleep. The sleep was so deep, so satisfying, so real, that David overslept for the first time since... well... ever. He lifted his head up. He was on his back, in the exact position he had been in a few hours earlier, and he let his head fall back to his pillow with a thud. He could probably lie there for three more days.

"Time to get up,"

It was his mom, making sure he was up for school. The fog of sleep made these thoughts come much slower than they normally would. Had he really been *that* tired? He rubbed his eyes and rolled over on his right side.

A dark blur on the floor slowly sharpened into the pile of clothes he'd shed before flopping into bed. It wasn't until then that his mind snapped into coherence and he remembered the night before.

Holy shit. It's really done.

"Hey. You up?" his mom asked from the other side of the door.

He half-jumped, half-fell out of bed and lunged for the clothes. He snatched them up and stuffed them under his bed.

"Yeah... yeah," David said. He stifled a yawn and shook his head clear.

Jesus Christ. What if Mom would have come in and seen them?

In reality, she wouldn't have noticed anything out of the ordinary. A pile of clothes on a 16-year-old boy's floor was evidence of nothing. The panic began to fade, and David glanced up at his clock.

7:50.

"Well, I'm off to work," Cathy Rowe said. "Just wanted to make sure you were up and going."

"Yeah, I'm up... sorry."

David grabbed a pair of shorts from his dresser and went looking for a t-shirt. He'd have to forego the shower today. Then he remembered the brake fluid on his hands. He whipped his hand up to his nose and smelled.

What did brake fluid smell like? Was that it? Was it something else? Or nothing?

David wasn't taking any chances. He looked back at the clock again. He could pull a quick shower. Just to be on the safe side.

He bolted out of his room and popped down the hallway. His mother was at the kitchen door, leaving for work when he came through on his way to the shower downstairs.

"Cutting it a little close today, huh?" She asked as he made his way down the stairs.

"Yeah, I overslept," he responded over his shoulder. "Sorry."

"Maybe you need to keep the T.V. off in bed," Cathy hollered down the steps, but David was already gone.

HE WAS OFF HIS BIKE and through the school doors by 8:25, breakfast be damned. As he walked down the hall, David was struck by just how normal everything was. He treaded towards his locker, bucking the tide of kids already headed to their first class of the day. By the time he was putting his backpack away the crowd had thinned considerably. Almost everyone was sitting in their first period classrooms, with the rest hustling down the hallways to get there.

As he reached up for his civics book, David caught sight of Carl and Russ Blake rounding the corner at the end of the row of lockers. His breath stopped, positive he would see Scott following right behind them. David had been keeping a paranoid eye out since he'd arrived at school, but hadn't seen any sign of him.

He wasn't with the Blake boys either. David let out the breath that had caught in his throat and closed his eyes. He pretended to be looking for something in his bag while Carl and Russ walked by his locker. They didn't seem any different than normal, so they must not have heard anything about their boss yet. After they passed by, David grabbed his books and shot down the hall to his first period class.

He ducked into Mr. Roderick's classroom as the daily announcements were ending. His teacher looked at David from behind his glasses, then glanced up at the clock, but said nothing. David slid into the closest open desk and plopped his textbook down.

Has it happened yet?
It must have.
But how do I know?
He's not here.
How do I know THAT?
Where else would he be?
Act natural. Act normal.

This was going to be a surreal day.

NOTHING WAS DIFFERENT throughout first period.

Or second.

Or third.

As the day drug on with no news, David grew more and more nervy. Between classes, he continually scanned the crowd for Scott. He walked past his locker three times, but there was no sign of him. Once, he was convinced he saw him heading down the stairwell, but it was somebody else. A sophomore. Or maybe just his imagination.

Of course it wasn't him. He wasn't here, and he isn't coming.

But the waiting was torture. The not knowing. It was going to drive him nuts.

Luckily, Matt was finishing up his final project for Government, so he took off for the library as soon as study hall started and saved David forty minutes of trying to act natural. Then again, after the last few months Matt was probably used to it by now.

The rumors started circulating in the lunch line. Somebody had been down in the office, and a whole bunch of people were in Principal Donald's office. Something big was going down, because one of the cops was there and the secretary was crying. That story spread through about half the cafeteria during lunch, but David hadn't caught a whiff of it when the intercom crackled to life.

"Attention students... please report to the auditorium for an assembly at 12:30. Thank you."

The announcement sent the rumor mill into overdrive. It also sent the butterflies that had set up camp in David's stomach into a frenzy.

Holy shit... this is it.

"What's that about?" Matt asked.

David looked across the table, trying to figure out what to say. His nerves were firing on all cylinders, but he also felt an odd excitement creeping up inside of him. There was no doubt about it now. Why else would they call an assembly?

"I dunno," David replied. He shoveled a forkful of diced peaches into his mouth in an attempt to look nonchalant. "Guess we'll find out in 15 minutes."

David went from picking at his food to wolfing it down. Whether his appetite came roaring back or he was just anxious to get to the auditorium he wasn't sure, but he did know one thing. This was almost over. As soon as Scott's death became public knowledge, the weight of secrecy pressing down on him would lift. Everyone would know what he did.

Well, not EVERYTHING.

But it would be enough. He'd be able to talk about it with people, and wouldn't have to hide what he knew. That would make the pressure go away. It would be like that week in fourth grade. That week everyone was happy.

It HAD to be.

The two boys finished up their lunches and dumped their trays before joining the herd headed towards the school's auditorium.

THE LMCHS AUDITORIUM was an odd relic. In keeping with school colors, the seats had been recently re-upholstered in a bright purple, but the walls and floor clashed with an ugly, faded green color that had been in place since the 1960s. The seats all slanted down towards the stage, which was raised about five feet and had steps leading down to the floor on each side. A group of teachers huddled together at the top of the steps on the left side, alternately talking to each other and looking out to see if the students were taking their places. David saw Principal Donald, Superintendent Beamer and both the high school and elementary guidance counselors amongst them.

"Wonder what the deal is?" Matt said, nodding towards the adults on stage. One of the town cops had walked through the stage door and said a few words to the superintendent before ducking back out.

All David could manage was a half shrug.

Students continued to pour into the seats, raising the volume of the room as they did. Mr. Roderick and Mr. Herman were walking the aisles, doing their best attempt at crowd control, herding the kids into the nearest empty seats and trying to keep the goofing around to a minimum. The crowd didn't seem too concerned about why they had been called together, content to enjoy the fact that this would surely cut into their sixth period class time.

At 12:30, Principal Donald disengaged from the group at the side of the stage and walked to the center with his hand raised to quiet the crowd. Mr. Roderick was standing in the center aisle, and David noticed that other teachers had fanned out in the aisles throughout the auditorium. The buzz dropped as Principal Donald tapped his microphone.

Here we go.

"Students," Mr. Donald began. "This morning, there has been a terrible accident. There was a car wreck just outside of town, and it has taken one of the most beloved members of our school from us."

A hushed murmur washed over the assembled students, knocking away any stray conversation that had been left over from lunch. Their attention locked on the stage. David almost laughed at the notion that Scott Alston was "beloved" at this school, but realized that everyone is beloved after a sudden death. A semi-martyrdom for Scott was a small price to pay for protecting society from a monster.

If you all only knew.

"As many of you know, Leah Peterson bravely fought cancer over the last year and was doing great in her fight. This morning, Leah and her mother, Kim, were headed down to Mason City for a doctor's appointment when they were involved in a tragic accident near Rice Lake."

The collective gasp took all the air out of the auditorium. David stared at the stage in utter disbelief.

What?

"The police have informed me that both Leah and her mother Kim were killed in the accident."

David's mind screamed a wall of white noise as the room went silent. He had been preparing himself to appropriately react to this 'tragic' news all morning, but now it had come in flipped on its head. He scanned the room in a rising panic, now expecting to see the back of Scott's head in the front row, putting his arm around Amy to comfort her.

How did this happen?

Sobbing broke from a group of volleyball players sitting together near the front of the auditorium. Voices quickly rose and created a din throughout the room. Principal Donald raised his hand in an attempt to quiet the crowd. Teachers were moving throughout the aisles, some kneeling down talking with students, some trying to keep things orderly. Mr. Burns, who also served as the volleyball coach, was hugging one of his players down front.

Principal Donald resumed speaking, but the static that filled David's head obscured everything that followed. Then a single thread pulled his mind back to the moment.

"It also appears that Scott Alston was involved in the accident."

The auditorium immediately quieted again. David snapped back to coherence, once again hanging on every word.

"Scott has been taken to Mercy Hospital by ambulance, but we don't know much about his condition right now except it is very serious."

Principal Donald continued to talk about losing one of our own, comfort in friends, strength in togetherness and counselors being available, but David heard none of it. Matt also tried to say something to him, but it passed right through.

The only thing David could hear was the nothingness in his head.

"Holy shit," Matt whispered.

The principal wrapped up, insisting that any student with the need talk to one of the counselors available. The students silently began to file out towards their sixth period classes. Matt stood and looked down at his friend, who was still staring at the stage.

"I can't believe it," Matt said. "I mean, how does this happen?"

David didn't hear him.

21

LAKE MILLS, IA - Tragedy struck Lake Mills Wednesday morning when a two-car accident took the life of 4-year-old Leah Peterson and her mother, Kim (30). The accident occurred on Winnebago County Road 34, approximately two miles south of Lake Mills.

The Peterson's were traveling east on CR 34 when they were struck head-on by another car. The driver, eighteen-year-old Scott Alston, was taken by ambulance to Mercy Hospital in Mason City, where he is listed in critical condition.

"It looks like the westbound vehicle was attempting to pass another car when he struck the oncoming vehicle in the eastbound lane," Winnebago County Sheriff Ed Schwab said.

John Charlson was driving along CR 34 and witnessed the accident.

"I saw that car come flying up in my rear-view mirror," the 71-year-old Lake Mills resident said. "I could tell there was no way he was going to make it around me, so I figured he was just going to (drive up to) my (car). Then as he got up to me he whipped into the lane and right into that van."

The accident remains under investigation by the Winnebago County Sheriff's Office.

Leah Peterson was well known in the Lake Mills community after fighting leukemia over the past year. Her "Team Leah" shirts, which were sold to raise money for her treatment, are commonly seen around town. She also served as an honorary captain for the Lake Mills High School volleyball team.

"Leah was just an amazing presence to be around," Lake Mills Elementary Principal Michael Timmerman said. "Throughout her fight, she was always upbeat and positive. Every day she was at school she brought an amazing light, no matter what she was going through with her treatment. Everybody was Leah's friend."

A memorial service for Leah and Kim Peterson will be held Friday evening at 5 p.m. in the LMCHS Gymnasium.

22

"ARE YOU GOING to that memorial tonight?"
The question hung suspended over the lunch table long enough that Matt would have believed David hadn't heard him, had he not been looking directly in his face when he said it.

Yup, find me and I'll save you a seat.
Not sure, gotta talk to my parents and see what the plan is.
Nah, It'll probably be really depressing.

Those would have been normal responses.

He was debating asking again when David blinked himself out of whatever conversation-killing trance he was in and re-joined the land of the speaking.

"Huh?"

Not exactly what Matt was looking for. He didn't bother repeating himself.

"I've got to go to that thing in the gym tonight with my mom and dad, but I'm thinking about heading uptown after. Wanna meet up there?"

David hesitated long enough that Matt thought he was going to ignore that question too.

"Nah, not tonight," he said. "Can't."

"You sure? I could pick you up. It's been a while since we shot some stick—I'll even let you win this time."

Matt watched as David rubbed his forehead with the back of his hand, still holding the fork he'd loaded with fruit cocktail three minutes ago.

"I'm just not feeling it," David said.

Matt considered his response as he reached down for his brownie. He'd gotten a corner piece, which in the LMHS cafeteria meant roughly one bite would be edible. The rest would be nothing short of petrified chocolate.

"I guess I thought you'd be in a better mood now, with all that's happened."

David's eyes snapped to Matt's for the first time.

"What the fuck does that mean?" David's voice was filled with an edge Matt hadn't heard before. He looked around, but the general roar of lunchtime drowned out any uptick in David's voice.

"I'm just saying, with all that's... happened..."

David dropped his fork with a clatter before Matt could finish. The two sat there in a long silence before David picked up his tray and dumped it on the way out, leaving Matt by himself at their regular spot trying to make sense of what just happened.

Maybe his friend felt guilty about the way they were talking about Scott before all this happened. Heck, just a few weeks back they all but wished he would get killed in some sort of accident.

It's not like that had any effect on anything—idle talk can't cause an accident—but a guy's conscience can be fickle. Who knows what kind of misplaced guilt David was feeling?

Probably shouldn't have mentioned the memorial.

23

MASON CITY, IA - Lake Mills High School student Scott Alston remains in a coma a week after a tragic accident that took the lives of 4-year-old Leah Peterson and her mother Kim.

Alston was attempting to pass on County Road 34 south of Lake Mills last Wednesday when he struck the Peterson van head-on. He was initially taken to Mercy Hospital, then transported to University of Iowa Hospitals and Clinics in Iowa City where he remains in a medically induced coma.

According to his father, Salem Lutheran Church Pastor Len Alston, his son suffered severe head injuries, along with two broken legs and various other injuries. The 18-year-old has undergone surgeries on both his legs since arriving in Iowa City, with more planned as he heals. He is listed in serious but stable condition.

"We pray every day for the Lord to place his healing hands on Scott," Pastor Alston said. "We know God is great and he will lead Scott through this. Through Him all things are possible."

The Winnebago County Sheriff's office says the accident is still under investigation and won't rule out charges being filed in the future.

24

ED SCHWAB WAS RESTLESS. He'd been waiting in this goddam office for 40 minutes, drumming his fingers on the wooden armrests of his chair, impatiently tugging on his thick, bushy moustache and bouncing his knee up and down. Ed's hulking 6-4 frame barely fit in the chair across from the giant desk littered with paperwork, so it hadn't taken him long to get up and wander the room. He passed the time by reading every worthless diploma displayed on the wall and the title of every book on the shelf, probably all of them unread.

Dr. Spencer's secretary had twice asked him if he wanted any coffee as he waited.

No, just remind Dr. *Spencer that* Sheriff *Schwab would like to speak with him, as soon as he finds the time in his preciously busy schedule.*

As Winnebago County Sheriff, this Peterson accident investigation was his responsibility, and it had been sitting on his desk for the past month. At this point, he knew all he needed to about what happened. This kid, whom everybody says loved to tear around the countryside in his muscle car, goes flying down the road and tries to pass an old codger in his truck. He's not paying attention, and he runs head-on into a van, killing that poor girl and her mother.

It was about as open and shut as it could be, and the only thing he was missing was an interview with Scott

Alston. It was just a formality, really. What was the kid going to say? There wasn't much of an excuse he could think of. The tox screen showed no drugs or alcohol, so the most they could hope for is a Class C felony, which would be up to ten years. Not enough for killing a little girl with cancer as far as Ed was concerned, but it would have to be good enough.

Unfortunately, he wasn't going to be able to do anything until the doctors let him talk. Ed had called the hospital the minute he heard Alston was out of his coma, but they said he wouldn't be able to come for at least a week.

Bullshit.

All he needed was the official statement from Alston and he could send it to the county attorney, who would charge him with vehicular homicide. Ed didn't care what some hospital bureaucrat said. He drove down to Iowa City first thing the following morning and camped out in the office of Tim Spencer, M.D., Ph. D, Chairman of Neurology and la-dee-frickin-da.

Ed was glaring at a framed picture of Spencer and three other jackasses dressed in ski gear on top of some mountain when the door opened and Dr. Spencer walked in. He was even shorter than Ed had imagined. Beady eyes, glasses. Just a little weasel of a guy.

Probably gets his thrills off making guys like me wait on him. I bet he was just sitting in his doctor lounge, chuckling with his doctor buddies.

"Sheriff, Tim Spencer," He said, heading across the room. It wasn't until he was behind his desk that he extended his hand. "Sorry to have kept you waiting, but I've got a full clinic this morning. What can I do for you?"

Ed took his hand in a firm grip. Dr. Spencer made no move to sit down, so Ed remained standing.

"As I'm sure you were told, I need to talk with Scott Alston."

The doctor broke off his gaze and settled back into his oversized leather chair. He crossed his legs and tented his fingers in front of him.

"And as I am sure you were told, that will not be possible today. Scott's condition is still delicate, and there is no way he is ready for visitors of any sort."

Ed bristled at the doctor's response and drew up his full height as he looked down at the small white coat in the chair.

"I'm not a visitor, Doctor, I'm a law enforcement officer. This young man was involved in an accident that killed two people, one of them a little girl, and I need to talk to him, immediately."

Dr. Spencer seemed unintimidated by the giant badge towering over him.

"Sheriff..." He let his eyes lift towards the ceiling and took a deep breath. "Scott Alston has just come out of a month-long coma. He has suffered severe brain trauma. His legs were shattered. You have to understand that he is still extremely weak and heavily medicated."

Ed was visibly frustrated. He stepped away from the desk and put his hand over his mouth, stroking his moustache with thumb and forefinger. He saw a line of pigeons on the roof outside the window behind Dr. Spencer's desk. Dirty birds. A single blast from his 12-gauge would probably take out the lot of them.

"When will he be ready?" he asked, still staring out the window.

"I don't know. Brain injuries are almost impossible to predict."

Ed looked down at the doctor in his chair.

"But you are the expert, right? Isn't that why you make the big money, to predict these things? Or am I thinking about somebody else?"

Dr. Spencer closed his eyes and shook his head in condescending amusement. It made Ed want to chuck him out the window.

"I wish it were that easy," he said. "I really do want to help you, Sheriff, but these things take time. Right now our focus is continuing to heal Scott's body and finding out where he is at mentally. We've begun some initial cognitive testing, and we'll continue as we are able to wean him off the painkillers he is on."

Ed could see this slipping away from him.

"Well, what if I went down to that old fashioned courthouse you guys have downtown and got myself a court order. Think I'd be able to see him then?"

Dr. Spencer didn't blink.

"Yes you would," he replied. "But as I've tried to explain to you, it would be pointless. Even if I let you in to see him right now, Scott is unable to string a pair of sentences together. He is *literally unable* to answer your questions. This is not just me keeping you out. You could sit at his bedside and pepper him all night with questions and you'd be lucky to get a confused look in response. The boy is broken, Sheriff."

"Well when is he going to be put back together?"

Dr. Spencer took a deep breath.

"As I've said, it's impossible to predict, but my guess is that if you come back in a week, you should be able to talk to him. How much you will actually get out of him, I have no idea, but by then he should be physically strong enough for you to see him."

Ed was seething. He could tell that there was no way he was going to see Scott Alston today, and nothing he was going to do would change that. What irritated him most was that he *wasn't* being kept out by some dumb hospital rule, but Dr. Spencer was probably telling the truth that Alston was in no condition to talk. The only thing worse than a weasely little bureaucrat was a weasely little bureaucrat who was right, and Ed knew Dr. Spencer loved being the one to tell him he'd come all the way down here on a pointless errand.

He closed his eyes and let out the breath he had been holding in.

"Next week," Ed said. "I *have* to speak with him next week."

Dr. Spencer looked up at him. His face didn't show it, but Ed assumed that behind that doctor façade he was dancing like a wide receiver in the end zone.

126

You haven't won anything, pal.

"Barring any setbacks, that should be fine," Dr. Spencer replied. "Again, I can't promise he'll be able to give you anything useful, but you should be able talk to him."

"Next week," Ed said and turned towards the door. He'd grabbed the handle and was halfway through when Dr. Spencer piped up from behind him.

"Sheriff," he said. "My schedule is pretty tight, but if you call ahead next time my secretary should be able to block out a time we can meet."

Ed continued to the hallway without breaking stride.

25

"MR. AND MRS. ALSTON..."

"Pastor," Len Alston interrupted.

"Excuse me?" asked Dr. Spencer. He was sitting across from Scott Alston's parents in a counseling room, just down the hall from where their son had lay for the last five weeks. The boy had undergone five surgeries since the crash that brought him here, two to relieve pressure on his brain, one to repair the massive amount of internal damage his organs had sustained and two on his broken legs. The guys over in orthopedics said each leg would need at least one more operation, and there was a good chance Scott would be at least an inch shorter when all was said and done. But that was inconsequential, and not his specialty. Dr. Spencer was here to talk about the boy's brain, and the news wasn't good.

"I'm a man of God," Len Alston replied. "I'm sure you understand, *Doctor*."

"Yes... yes," Dr. Spencer replied. This was already off to a rough start. "Of course, Pastor Alston. My apologies."

A curt nod was his only response.

"Anyway, I wanted to go over the neurological tests we have been performing this week. As you know, Scott suffered severe brain trauma in the accident. When he arrived here, there was swelling around both his frontal and temporal lobes, which, if you'll remember, is what we attempted to relieve with that first surgery. We knew there was going to be some damage, but did not know the amount."

Pastor Alston looked at him stoically, almost disinterested, while Mrs. Alston sat with wide-eyed optimism, seemingly hanging on every word he said.

"After looking at the results of the CT scans we've taken, we can confirm that Scott has had significant damages to both regions."

Mrs. Alston put her hand to her mouth.

"Now while this is not necessarily good news, there is a silver lining here. Scott has already regained much of his motor skills and speech, and we feel very confident that he will continue to make an almost full recovery in these areas.

"Where the damage was greatest, however, is in the cognitive areas, specifically his memory."

Mrs. Alston returned her hand to the table, where it sat folded with the other in front of her. She looked at Dr. Spencer quizzically. Her husband's look hadn't changed.

"The damage to the temporal lobe, which is this part here..." Dr. Spencer pointed to a dark area on one of the scans of Scott's brain lying on the table. "... has caused Scott a strong case of retrograde amnesia, which means he is having trouble remembering many stored memories from before the accident. I'm sure you've noticed this during your visits with him."

Mrs. Alston looked at him earnestly.

"But Scott knew both of us," she said. "He called me Mom."

She turned to her husband, "You heard him, didn't you. He called me Mom."

Pastor Alston looked over at his wife with the thinly veiled contempt he would give a hysterical woman on the street.

"Not right away, honey," He said. "He didn't know anybody right away."

"But he knew me," she said, then turned to Dr. Spencer. "He knew me. He called me Mom."

"Yes, he did," Dr. Spencer replied as comfortingly as he could. "And there is a real chance that he did recognize you, even if he didn't actually remember you."

"What does that mean?" Mrs. Alston asked.

"Well, memory is a complicated thing," Dr. Spencer explained. "Some patients with retrograde amnesia remember nothing from before their trauma, for some it is more selective. Sometimes memories start coming back within a few days, sometimes they never do. We're learning more about the brain every day, but every day we are also presented with something that we can't explain yet.

"Right now with Scott, it seems like his memory from before the accident is extremely limited. While it appears he may recognize you as his mother, we have yet to find any other memories he is recalling. Many times, memories resurface over time. We hope that will be the case with Scott. There are also things that can be done psychologically to help bring back memories that are buried in his brain, but that will be more down the road.

"But there was also damage to his frontal lobe. And while this won't affect his memory, this can change how Scott will react to different situations." Dr. Spencer went into the specifics of the damage to Scott's frontal lobe, but could tell by the looks on the faces across from him that nothing was getting through. Pastor Alston seemed as disinterested as his wife seemed incapable of comprehending their son's condition.

"In plain terms," He stated. "The Scott you knew may not be the Scott that comes home from the hospital with you."

Mrs. Alston again put her hand over her mouth, this time adding a shocked whimper.

"But... my Scotty..." she said.

"Ideally, we'd love to get both his memories and personality back to where they were before the accident, but realistically, a complete recovery like that may be more of a goal than an expectation."

Dr. Spencer conferred with Pastor and Mrs. Alston for the next 20 minutes, going over what they could do to help, what they might realistically expect, and potential rehab therapy for Scott once he left the hospital. What he didn't mention was his conversations with Sheriff Schwab, who was scheduled to meet with Scott at 1 p.m. that afternoon. He was probably already in the building, badgering the nurses to let him in.

Dr. Spencer had taken two phone calls from the sheriff this week and avoided countless more. He had finally run out of reasons to hold him off, so they set up a meeting for today. What the sheriff would get out of that, Tim was dubious. Scott truly had no memory of the accident, but he could tell that the interview was much less about fact finding than it was about formality. Ed Schwab had one more box to check off on his investigation "to-do" list, and he was hell bent on getting that done so he could pass it along to the County Attorney. After that, who knew. If Scott was arrested like Ed Schwab so desperately seemed to want, all the rehab options he had just gone over with Scott's parents would be moot. His care would be turned over to the state, where there would be very little interest in healing Scott's brain. If his body was stable, that was good enough for them.

But it wasn't his place to go over that scenario.

Let Ed Schwab do it.

26

SCOTT ALSTON LAY UPRIGHT in his hospital bed with a rolling tray still across his lap from lunch. His plate was gone, but a large plastic mug with a bendy straw sticking out the top remained. Probably water. There was an old bouquet of flowers on the corner table, with a pair of silver "Get Well Soon" balloons hovering above. They must have been there a while, because one was losing altitude.

Sheriff Schwab introduced himself to Scott's mother first. Pastor Alston sat in the green vinyl chair by the window. While Scott Alston was 18 and legally an adult, Ed allowed the parents to remain. Since they had already waived their right to a lawyer, he didn't want to give a defense attorney any potential ammunition when this ends up in court. He explained that he was investigating the accident and had a few questions for Scott about what happened that day.

"Karen, why don't you step outside," Pastor Alston said from his chair. Without a word, his wife immediately left.

Ed Schwab wasn't surprised. He knew Pastor Alston from various functions back home, and always saw him as a very old fashioned kind of guy. Nothing wrong with traditional values.

He turned to Scott, who was lazily sipping from his water, and pulled up a chair.

"Scott," Ed began. He was using his interview voice now, which was a time-tested combination of warmth and authority. Make them trust you, but also be afraid to lie to you. It was a balancing act Ed had gotten good at over the years. "What can you tell me about the accident?"

"Nothing really, sir," Scott said. "I don't have anything from then."

He motioned over towards his step-dad. "As these guys will tell you... I mean my parents. Mom and Dad. I don't really remember anything from before being here."

Ed looked Scott in the eyes. He'd done a lot of interviews, including scores with high school kids. The one thing he learned from 15 years in the sheriff's office was kids were shitty liars. Always. Every kid that had told him he hadn't been drinking, there was no more beer at the party, yes sir I was wearing my seatbelt. All liars and all easy to spot.

Scott Alston wasn't lying.

That also meant that his egghead doctor wasn't lying. The kid really didn't know what happened that day. That's OK. There was still plenty of evidence for the County Attorney to charge him. They didn't need a confession. All they needed was an interview, and Ed would get that now whether the kid knew anything or not.

"What about earlier that day?" Ed pried. "What do you remember about the time before the accident? Where were you going?"

"Nothing." Scott said, shaking his head. "Anything before the hospital is just dark. I mean, I think back on it and there's just nothing."

Ed thought that how calm Scott was seemed off. For someone who woke up in a hospital with almost no memory from the time before, he was really taking it in stride. But this appeared to be going nowhere, just as Dr. Spencer had said it would. Still, he needed to give Scott Alston every chance to defend himself.

"OK Scott, I understand this is hard," Ed said, reassuringly. "But, if you can, I need you to tell me anything you can remember about the accident. I'm working up a report, as we always do, and I'd love to put in absolutely anything you can tell me about what happened. Your account is the only one we don't have yet."

"I mean, aside from the fact that I crashed head-on into the other car, I don't know anything."

Ed straightened up.

"So you remember hitting the other car?" He asked.

"Well, that's what the doctors said happened," Scott replied sheepishly. "It's how I ended up here. So I know that."

Ed's expression slumped. He looked at Scott with a serious face.

"Now Scott, is this something that you remember happening, or is this something that you have been told? I've talked to the doctors, so I know what they said. I need to know what *you* remember."

"It's what the doctors said," Scott replied.

Ed nodded sympathetically.

"That's OK son," Ed couldn't help but feel a bit sorry for the kid. Without any sort of defense, this would be an open and shut case. The boy was going to jail for something he didn't even remember doing. Tough, but it didn't change the fact that he still did it.

"I tell you what. I'll leave my card with your Dad, and if you can think of anything you want to tell me, he can give me a call and I'll come back. How's that?"

"Fine," Scott said.

Ed rose from his chair and looked over towards Pastor Alston. He crossed the room and held his hand out to Scott's stepfather, who was getting out of his seat for the first time. He extended his hand and offered his card.

"Thank you very much for meeting with me Pastor Alston," Ed said, shaking his hand. "If anything comes back to him, feel free to give me a call."

Pastor Alston returned Ed's firm handshake and asked to speak with him in the hallway. When they were out of the hospital room, he turned to Sheriff Schwab.

"So what is to come of this?"

The hallway had that bright, fluorescent illumination hospitals always seemed to have. Nurses wandered in and out of rooms, when they weren't eating muffins at the nurse's station towards the end of the hallway. And then there was that antiseptic hospital smell. Like somebody tried to cover the smell of sickness with 15 gallons of bleach.

"It's all just part of the investigation, Pastor Alston," Ed replied. "We need to talk with everybody involved.

"To what end?" Ed did not like the tone Len Alston was taking. "This was just a horrible accident. I guess I don't understand why law enforcement needs to be involved at all."

As a rural county sheriff, Ed Schwab had been in pissing contests before, and he knew he better start loading up on water. Len Alston had a very authoritarian reputation amongst his congregation, but Ed could tell he may need a reminder that his influence didn't extend much further than the last row of pews.

"Well Len," Ed used his first name on purpose. "Law enforcement is involved anytime we are called to an accident scene—even if there is no loss of life, which there was in this case. By law, we have to do a thorough investigation to see if anybody is at fault, then we pass that information along to the county attorney."

"And what do you plan on telling the county attorney?" Pastor Alston bristled.

A janitor made his way past the two men, pushing a cart full of cleaning supplies. Ed waited until he was gone to reply. It also gave him a few seconds to consider his response. Ed was getting very sick of people questioning his authority in this investigation, but getting into a shouting match with Len Alston wasn't going to do him any good, no matter how satisfying it would be. He wanted to tell Pastor Alston that memory or not, his little boy was going to be charged with vehicular homicide and there was nothing he could do about it. But, again, he couldn't seem prejudiced.

"Everything we find," Ed replied. "Then it's out of our hands."

The artificial light did no favors to Len Alston's face. Every wrinkle and frown line was accented, making him look like a grizzled, pissed off prospector with a haircut and oxford shirt. Ed decided he was done with this, and turned down the hall towards the elevators by the nurse's station. He wasn't two steps away when Len Alston spoke up one more time.

"Are you planning on running for re-election next year *Sheriff*?"

Ed kept walking, turning his shoulder to squeeze between two nurses gabbing in the middle of the hallway.

He was going to enjoy putting Len Alston's kid in jail.

27

FOREST CITY, IA - Scott Alston has been charged with two counts of vehicular homicide in the deaths of Leah and Kim Peterson, reckless driving and various other traffic violations. Police allege that on May 25, Alston swerved into the oncoming lane while attempting to pass another vehicle and struck the Peterson van head-on.

Alston (18) was in a coma for 28 days following the accident, which delayed charges being filed. Further complicating the case, Alston's family claims he has no memory of the accident or anything before.

"While it is unfortunate for Mr. Alston that he apparently has no memory of the accident, there was plenty of evidence taken from both eyewitnesses and the scene of the accident for charges to be filed," Winnebago County Sheriff Ed Schwab said at a news conference announcing the charges.

When asked if Alston's alleged amnesia affected the charges brought, or could affect the trial, Winnebago County Attorney Brian Lentz demurred.

"(Alston's memory) had no bearing whatsoever on the decision to bring charges," Lentz said. "Nor should it have an effect in court."

After the charges were announced, the Alston family released a statement through their attorney.

"Our prayers still go out to the Peterson family," said Alston's father Len, Pastor of the Salem Lutheran

Church in Lake Mills. "We are saddened that the Sheriff's Office and the County Attorney have decided to file charges against Scott without being able to get his side of the story, but we look forward to facing them in court."

Alston posted $10,000 bond and remains in an Iowa City rehabilitation facility, where he continues to receive treatment for injuries suffered in the crash.

No trial date has been set.

28

MATT'S EYES RACED over the newspaper article, taking it in for a second time.

Whoa.

His Saturday morning breakfast, toast with American cheese, lay on his plate. He'd only gotten one bite out of it before he saw the paper lying on the table. Since school had let out three weeks back, Matt was removed from the rumor mill and hadn't heard much about Scott Alston. He certainly hadn't heard that charges could be filed against him.

Matt reached over to the counter and grabbed the phone. He dialed David's number.

"Hello," It was David's mom.

"Hi Cathy, it's Matt. Is David there?"

"Yeah, but he's still in bed," Cathy answered.

He looked at the clock above the sink. It was just after ten.

"You want me to go wake him?"

Matt considered that. Last summer, David was always the one rousting him from bed, itching to get out to the course before it filled up with old guys. Except he never used a phone call, but biked over and came barging in his room, kicking the foot of his mattress. This summer, he'd barely seen his friend since school let out. Matt was starting to think he'd done something to piss him off.

He wondered if David had heard about Scott. He'd always talked about there were never any consequences, how nobody else seemed to care what Scott did. Maybe the news would pull him out of whatever funk he was in.

"No, that's OK," he said. "But tell him to give me a call when he gets up, OK?"

"Will do," David's mom said. They exchanged goodbyes and Matt put the receiver back down on the counter. He finished up his breakfast and dropped his plate next to the sink.

He considered flipping on the TV for a bit, but put his shoes on and headed out the door instead. Matt threw his leg over his bike and headed out to the driving range.

Whether he admitted it or not, Matt knew if he stayed he'd just be waiting for a call that wouldn't come.

As he coasted out of town, Matt found himself wondering if (*hoping*) Shana would be working today. Aside from buying a Gatorade off her cart on the back nine, he'd never talked to her much until last weekend when he'd wandered up to the Wreck on his own.

She was actually pretty funny. And watched Seinfeld. She was only a sophomore, but was already on the varsity golf squad.

Maybe she wants to hit the links sometime?

2015

29

THE SIGN ON THE SIDE OF THE ROAD was almost taunting him.

Welcome to Lake Mills - A good place to call home!

Matt sped past in his old Toyota Camry. How many times had he ridden past that sign on his bike, coming back from Rice Lake Golf Course? Only this time, cardboard boxes containing half his worldly possessions filled the backseat. The rest of his stuff was in a storage locker in Des Moines.

How the hell did I end up back here?

Starting a career in a dying industry, probably. Print journalism wasn't just dying, it was brain dead, hooked up to a respirator and taking its food through a tube. Matt had survived two rounds of cuts as the statehouse correspondent at the Cedar Rapids *Gazette*, but when he was called into his editor's office after a partnership with the *Des Moines Register* was announced, he knew there was no chance of sticking around. Bob had nothing but good things to say about his work, but the budget is an uncaring bitch.

Whether it was arrogance or ignorance, Matt hadn't been too concerned. He figured he was young and a damn good reporter. He'd latch on somewhere. Granted, many of his friends and colleagues who had been sent packing in the first two rounds of cuts were either still looking or had left the business altogether—he'd even seen Greg Wallace working at Best Buy—but he had broken the story on the government misdirection of recovery funds after the flood for crying out loud. That story alone won four Iowa Newspaper Association awards. He'd interviewed presidential candidates, called up congressmen at their homes and knew the Governor on a first-name basis.

Yet here he was, moving back to Lake Mills.

The job search had been a brutal wake-up call.

He had gone through his contact list, checking in with everybody he knew in the business—the ones that still had jobs, anyway. Many had suffered the same fate he had. The story was the same everywhere. Not only were they not hiring, they were worried about their own jobs.

Months passed with nothing, and Matt was beyond desperate. Best Buy was starting to look good when an old name that Matt had dropped from his contact list long ago came through with an unsolicited phone call.

"Hello, Matt. Bill Harris here."

Honestly, Matt didn't know how the old guy was still alive. Mr. Harris (*he'd always be Mr. Harris*) had been the Editor/Publisher/Writer/Photographer/Ad Salesman and just about everything else for the *Lake Mills Graphic-Glimpse* for at least 50 years, and he'd given Matt his first job covering the boys' and girls' basketball teams during his senior year. That turned into a journalistic crash-course where he learned to write, interview, take pictures, develop film, edit copy and lay out a page. By the time he attended the University of Iowa, his job as a reporter at the student paper seemed easy. All he had to do there was write.

Mr. Harris had kept tabs on Matt over the years, and he knew his success in the business was a real badge of honor for the small-town newspaperman, who saw him as a protégé.

He'd heard about the layoff from Matt's father.

"I've been giving some real thought to hanging up my cap lately, so I was wondering if you would be interested in lightening my load."

Matt's initial reaction was 'no way'. He had been the political reporter for the second-largest paper in the state. He wrote stories about pending legislation and senate races, not bake sales.

He wasn't *that* desperate.

"You can come in while I'm still here. I'll stay on as publisher, but I'll give you the run of the place."

Matt paused. It *would* keep his byline in print while he looked for a real job, and it would look better on his resume than Best Buy. Maybe even score him points for 'saving' a small-town weekly.

So here Matt was, pulling into the driveway at his Dad's house with his bags packed.

As he put the Camry in park, Matt looked up and saw his dad walking down the front steps. Even though he hadn't said as much, Matt thought Dad was pretty excited about him coming home. His mom had died after a battle with ovarian cancer four years ago, and his brother lived with his wife and son on a Naval base in Connecticut. Even though he'd been only two hours from Lake Mills, Matt's job had kept him from visiting as much as he should. It was probably nice for the old man to have some company.

"Welcome home," Jon said.

30

"OK THEN, HIT 'SEND FILE' and you're done." Mr. Harris said, clapping Matt on the shoulder as he stood up. "Easy peasy, eh?"

Matt leaned back in his chair across from the iMac and rubbed his palms on his eyes. He looked up at the old clock hanging on the back wall. It looked like something out of a schoolroom, but thankfully didn't have the audible ticking marking each second. That came from his head, memories of a 10th grade classroom.

8:26

His first issue of the Lake Mills Graphic-Glimpse was off to the printer with a combination of relief and dread. It was the 'tightrope without a net' feeling that came from being the last line of defense that sat in the pit of his stomach. There was no copy desk, no editor between him and the press. Every mistake in the entire issue would be his, and there would be mistakes. Even a staff of dozens couldn't catch everything, how was he supposed to do it all by himself? Especially when most of the copy that came in from the stringers, or as Mr. Harris jokingly called them 'correspondents', was brutal. Matt had spent a full 40 minutes on Monday editing a story Judy Gilmore had brought in about a Girl Scout fundraiser before Mr. Harris stuck his head in and told him to stop.

"It's not the *Times*," he said. "Your job is to make it grammatically correct and readable. It doesn't have to win a Pulitzer."

Matt looked up from the maze of red ink he had scribbled over the printed out copy.

"Yeah, but..."

Harris cut him off.

"I get it," he said. "I've been reading Judy's stories for years, and she can't write a lick. But if you work it up too much, she's going to be in here with her knickers in a twist Thursday morning."

Bill broke into a high-pitched squeak.

"Why did you change my story?" He laughed at his own imitation. "Then *you're* going to be the one out finding stuff to fill space. Judy's copy might be rough, but she's good for about 10 inches and a picture every week. And I tell ya what, that's the stuff the people read most. They don't care how it's written, they care that their kid's name is in the paper."

And so it went. Mr. Harris had plenty of stuff lined up for the week, so Matt only had his byline over a pair of stories.

"Now what?" Matt asked.

"Now, we shut this place down, head over to Frank's and I buy you a beer."

Matt smiled as he powered the computer down.

"Sounds good to me."

They locked up and made their way down the sidewalk. Matt's eyes were drawn across the street towards the old Wreck, now sporting a sign that said "Silver Moon Saloon".

"Is that new?" Matt asked, nodding across the way.

Mr. Harris looked over and squinted his eyes as if he had to double check to make sure he knew which building Matt was talking about.

"No, it's been that for a while now," he said. "Some guy from Albert Lea owns it. Mostly second and third shifters in there now."

That explained why they weren't going there. Night shift workers were the underclass of small town life. Many lived out of town, which, combined with their nocturnal schedule, didn't allow them to integrate into the community much. Small town life could be extremely cliquey, even for grownups.

"It was a place for kids when I was in high school," Matt said as they arrived at Frank's Place.

"Yeah, I remember that," Mr. Harris said with an odd note of shame in his voice. He held the door open for Matt. "That wasn't a very good idea."

FRANK'S PLACE WAS EVERY BIT of a townie bar — dark, quiet and mostly empty. The pink and blue light from the neon beer signs that blared out from the window seeped into the front of the bar, tinting the haze of smoke that had been hanging there for 30 years.

Bill eased himself onto stool as the bartender placed a can of Busch Light in front of him.

"I'll need another for my friend, Marty."

The bartender pulled another can from under the bar and popped the top. Matt watched the foam ooze out as he tried to remember the last time he'd been served cheap beer in a can.

Bill offered a toast to Matt's new career and Matt was nice enough to force a smile. The two men drank, segueing into the traditional topics of work, family and the weather. It was nice, and while Matt would never consider making it his career, he began to understand the charm of a small-town newspaper's low-key schedule.

Bill had barely finished his beer when he dropped a five on the bar and announced his departure.

"Us old guys can't stay out all night."

Matt thanked him for the beer and was turning to follow him out when David Rowe walked in the front door.

Matt was taken aback. He'd barely seen David since they graduated from high school, and it had been at least 15 years since their last brief encounter. Matt thought back to their first few years of high school when they had been almost inseparable. Then, during their senior year, the two had drifted apart. Matt had gotten his first job at the *Graphic-*

Glimpse, then his first girlfriend, both of which began to dominate his social schedule. He also remembered David growing more distant, probably a reaction to his best friend's divided attentions. After graduation, Matt headed to the University of Iowa while David ended up in community college. They saw each other a few times when Matt came home that first summer, but after that his job at the student paper kept him in Iowa City most of the time. There was never any 'official' ending. Like many high school relationships, the friendship just kind of died on the vine.

He hadn't even considered the fact that David might be living in Lake Mills.

"Well look at you," David said. "I'd heard somebody say you were back in town." His tone was slightly flat, but friendly. Matt met him with a smile and extended his hand.

"How you doing buddy?" Matt asked. "Long time no see, eh?"

David's hands were callused and worn with that perpetually dirty look that came from manual labor. He had a good bit of patchy stubble on his chin. Not quite a beard, but more than just missing a day of shaving. He was wearing a severely broken-in Lake Mills Lumber cap and faded jeans. He reminded Matt of a backyard swingset after the kids had gone to college. The years had worn on David, no question.

"Yeah, it's been a while," David said, keeping his eyes on the bartender until he was noticed. He gave a slight nod and turned back towards Matt. "So what brings you back?"

"Well, I was working for the Cedar Rapids *Gazette* down in Des Moines, covering the Statehouse, the Governor, then doing a bunch of election stuff during the caucuses—interviewing the candidates, covering events," Matt was beginning to notice how he always began listing his credentials whenever asked about what brought him back to Lake Mills.

"But, anyway, they ended up cutting quite a bit of staff and I got laid off. The newspaper business is pretty rough right now, cuts everywhere."

As Matt talked, the bartender placed a Jack and Coke in front of David and walked back to the end of the bar without a word.

"Yeah, things are rough all over," David said, taking a long pull from his drink.

"So, anyway, there aren't any papers hiring right now, no matter what your credentials are," Matt said. "But eventually I got a call from Bill Harris, and it ended up working out. Here I am."

David downed the rest of his drink and set the glass back on the bar. The ice had barely gotten a chance to melt.

"Home, sweet home, eh?" David said.

"I guess so," Matt said. It was slightly awkward talking to David again after all these years, but he couldn't quite pinpoint why. Maybe David resented Matt getting out and leaving him behind. Is that why he came over? To gloat that Matt got sucked back in? Seemed a little paranoid. He probably just came over to talk to an old friend. Wouldn't he have done the same had they run into each other in Des Moines?

"So what have you been up to?" Matt asked.

"Nothing much," David responded, staring ahead behind the bar. "Same old shit. Getting some hours at the lumberyard."

"So you're working down at the lumberyard, huh?"

"I work at the school, actually," David said. "Custodian. But I work part-time down at the lumberyard during the summer."

"Ah," Matt said.

The silence hung a beat too long for Matt, who rushed to fill it.

"Married? Any kids?"

"Divorced a few years back," David said. "No kids."

David offered no follow-up information, and Matt didn't want to pry. It had been too long since they had been close enough to delve into what could be an awkward personal situation.

So he didn't.

"No on both for me," Matt said. It was all he could think of. "Never had the time to get close enough with anybody to get serious—that was my excuse anyway."

While Matt chuckled at his lame attempt at a joke, the empty glass on the bar was swapped for a fresh drink. Matt wondered if David was in here every night. He at least had become a regular, and not the one beer, once-a-week type that Bill Harris was. The guy behind the bar obviously knew what David wanted, but hadn't said as much as 'hello' to him since he came in.

The conversation got easier as the night went on, with Matt doing most of the talking. Maybe it was a journalist's natural inclination as a storyteller, maybe it was that subconscious need to be seen as a success, or maybe it was the third beer, but it didn't take long for Matt to be re-telling the tales of meetings with failed and successful Presidential candidates, opinions of how screwed-up the legislature was and the Governor's notoriously foul-mouth.

David mostly sat and listened, laughing at the appropriate times and even asking a few follow-up questions. Matt could feel the awkwardness that had started their meeting melt away. It felt good having his old friend around. Maybe they'd be able to jump back to where they left off as high school kids. It would be nice to have somebody to hang out with, especially if his nights were going to be free like this. He wouldn't know what to do with himself and a once-a-week 8 p.m. deadline.

Around 10 o'clock, Matt fished in his pocket so he could settle his tab. David put his hand down on the bar in front of him and refused.

"I've got it," he said.

"No, that's OK man, I can…"

"I've got it," David repeated. "Welcome back."

Matt paused for a second, considering another refusal, but didn't want to insult his friend.

"Well, I've got next time then," Matt said.

"No problem," David replied.

"It was really good to see you," Matt said, standing up. "We'll have to do it again soon. Maybe even hit the links sometime, what do you say?"

David looked up at Matt, remaining on his stool.

"I don't really golf anymore," David said. "But I'll be around."

"OK then, sounds good. I'll see you around," Matt turned to leave as the bartender put another Jack and Coke in front of David.

31

The score remained knotted at 14 until Bulldog halfback Jonny Pederson broke through the line and scampered for a...

Matt looked down at his notebook and deciphered what he had written the night before. His normal reporter's handwriting was even worse, as the temperature had dropped precipitously after kickoff and he had neglected to bring a pair of gloves. Who knew fall would come so quickly this year? He spotted the number he was looking for and continued writing.

...42-yard touchdown with just under two minutes left in the third quarter.

Matt leaned back against the hard kitchen chair and pressed his hands against his eyes. He could have written this last night after the game, but with the paper not going to print until Wednesday, why bother? It was just as easy to do the next day. He thought about the pictures he took along the sidelines, wondering if he had a shot of the Pederson kid. Matt knew he didn't have one of his big run — he'd only shot during the second quarter before returning to the stands — but he thought he'd gotten a decent pic of him carrying the ball at some point. That would be fine.

He was almost done with his recap of the big Bulldog win when his cell phone sprang to life. He pushed back from the kitchen table and walked over to where his phone sat charging on the counter. He looked at the caller ID as he detached it from the cord.

Bill Harris.

"Hello."

"Matt it's Bill," his boss's voice came back. Matt thought it a bit curious Bill was calling him on a Saturday morning. To be honest, he couldn't remember a time Bill had called him at home since he had started working for him. The *Graphic-Glimpse* didn't require a lot of off-hours work.

"Hey Bill, what's up?"

"There's something going on south of town."

Matt's reporter's instincts, long dormant after months of covering Lake Mills High School football games and charity bake sales, took notice.

"OK."

"I got a call about a fire out at Steve Stamp's place a few minutes ago. You know where that is?"

Matt glanced down at his watch, then immediately turned around to grab his notebook. He could feel the adrenaline trickling into his veins. It was good to know a story could still get his juices flowing.

His hometown hadn't beaten him yet.

"Um... no."

"Just head out on 225 a couple miles, go past the Rice Lake turnoff and take the first gravel road after the big curve. Should be the first house on the south side."

"Gotcha. I'm there." Cell phone still pressed against his ear, Matt tore the top three pages of football notes out, placed them on the keyboard of his laptop and scooped up his mini recorder.

Matt grabbed his keys off the counter and was two steps from the door when Bill spoke again.

"Be careful out there. I called the sheriff's office, and they are already on the scene. Tread lightly around Ed Schwab. I've known him a long time, and he's surly. Get under his skin and he'll fight you every step of the way.

Don't get in the way. But we do have a job to do, as well, so take the camera."

"Will do, Bill," Matt replied, doubling back for the digital camera he'd used at the football game the night before. Even if it was a legitimate news story, he'd still have to shoot his own pictures.

Matt flicked it on, checking the charge and the amount of storage space left. He was out the door and into his car as Bill finished up.

"Give me a call when you get back, and we'll talk it over."

AS SOON AS MATT WAS PAST the city limits, he hit the accelerator on the Camry and sped south. The morning was thick with a damp grey haze that hung over the countryside. It wasn't raining, but it was one of those days where the mist just seemed to grow on your coat as you walked through it.

Matt passed the quarter mile turnoff and eased off the gas as he entered the giant 'S' curves south of town. He turned west on the first gravel road and continued on up a hill. There were cornfields on both sides of the road.

As he crested the hill, he could see the Stamp farm in the distance. The house was white with brown trim and certainly hadn't burned down. In fact, there seemed to be hardly any activity at all near the house. But along the gravel road leading to it were three police cars with lights spinning, an ambulance and a trio of Lake Mills fire trucks. Various law enforcement and emergency personnel were milling about, although not as many as the number of vehicles would suggest.

Each one probably drove out by themselves, all excited to have an excuse to turn on the lights and drive fast.

He immediately felt duped into thinking this could be a big story. Then again, this probably *was* a big story here. He could envision the headline already.

BRUSH FIRE BURNS BRUSH
Hero firefighters save corn from blaze

Matt pulled his Camry up behind the first police car and put it in park. He got out of the car, then immediately reached back inside for the camera.

If they were going to send every emergency responder in a 10-mile radius out here, they'd want pictures proving their heroism. Matt leaned over the open driver's side door and snapped a few pictures of the emergency vehicles alongside the field. He slung the camera's shoulder strap around the back of his neck and grabbed his notebook before closing the door.

"Hey," a voice came from behind. "Can I help you?"

The tone was not that of someone offering help. Matt turned around to see a man in full firefighter regalia approaching him from one of the engines.

"Hey," Matt said, turned back to meet the firefighter and extended his hand. He recognized him as Larry Van Abel, who ran the seed house on the north side of town. His son was one of the linemen on the LMCHS football team. "Matt Carlton. I'm with the paper. Bill Harris sent me out here. Said there was a fire, but I'd assumed it was the house."

"Jeez," Larry said, taking his oversized helmet off. "Goddam awful."

"Back there?" Matt asked, following his eyes towards the corner of the field he had been headed towards. The stalks were at least seven feet high and had taken on quite a bit of brown, although a few streaks of green were visible amongst the broadleaves. They hid whatever had drawn the fire department out here this morning. A sheriff's deputy was standing near the corner of the field, talking with a pair of firefighters hauling hoses back up towards the trucks.

As the firefighter gave a slight nod, Matt could tell this was more than just a little fire in the grass. A jolt of reporter's passion hit him again.

"What burned?" Matt asked, flicking on his recorder.

Larry Van Abel's face turned back to Matt. The stern look he'd worn as he approached was gone. He ran his hand through the dampening hair on his head and snuck a glance at the field one more time as he looked back to Matt. He opened his mouth to say something, but hesitated and just drew in a big breath instead.

"You need to talk to the sheriff. I'm not... you just need to talk to the sheriff."

Matt's instincts were all firing now. The look on Larry's face said this was anything but ordinary.

"OK, thanks. Where can I find him?"

Larry nodded towards the field. Matt thanked him again and set out past the front of the fire truck. A pair of tire ruts ran down the inlet where the deputy had been standing just moments ago. There was no sign of him, but now that Matt was around the corner of cornstalks, he could see a gaggle of emergency personnel gathered amongst some tall grass near the split-rail fence that separated the Stamp's yard from the corn. Matt followed the path that had been trampled through the grass that morning.

As he approached, Matt recognized Sheriff Ed Schwab talking with a pair of deputies and one of the Lake Mills firemen. A mountain of a man, the Sheriff dominated the clearing. He had added at least 50 pounds to his bulky frame since Matt had seen him last, which was probably in high school. His hair had greyed considerably, but the large, bushy mustache stretched under his nose was still as dark as it had been years ago.

The sheriff saw the notebook in his hand and camera around his neck and stepped over to him.

"Who're you?" He asked.

"Matt Carlton," he answered, extending his hand. "I'm with Bill Harris at the *Graphic-Glimpse*."

Ed Schwab ignored his hand.

"Jesus Christ," he said. "Where the hell is Bill? He send you out here?"

A small pause as Matt considered his options. He did everything he could to see beyond the Sheriff, but it was impossible without being obvious, and he didn't want to make any waves yet.

"Bill hired me to take on the bulk of the work at the paper. He's phasing into retirement."

The sheriff did not look pleased, but Matt re-extended his hand anyway. After a moment's consideration, he took it in a vice-like grip. Matt made every effort not to wince as his knuckles were ground together.

One of the deputies approached from behind and tapped him on the shoulder, causing him to let go. As the sheriff turned to talk, Matt got his first view of what had brought them out here.

A large, black patch of charred grass amidst the dirt. In the middle was something covered by a yellow sheet. Two men who looked like EMTs were kneeling down around it. One was holding the sheet up while the other poked around underneath.

"Jesus, is that a body?" Matt asked, the question out of his mouth before he could pull it back. He was furious at himself for acting like a rookie. Maybe he was a little rustier than he'd thought.

The sheriff whipped around to look back at Matt. His mammoth frame took up the entire ribbon of trampled grasses that led from the road, blocking out the view of the scene behind.

"We don't know anything yet," the sheriff said, more than a touch of warning in his voice.

Matt tried to see around the sheriff where the body lay, but it was pointless. The Deputy read his boss's body language and had stepped forward to form a human blockade. The look in his eye showed he was ready and willing to kick a nosey reporter back to Lake Mills the second the word was given.

Matt needed damage control or the only information he'd get was fourth-hand gossip. He could hear Bill lecturing him about Ed Schwab's temperament.

"Of course, sheriff," Matt said, pulling out every bit of composure and reporter's gravitas. "I'm sorry. I just had no idea when I came out here there was a victim involved. I didn't mean to be disrespectful."

The sheriff eyed him suspiciously, but Matt plowed on.

"Do you have any idea how this happened?"

The deputy stepped past the sheriff, tramping down more of the knee-high grass that stretched from the fence to the field.

"You're gonna need to..."

Sheriff Schwab put the back of his hand across the deputy's chest.

"Don't worry Roger," he said, lowering his hand back to his side. "Why don't you check with Denny and see if they're ready to pull out of here, OK?"

The deputy gave Matt an unsympathetic look before turning back towards a trio of firemen standing near the clearing. He shook it off and looked back at the Sheriff, who still looked stern, but had lost the outright hostility he'd shown before.

Matt figured he would start slow. Most of the time if you could get a subject to start talking, they won't stop.

But the hard part was to get them to start.

"When did you get the call?"

The pause hung long enough that Matt didn't know if he was going to get an answer or not.

"Around seven this morning."

Matt started writing in his notebook, despite the fact that his recorder was out and running. Never trust the tape, because there aren't any re-dos when you go back to the office and find out your batteries died or you accidentally hit the mute button.

"Who called it in?"

Sheriff Schwab looked back towards the Stamp house, keeping his gaze there as he spoke.

"Steve did. They got up this morning and realized their daughter's not there. She'd been out last night and they never heard her come home."

The Sheriff moved his eyes back to Matt, who was frantically dictating.

"Looked all over the house, then go outside and see her car in the driveway. Steve looks around the yard and sees smoke over by his field, so he goes to check it out and finds this."

159

Matt looked up from his notebook. This wasn't a question you asked with your nose buried in a page full of quasi-coherent scratchings.

"Is that her?" He made no motion behind the Sheriff, but he didn't need to. Ed Schwab looked back over his shoulder, as if asking the girl for permission to talk. He turned back and gave a curt nod. The information swirled through Matt's head. Teenage girl's body found burned about 200 feet from her own house on a Saturday morning... he was trying to find any scenario where this was some sort of accident and coming up empty.

"Do you suspect foul play?" Even as the words came out of Matt's mouth, he thought they sounded like they belonged in some lame network cop show. But it had to be asked, and they got the point across well enough.

"We don't know how this happened yet," Sheriff Schwab said.

In the background, Matt saw the medical examiner had pulled back the sheet and exposed the upper half of the body underneath. He'd done a turn or two on the city beat for the *Gazette*, and had visited a few crime scenes in Cedar Rapids, but he had never seen a dead body on the job. The only ones he could remember seeing were his grandmother when he was seven years old and his mother a few years back, but that was totally different. Those were open casket funerals, with the bodies made up to look as lifelike and beautiful as possible in their death.

The fire had done no such favors.

The face was covered in a grotesque black char, with the remaining flesh beneath the color of pumpkin pie. The hair on the front half of her skull, along with her eyebrows and all the skin on her forehead had been singed off. Even from across the clearing, Matt could tell it was a female body. Her sweater was mostly burned away in the front, with patches that remained seemingly melted to the body.

Ed Schwab followed Matt's stare.

"What was her name?"

32

MATT HAD HIS PHONE OUT and was dialing Bill the second he was back in his car. He mentally arranged the story as he waited for his boss to pick up. While Sheriff Schwab wouldn't officially confirm the body was that of Mackenzie Stamp, Matt could tell there were no doubts. The odds of a girl going missing the same morning a different girl's body was found burned in a nearby field were astronomical. Even more so in such a small community with a crime rate barely above zero.

The Sheriff wouldn't give (or speculate on) any potential motives for why someone would do this to a small-town high school girl, but every possibility filtered through Matt's head as he turned his car around. This seemed mighty extreme for a jealous boyfriend or jilted lover. Small towns across the Midwest had been dealing with a creeping methamphetamine epidemic, but Matt struggled to figure out how a supposedly clean-cut girl could get caught up in that to the extent she ended up burned in a field.

"Hello?"

"Bill, it's Matt. This is a major story."

Matt filled his boss in on what Ed Schwab had (and hadn't) told him as he drove through town towards the *Graphic-Glimpse* office. Even on an overcast fall day, he saw all the requisite people milling around town.

How long until the Lake Mills rumor mill picked up on the story?

It would turn the place upside down.

As soon as Matt got into the office, he started up the computer and pressed play on his recorder. He jotted down a few notes in his notebook as he waited for the computer to boot up.

Matt had barely started typing when he heard the front door open. He looked up to see Bill Harris enter.

"So where are we at?" he asked.

Matt briefly looked down at his notes, then back at his publisher. He must have hopped in his car the minute he hung up the phone.

"I still haven't transcribed my quotes yet, but I could have copy in 45 minutes."

Bill grabbed the back of a chair by the layout board and wheeled it over towards where Matt was sitting.

"Slow down," He said. "There is no hurry. Remember, we've got four days and I'm sure things will change quite a bit until this goes out."

Matt gave his boss a quizzical look. He'd completely forgotten he was working for a weekly paper.

"Bill, I don't think we can wait for Wednesday on this," Matt said. "This is huge, and I think we need to get something out today."

"Today?" Bill said the word as if the thought had never occurred to him.

"We can put it up on the web," Matt said.

"That's not really how we do things here."

The thought of letting this story sit four days made Matt's soul hurt. His reporter's juices were flowing again, and he wouldn't let it pass. News outlets across the state, possibly even across the Midwest would be on this story. Dead girls begat readers and eyeballs, and leading on a story like this could get his name out again in a big way. If he waited until Wednesday, anything he put out would be the journalistic equivalent of microwaved leftovers.

He had to find a way to change the old man's mind.

"This is going to be all over town in a few hours—if it isn't already. There needs to be a legitimate account that people can refer to—something that has facts, not gossip. The Stamps deserve that, don't they?"

Bill leaned back in his chair, rubbed his temples and lifted his eyes to the ceiling.

"I need to talk with the Sheriff," Bill said.

"About what?" Matt asked.

"I want to make sure the family knows."

"She was burned in their front yard," Matt said. It came out much more petulant than he wanted. Bill gave him the 'not mad but disappointed' look only 80-year-olds can pull off.

"There's more family than the ones in that house. There's Stamps all over around here, and I don't want a single one of them to find out what happened to that girl from *my* paper."

The silence hung as Bill went to his office to make the call.

DESPITE THE CHARRED REMAINS, Steve Stamp officially identified his daughter's body around noon and the sheriff's department immediately started investigating Mackenzie Stamp's death as a homicide.

Matt's first story hit the Internet around 4 pm Saturday, after Bill had talked with Sheriff Schwab and finally given the green light.

Matt was amazed at how many hits his story got that first night alone, going the small, rural community's version of viral within a few hours. As word filtered out, the local television affiliates all sent trucks to Lake Mills, but their reports consisted of little more than a windbreaker standing near a field rehashing what Matt had put in his story.

He even heard an "According to the Lake Mills *Graphic-Glimpse…*"

For the first time since he had been let go by the *Gazette*, Matt felt like a real reporter. From the confines of a small-town weekly newspaper, he had scooped everybody on a major story that could get statewide play.

Now's not the time for a victory lap.

In reality, he'd been lucky. The story fell directly in his lap. He'd had a massive head start, but now all the other news outlets were in the race too. If he slowed down, they'd all blow by him. He needed to keep on this, keep out in front. Through Bill's relationships with seemingly everybody in town, Matt had access that no other journalist would have. He'd just have to find a way to use it.

Assuming Bill lets me.

33

MATT CALLED BILL'S HOUSE early Sunday morning hoping to catch him before he left for church, but he was too late and left a message. As the morning drug on, he poured over his notes from the day before, trying to piece together how this could have happened to Mackenzie Stamp.

Unable to wait for Bill's stamp of approval, Matt called the Sheriff's office. The receptionist he spoke with said Sheriff Schwab was off duty, and all on-duty deputies were out and unavailable. She wouldn't confirm whether they were out investigating the Stamp case or not, and she was adamant that no public statements would be coming from the department anytime soon.

Frustrated, Matt hung up his phone and hung his head. His reporter's itch was screaming up the back of his neck, and he didn't know how much longer he could just sit and wait.

Screw it.

He grabbed his notebook and recorder, then bolted out the front door. Matt hopped behind the wheel of his Camry and backed out of the driveway. Sitting around his dad's house wasn't going to get anything done. The Sheriff's office was in Forest City, which should be about 15 minutes away.

By the time Matt arrived, Ed Schwab was in his office. He was still dressed in his church clothes, white oxford shirt and brown patterned tie, but the top button was undone. It was the first time Matt had seen the sheriff out of his uniform. He looked a bit disheveled behind the desk when he motioned for Matt to sit down. Matt was surprised. He'd half expected Schwab to show him the door with an unoriginal obscenity the minute he walked in.

"Get your notebook out and write this down," The Sheriff said before Matt was in his seat. "Anybody who knows anything about this needs to call me right now. They can do it anonymously if they want, but they need to call immediately."

"I take that to mean you have no suspects?"

Schwab's eyes hardened. "We'll find this sonofabitch."

"Of course," Matt said as sincerely as he could. "Just making sure I have the facts correct. This is a horrible situation, and I don't want to get anything wrong. I definitely don't want to hurt your investigation any."

Before Sheriff Schwab could respond, Matt jumped in with his questions.

"What do you know about what happened Friday night?"

A few seconds hung where Matt thought he'd get nothing, then the information started to drip out.

"It looks like she was attacked from behind as she got out of her car, then moved across the yard to where we found her."

"So whoever killed her was waiting out in the yard?"

The Sheriff nodded.

"Could it have been anyone in the family?"

"No," Sheriff Schwab said. "Steve was the one who found her and called it in. Other than that it's just the wife and boy out there."

Matt assumed Steve was Mackenzie's father and wasn't so ready to throw him aside as a suspect.

"Why do you think the father couldn't have done it?"

"Nobody ever had a bad thing to say about Steve Stamp. Everyone in the family says they got along perfect. Besides, domestic cases don't end up burning in the front yard."

Matt wasn't convinced, and it must have shown on his face.

"We're looking at everything, but I'm telling you it wasn't him," The sheriff continued. "I talked to him myself, and that man is devastated."

"How old is the brother?"

"Nine."

"What about the mother?"

"The girl's skull was cracked and she was drug 100 yards, and Heather Stamp weighs 100 pounds soaking wet."

Matt wasn't willing to write off anyone yet, but he had to admit the Sheriff's reasoning was probably solid.

"Any boyfriends?" Matt asked.

"Yeah, but he's clear. They were watching movies at his house Friday night. Mom says she left just before midnight and he went to bed."

Matt kept the Sheriff talking and dictating all the details he could.

Heather Stamp realized her daughter hadn't come home Saturday morning when she saw the folded clothes she had put on her bed the previous afternoon undisturbed. Her husband headed outside and found Mackenzie's car parked in the driveway, then saw smoke coming from near his field. The fire had mostly died away, leaving him to find the charred remains of his oldest daughter. The amount of burn damage to the body made investigators believe that an accelerant was used, most likely gasoline or lighter fluid.

"I don't expect any of the gory stuff to be in the paper, understand?" Ed said, boring his tired eyes into Matt's.

"Of course," Matt replied. He was getting tired of people explaining how to do his job. "I'm just trying to get the facts straight, Sheriff. I'm not trying to sensationalize anything."

Matt looked down at his notes before continuing.

"So you've more or less cleared the family and the boyfriend. Is there anyone else who you know would have a reason to hurt her?"

"Somebody out there knows something." The sheriff came back quickly. "You tell them to call me. They don't have to give their name, I don't care, but somebody has to know something."

34

A FTER MACKENZIE'S BODY was released to the family, a funeral was held at Salem Lutheran Church. By the time Matt arrived, every pew was filled with family, friends from school and members of the community. Unable to find a seat, he stood behind the back row with the rest of the overflow.

Matt recognized a number of faces from around town. He spotted Bill and his wife Ellie seated just off the right aisle, along with Sheriff Schwab and his wife a few pews behind them. Seemingly everyone from the school was there, from students to teachers. Matt even saw his old teacher, Mr. Roderick. His beard was thick as it ever was, only now streaked with gray, and somehow he'd found glasses even thicker than the ones he used to glare through when you waltzed into his classroom three minutes late.

As Matt marveled at how many people were here, he thought back to his mother's funeral. It too had been held at Salem, but barely had a quarter of the people here. The only time he had seen anything like this was when he had been in high school and that little girl died in a car wreck.

The thought was barely in his head when his eyes came across an anomaly in the sea of mourning faces, almost as if it had been planted there for him to see at that exact moment.

The dirty blonde hair was shorter and the face was thinner. Not quite gaunt, but not with the youthful flush he remembered. Matt stared at him, memories flooding back. God, he hadn't thought about Scott Alston since high school.

Back when he killed that little girl.

Matt couldn't figure out why someone who had filled up a church himself once upon a time would come take a spot the next time a dead girl brought out the mourning masses. It's just a way to kick up a lot of bad memories and connotations.

Even in a coma, Scott was a pariah after that accident. No matter how much the citizens of Lake Mills loved their Christian values, there was no forgiveness for killing a little girl with cancer. After he had been sentenced and sent away, the town took the one bit of revenge they could.

They forgot about him. Scrubbed him from the record. Deleted all files.

Matt had been amazed at how quickly Scott had gone from the topic of almost all conversation to completely disregarded.

He who must not be named.

It wasn't just him, either. Attendance at his father's church, the one he was sitting in right now, dropped dramatically after Scott's sentencing. It got so bad that the Church Board voted to replace Pastor Alston the following year. If Matt remembered correctly, he'd planned on opening a church in the old hardware store downtown, but dropped dead of a heart attack while helping with the renovations.

Scott sat stoically in a plain white shirt next to his mother, who dabbed tears away from her cheeks with a lacy handkerchief. He didn't seem too affected by her weeping, or any of the sadness around him, for that matter. Just stared straight ahead with a blank look. He could easily have been a commuter taking that 45-minute train home after another 10-hour day at the office.

So why come here?

Music started up as the Stamp's and their extended family took the first five pews. Mackenzie's white casket lay in front of the altar. Flowers covered the top, then flowed off like a floral waterfall and spread all over the front of the church.

The service started, but Matt's mind was flooded with memories from high school. He saw the back of Scott's head as he squeezed his girlfriend's throat behind the Wreck. He heard David explaining all the traits Scott shared with serial killers.

Serial Killer?

The thought was both ridiculous and completely logical. That girl up in front of the church was killed in a grisly fashion and there were no suspects. Cop shows always talked about killers who would return to the scene of their crimes—even attend the funerals of their victims.

And there was Scott Alston.

But that's movie stuff, right?

The service continued for at least an hour, and not a single speaker was able to get through their respective piece without being reduced to tears. But it was all background noise to Matt, who was unable to quiet the squabble in his head.

As the ceremony ended, a large contingent of the Lake Mills senior class escorted Mackenzie's casket to the back of the church, where they waited for people to file past and pay their final respects. As they exited the church, people lined the steps of the church, spilling out into the sidewalk as Mackenzie's classmates walked out with the casket. Outside, the white coffin seemed to glow in the early afternoon sunlight as it was placed in the back of the hearse.

Matt hung towards the back of the crowd, surveying the faces. Most looked teary-eyed as the hearse drove away towards the cemetery where the Stamp family would have a private burial service. He spotted Scott walking his mother to their car and found himself following. Matt had to fight the current of seemingly everyone Mackenzie had come in contact with during her 17 years in an effort to catch up. He had no plan, just an odd compulsion to follow.

The crowd was still thick when Karen Alston stopped to look in her purse. Not wanting to blow his cover, Matt kept walking. As he passed by, a toddler darted in front of him and forced him right into Scott's mother.

"Oh, I'm sorry ma'am," Matt said. He reached out to steady her only to put his hand on top of Scott's, which was already on his mother's shoulder. Matt reacted as if he'd touched a stove before Scott's gaze caught him.

Karen Alston straightened up, oblivious to the river of people she was standing amongst.

"That's OK young man, no harm done," she said. She gave Matt a quick up-and-down. "Do I know you?"

Matt looked down to her but could still feel Scott's eyes on him.

"No ma'am. I'm Matt Carlton. I work for the *Graphic-Glimpse.*"

Her face brightened.

"So you're the new guy at the paper," she said in an excited tone foreign to funerals. "You do such a good job there. I read everything you write *every* week."

"Well thank you," Matt said. He looked over at Scott and offered his hand. "Hello Scott."

"Do you know each other?" Karen asked.

"We went to school together," Matt kept his eyes on Scott, looking for any sign of recognition. He found none.

"That's wonderful," Karen said. "Do you remember Matt, Scotty?"

Scott's expression remained blank. "Sorry."

"It's OK, honey," She said. "It's OK.

"Scott had an accident a while back and isn't able to remember much from back then, but that's OK. The doctors always said it could all come flooding back someday, even all these years later, which is why I always get excited to meet people from back then. You never know what may do it, right Scotty."

He gave his mother a polite smile. It must be one he must use often, because to Matt it looked wooden. Practiced.

"It was very nice to meet you anyway," Karen said, eyes drifting back to the church. "Such a shame about that girl."

Matt was taken aback at the abrupt shift in tone from Mrs. Alston, jumping from delight to morose in a single sentence.

"Yes it is. Did you know her?"

"I used to watch over her," Mrs. Alston said. Tears suddenly appeared in her eyes. "After my husband died, I'd have kids out to the house when the parents worked. She was such a bright girl, wasn't she Scotty?"

The lace handkerchief appeared again as Karen Alston sobbed softly. Scott took his mother's elbow and led her away without a word.

Matt watched Scott help his mom to their car, unease boiling up from his stomach.

"WHAT DO YOU KNOW about Scott Alston?"

Matt stood in the doorway of Bill's office. He'd waited until their receptionist had left for lunch and he had his boss alone to ask.

"The Alston kid?" Bill asked, because when you are pushing 80 everyone is a kid. "What do you mean?"

Matt hadn't been sure how to approach this, but seeing Scott at the funeral planted a seed that was growing every day that passed without a suspect in Mackenzie Stamp's murder. He tried to dismiss it as ridiculousness, coincidence, but it wasn't going anywhere. He had to ask, partly hoping he would be told he was crazy.

"I ran into him a few days ago. We were in high school together."

Bill leaned back in his chair with a slight smile.

"Didn't know you, did he?"

Bill's insight amazed Matt, although it shouldn't have. Run a newspaper in a small town for your whole life and you probably know everything about everybody.

"No, he didn't."

"If you were in high school with him, you remember that accident he was in."

Matt nodded.

"Terrible thing," Bill continued. "A little girl and her mom died, and Scott almost did, but it just ended up scrambling his brain pretty good. Amnesia. Didn't remember a thing from before."

"That's what his mom said. But is that even possible? Nothing's come back after all these years?"

"I'm no doctor, but that's what they say," Bill said. "Why do you ask?"

Matt hesitated before responding. The stuff swirling in his head made for great hypothetical thoughts, but he knew it would sound exponentially more ridiculous when said aloud.

"It's just that when I talked to him he seemed different. Back in high school he was the kind of guy who was a little intimidating. He seemed much more... reserved. Is it possible he's changed that much?"

Bill smiled and got up from behind his desk.

"Yeah, he's a quiet guy," Bill said, putting his hand on Matt's shoulder and stepping through the doorway. "Keeps to himself and takes care of his mother. Ellie plays cards with Mrs. Alston, so we know them a little bit.

"I'm going to get some lunch. Want to come?"

Matt remained fixed to the doorway. "No thanks. I've got some stuff to do."

"Suit yourself," Bill said with a smile. "I wouldn't worry too much about Scott Alston. He may have been a pill in high school, but he's different now. Heck, maybe that accident was in some way a blessing for him."

Bill said goodbye and left, leaving Matt to wander back to his desk and sort out a head full of craziness on his own. Based on what he saw in high school, Scott should be the first suspect in a case like this. But if what Bill said is true, he's a completely different person now.

An accident can't fundamentally change who you are, right?

He minimized his desktop publishing program and opened an internet browser. He typed in 'amnesia' and looked with wonder as all the different hits came up. He spent the rest of the afternoon reading everything from the

Mayo Clinic website to Wikipedia, and what he found just brought up more questions.

Complete memory loss, or retrograde amnesia, is apparently not as common as soap operas will have you believe. It can be caused by traumatic brain injury, strokes, viruses or psychologically traumatic events, but is usually a temporary occurrence. Most people suffering from retrograde amnesia get their memories back in weeks or months. There are also various therapies that can be used to help people recover their memories. A complete blank slate was extremely rare and hotly debated among doctors and scientists.

Matt found quite a few stories about a man who claimed he woke up on a New York subway car one day with no memory of himself or his life. Complete memory loss—pretty much what Scott was claiming. His story was made into a documentary, although he found many articles that claimed it was an elaborate hoax and that the guy was faking the whole thing.

Could Scott have been faking this whole time?

It made sense—as much as anything in this case did, anyway. The kind of memory loss he was claiming was at best exceedingly rare, and according to many researchers impossible. Maybe he faked the amnesia from the beginning in hopes of a lighter sentence. Even if he hadn't, it was entirely plausible that if his memories did eventually come back he would keep up the story as a way to gain sympathy from the town. Or at least to blunt the hostility he'd faced after the accident.

It also made for a perfect cover if he wanted to hide his true personality.

The more Matt read, the more skeptical of Scott's story he became. He continued his research throughout the afternoon, and it wasn't until their secretary hollered back that she was leaving for the day that he realized what time it was. He printed off a few of the articles he had been reading and stuffed them into a manila folder that was sitting near the printer.

A WEEK PASSED WITHOUT any official developments. Matt talked with Ed Schwab a few times, but there was no new information or theories in the Stamp investigation. Matt followed up with an article after their second talk, basically saying how the police had no suspects, no leads, and once again asked the public for help.

Matt scoured the web looking for similar cases in other parts of the country. Naturally, there were a few missing teenage girls in the state, but nothing that screamed out a link to what happened with Mackenzie. There were some cases of bodies being burned out in Arizona, although that was part of the drug war raging along the border. Matt was fairly certain Mackenzie Stamp wasn't involved there.

With nothing else to latch onto, he kept coming back to Scott Alston. As subtly as he could in such a small town, Matt asked around about him. Nobody had much to say, and when they did it was just as Bill said.

Quiet.

Keeps to himself.

A changed man.

Since he'd gotten out of jail, Scott worked the second shift making storm doors and didn't have any friends. It was as if he and the town came to an agreement—you keep quiet and stay out of sight and we'll forget about that little accident you caused.

Matt had no idea what to think. Despite not getting anyone to corroborate his theory about Scott, he couldn't sweep it out of his head completely.

Maybe I'm the crazy one.

He was beginning to think the trail, and therefore his story, had gone cold, when an early morning phone call rousted him out of bed.

"Matt, there's been another one."

35

MATT TRIED TO SHAKE THE SLEEP from his head as he propped himself up on an elbow. He'd seen 7:09 on his alarm clock as he had reached for the phone lying next to it on his bedside table. His head was still too cloudy to understand what Bill was saying.

"What?"

"Another girl. Out by Rice Lake. Ed Schwab just called."

Matt bolted upright in his bed.

"What do you mean?" he asked. "You mean missing, or like, another body?"

"A body. Out at the north side boat ramp. You know where that is?"

Kids had been partying at that boat ramp for years—probably since Bill Harris was in school. They called it the North Shore. Surrounded by woods, there was a gravel road leading in through the trees, which opened up into a large clearing with an old boat ramp where the public could get their boats in and out of Rice Lake. Kids would park by the ramp, then follow a short path parallel to the shore to a second opening that looked out over the lake. For a 17-year-old kid, it was really a perfect place to bring a six-pack or bottle of Boone's Farm wine and hang out. As well known as it was—every kid was always shocked to find out their parents not only knew about it but also drank out there 25 years before—there were usually never any big, organized

---

parties. Too easy to bust. But it was a place where more often than not small groups of friends would end up finding each other, each toting a six-pack, and before the night was over half the kids in town were there.

"Yeah," Matt said. "North Shore."

"Right," Bill said.

"I'm on my way," Matt said. "You want to meet me there?"

"No," Bill responded. "You don't need me out there. Just call when you are on your way back."

"Will do," Matt said, and hung up. He hurriedly threw on some clothes and tore out his bedroom door. His dad was sitting at the kitchen table drinking a cup of coffee.

"What's wrong?"

Matt grabbed his messenger bag from the kitchen chair and dug through it looking for his recorder and notebook.

"They found another body," he said. "Bill just called. I'm heading out there now."

Jon closed his eyes and set his coffee down.

"Good God," he muttered.

"Yeah, this is fucked up," Matt said, not stopping to realize this was the first time he had used the 'f-word' in front of his dad. "Bill didn't know much, but it sounds like it may be the same thing as Mackenzie Stamp."

Matt tossed his notebook on the table, then finally found his recorder at the bottom of the bag's side pocket.

"Who's doing this?" Jon asked, probably more to himself than anything.

The question made a thought pass through Matt's mind, but he forced it down. Another victim was a game-changer. There would be tons of new information, new clues, any of which could turn his "theory" on its head.

Or confirm it.

No, he had to go out with an open mind. Reporters follow facts, not half-baked notions.

"I gotta go," Matt said, bolting for the door.

"You need the camera?" Jon asked.

"Shit," Matt replied, wheeling away from the door. The Nikon was sitting on the counter, its lithium ion battery charging in the outlet under the cabinet.

"Yeah," he said, slapping the battery back in. "Thanks."

Matt slung the neckstrap over his shoulder and headed back out.

"Be careful," Jon called after him.

THE SCENE AT THE NORTH SHORE was unlike anything Matt had seen. Well, it would have been, had Matt been allowed anywhere close enough to see it. He could see the lights as he got within a half mile of the turnoff towards the boat ramp. Seemingly every fire truck and police car in northern Iowa lined the road, and the road leading through the woods towards the North Shore was already blocked off. As he approached, an officer he didn't recognize standing in the middle of the road started walking towards him, motioning for him to turn around.

Matt stopped and rolled down his window as the officer approached, pointing back towards the way Matt came the whole time.

"Gotta turn around," he said, "Road's closed."

"Hi," Matt said. "I'm supposed to meet with Sheriff Schwab."

The cop looked at him skeptically.

"And you are?"

Damn, Matt thought. Anything short of an official title was going to do him no good.

"He called me, told me to come out," Matt lied. But it was partially true—he *had* called Bill.

The officer looked him over with a cynical eye before he caught sight of the camera on the passenger seat.

"What's your name?"

"Matt Carlton."

As they talked, Matt recognized Ben Jacobs approaching from behind.

"What's going on?" Deputy Jacobs asked.

The cop turned and spoke before Matt could say anything.

"Guy says he's here to see the Sheriff," he said, tilting his head towards Matt's car.

Deputy Jacobs leaned down to peer in Matt's windshield.

Shit, Matt thought, tightening his grip on the steering wheel.

"Sheriff's pretty busy right now, as you could probably imagine" the deputy said to Matt. "Not doing any interviews. Why don't you turn around."

Matt knew it wasn't a request, but tried anyway. "Hey, deputy, I was..."

"Turn around now," Jacobs said. "Right now."

"Fine, fine," Matt said. "Would you tell the sheriff I'm here?"

The deputy's face darkened as he looked down into Matt's car.

"I don't think he gives a rat's ass about you right now. Now turn around and get out of our way."

His tone left little room for negotiation, so Matt backed out. He followed the row of fire trucks and pulled to the side of the road after the last one. He put his car in park and considered his next move. There was no way Jacobs and his crew were going to let him back anywhere near North Shore. He opened the door and stepped out onto the road. Matt leaned against his front bumper and surveyed the area. He was dying to see what was going on, but saw no way to get back there without not only getting kicked out, but burning every bridge Bill had managed to build for him.

He pulled out his phone and called his boss.

"Hey Bill, it's Matt. I'm out by North Shore, but I'm pretty well shut out. They're not letting anyone back there."

"Yeah, I'm not surprised," Bill sighed. "What's it like out there?"

"It's a zoo," Matt responded. "Law enforcement and emergency responders everywhere. What did Schwab say?"

"Not much, just that there was another victim," Bill said. "Sounds like it's a very similar situation to Mackenzie Stamp, although he wouldn't come out and say it."

Matt's head was swimming. He looked back down the road towards the plethora of lights, people and vehicles all swarming around the road towards the North Shore. The response alone proved there was now a lot more on the table than just a dead girl.

"This changes everything. Two girls in the same town in a matter of weeks? We've got to be talking about some kind of serial killer operating here," No matter what he had thought before, Matt still couldn't believe he was saying those words out loud.

"Just slow down, Matt," Bill said. "We don't really know anything yet, and we need to get facts before we go flying off the handle."

"I understand, but if this ends up being the same as Mackenzie Stamp, there's no way that can be a coincidence, right? No chance, especially in a town like this. No way that's chance."

There was silence on the other end. Matt's brain was whirling, trying to wrap itself around the possibilities. A serial killer, in a small town, preying on high school girls — this was exactly the type of story that could go national. Network news. CNN. Nancy Grace's head would explode. As his mind raced, he thought about how the coverage would shape up. Worst case, the networks and the 24-hour news channels would all need interviews with people on the ground, and a local reporter who had been on top of the story from day one would fit the bill nicely.

And if he was the one who broke the story? True crime books were always popular, weren't they? Careers were made on stories like this.

"I need to talk with Sheriff Schwab," Matt said. "Can you call him and get me back there?"

"Matt, there's no way the Sheriff is going to let you back there during the investigation."

"Call him and find out. We've got to get on this."

"I'm not calling him now. He wouldn't answer anyway. We're just going to have to wait."

"I can't wait. This is too big. We've got a few hours before everyone else is out here on it too, so I've got to go now."

"No," Bill said sharply. "Listen to me, Matt. It's not happening. And I'm telling you right now, you're not to do anything stupid out there, you understand? Stop and think. You're right, there will be other news people out there. Probably soon. So any bits of little information you get now would be yours for, what, three hours? Being first isn't the only thing. It's not worth it."

"But..." Matt interjected.

"No," Bill snapped. "Think about this for a second. Being first is not something we are made for. The big boys will always have us there. BUT, that doesn't mean we don't have advantages."

Matt was steamed by this point. This was his shot. His best chance for something big. Stories like this didn't come around in a small town—ever. And the old man was going to block him from it.

This is my ticket out.

"What," Matt asked. He was upset enough that he didn't even regret the sarcastic tone he took.

"Well, think," Bill said in a tone Matt hadn't heard in 25 years. "Ed Schwab called me before heading out to the scene, and Ed Schwab is a prick. But he's loyal, and I've been dealing with him for about 25 years. I can't think of anything Ed would like more than to tell some big shot from CNN to go to hell. But he called me this morning."

Matt listened, waiting to see where Bill was going with this.

"If Ed will talk with me, we'll get information straight from the investigation. Stuff nobody else has. We may not always be first, but we can be best, and that's much more important in the long run."

Matt took a deep breath. Bill was right. As hard as it was to swallow, the man had a point. And while Matt would argue that they should strive to be first *and* best, the

181

obstacles they faced were indeed monumental. What chance could a small town weekly hope to have in scooping a network?

Besides, if he had information nobody else had, they would have to come to him to get it. Maybe he could be the face of this story after all.

"Fine," Matt conceded. "But I'm going to stay out here and see what I can get. I'm not going to get in the way, but I've got to get enough for a story for today."

"That's fine," Bill said.

"And you need to call the Sheriff," Matt said. "We need to talk to him *today*."

"Fine. I'll let you know if he gets back to me."

Matt spent the next three hours waiting, wandering up the road and talking to everybody who would look at him. He made no move to go down the road towards North Shore, which was now blocked by a pair of wooden sawhorses and police tape. Police, fire and sheriff vehicles came and went at a steady pace.

Despite repeatedly explaining the concept of "off the record", Matt had trouble getting much information from the various fire and law enforcement officers milling about. After about two hours of questions and eavesdropping, he was able to put together what was going on.

A young girl's body had been found early this morning, burned, at North Shore. It sounded to be exactly like what happened to Mackenzie Stamp.

Matt thought back to that day in the park all those years ago, his friend pulling out a magazine that showed the 14 signs of a serial killer, then telling him stories. Awful stories. Stuff kids shouldn't have to deal with. Assuming this was a similar situation, a serial killer was the most logical answer, as ridiculous as that statement sounded. With that as a starting point, there was only one place that path kept leading him.

The more he thought about it, the more excited he got.

Around 11 o'clock, a local news van pulled up. A reporter who looked like she was about 21-years-old jumped out and anxiously surveyed the scene. Her cameraman, a skinny, middle-aged guy with a scraggly goatee and torn blue jeans came out from behind the wheel and pulled a worn shoulder-camera out of the back of the van.

While the cameraman prepped for her stand-up, the reporter had pulled out a comically oversized notepad and walked down towards the barricade. Matt watched from a distance as she was re-buffed by Ben Jacobs, two guys in firemen's jackets and a paramedic. Despite the fact that he hadn't gotten a whole lot further, Matt couldn't help but chuckle.

She trekked back towards the van, looking like a kid that couldn't get into a kickball game at recess, and shot a short stand-up. After finishing, they packed up and headed out.

Matt remained through the early afternoon, chewing over his theories and occasionally checking in with Deputy Jacobs to see if any new developments were coming out. Expectedly, he got nothing, and by the third time he could tell the deputy was plenty sick of Matt's inquiries.

As he was walking back towards his car, Matt's phone rang.

It was Bill, letting him know he'd heard from the Sheriff.

"There's going to be a press conference at 5 p.m.," Bill said.

36

AROUND FOUR O'CLOCK, Matt drove out to Bill Harris's house, located on a hill just a couple minutes outside of town. The turnoff to the drive was marked by an old Heidelberg Windmill printing press, which Bill had stuck a mailbox on the end of. Very fitting for the old newspaperman.

Ellie Harris greeted Matt at the door with a smile and hug. She was just a little thing, barely topping five feet, but her eyes showed the spark that Bill was always talking about. Combined with the slender build she maintained from walking three miles every day, she was in remarkable shape for a woman who had to be on her way to 80.

She ushered Matt into the kitchen, where Bill sat at the table with a pile of newspapers in front of him. Matt looked down and saw the last few issues of the *Graphic-Glimpse*, along with the Mason City *Globe Gazette* and the *Des Moines Register*. All were opened to stories about Mackenzie Stamp.

Bill stood up from his chair. "Well, shall we?"

"Sounds good," Matt replied.

As Bill stepped away from the table, Ellie swooped down and started gathering the papers together.

"We can take my car, if you want," Matt offered.

"That's OK, I can drive," Bill said. He turned back towards Ellie. "I should be back in a couple hours, OK hon? Hopefully not too late."

Ellie Harris stacked the newspapers in a pile on the edge of the table and gave her husband a quick peck on the lips.

"That's fine," she replied. "What are you two going to do about dinner?"

"Depends on how long things last."

"We can grab something over in Forest City," Matt offered.

The thought of fast food brought a grandmotherly scowl to Ellie's face.

"Nonsense," she said. "I'll have leftovers here. It heats up just fine. You two can come out for sandwiches."

Matt looked at Bill. There was no way he'd have time for a dinner visit tonight. He started to open his mouth for what he hoped was a polite denial when Bill spoke up.

"We'll see, OK hon? But right now, we've got to go. Love you," Bill said.

"Love you too," Ellie responded. She'd taken the hint and backed off. "Take care you two. It was good to see you Matt."

Matt smiled back.

"You too Ellie."

Bill led Matt through the kitchen and out the door into the garage. They got into Bill's red Ford Explorer and backed out.

"So what's he going to tell us?" Matt asked.

Bill turned around in the driveway and pulled out towards the road.

"Honestly, I don't know." he said.

Matt had debated telling Bill about his theory about Scott since it had first invaded his thoughts, and he batted it around the entire drive to Forest City. By the time he'd made his decision, they'd arrived.

LIVE SATELLITE TRUCKS from Channel 3 and Channel 6 were already parked outside the sheriff's department when Bill and Matt pulled up. Each had tripods set up for live shots with the county courthouse as the backdrop.

The media briefing was held in a conference room at the Sheriff's office, which was much more comfortable holding meetings than press conferences. Just after five, a group of men in suits walked in with Ed Schwab trailing behind, sporting a look of poorly contained frustration. His deputies followed the group in and hung back around the door. The room suddenly felt very cramped.

"Thank you all for coming out," one of the suits said into the bank of microphones, using the smooth delivery of somebody used to public speaking. "I realize it was kind of short notice on a Sunday evening, but we felt it was important to put out some information tonight, in regards to the situation earlier today at Rice Lake."

Situation? Is that what we call the second murder this month?

"Anyway, I am Agent Lee Terry with the Iowa Department of Criminal Investigation," he continued. "Late last night, the Winnebago County Sheriff's office got a call about a fire and potential body found by the north boat ramp at Rice Lake, a few miles outside of Lake Mills. Dispatch then contacted the Lake Mills Volunteer Fire Department and sent both on-duty officers to investigate.

"When they arrived at Rice Lake, the deputies found the fire burnt out and the body of what appeared to be a high school-aged female. They immediately cleared and secured the scene, then reported in to Sheriff Ed Schwab, who then contacted the DCI.

"The body was identified as 16-year-old Jillian Dayton of Lake Mills."

While Matt furiously scribbled in his notepad, Bill sat with his elbows propped on the table, content to take in every word himself. Before Matt could get a question in, a voice from the back came in.

"Was this an accident or do you suspect foul play?"

Leave it to a TV guy to make the first question a dumb one.

"We're obviously looking at everything, but this is being handled as a homicide investigation," Terry responded.

"What was the cause of death?" a reporter across the table asked.

"Right now, the medical examiner has the body and will be performing an autopsy to determine the cause of death."

"Was it the fire?"

"We don't know if the fire was the cause of death or if it was done post-mortem. That's something we expect the medical examiner to tell us."

Matt continued to dictate what was said, no matter how ridiculous he thought the questions were, until he caught up enough to fire one of his own.

"What connection does this have to Mackenzie Stamp?"

Agent Terry quickly glanced back at the two other men in suits along the wall behind him before answering in a very measured tone.

"We're looking at all possibilities," he said. "As of now we know of none."

"Is there any known connection between the two girls?" Matt asked.

"Nothing beyond the obvious—they attended high school together and assumedly knew each other, but they were not friends and had no connection out of the ordinary that we know of."

Matt could tell the DCI was doing all it could to avoid anything sensational, so he would have to be direct.

"Do you think there is a serial killer in Lake Mills?"

The buzz in the room disappeared as the question hung unanswered. Agent Terry looked like his brain was digging for the appropriate 'official' response, while whatever animosity Sheriff Schwab had towards the suits he was forced to work with was transferred to the glare that bore into Matt from across the room.

"We aren't ready to make any assumptions at this time."

"Assumptions?" Matt asked. "You have two teenage girls killed in the exact same way two weeks apart. You aren't trying to say that is a coincidence, are you?"

Sheriff Schwab stepped in front of Agent Terry and grabbed one of the microphones off the podium.

"Nobody's saying anything right now, and nobody's making any assumptions about anything," the Sheriff said. Matt could see the hate boil off the top of his head. "And if you had any clue how to do your job, you won't be jumping to any rash conclusions either."

Agent Terry shouldered his way back in front of the podium and shot daggers at Schwab for hijacking his press conference.

"Right now the most important thing is for the public to stay calm and know we are looking into everything."

Bill sat stoically in the chair next to him, and Matt could feel the disapproval coming off his boss in waves. Questions continued from around the room, but Matt couldn't get Agent Terry to even look in his direction, so he resorted to stenographer mode. The heat of the Sheriff's glare was palpable as he took notes.

Jillian Dayton had attended a party Friday night at North Shore with some friends, who last remembered seeing her around 11:30. When the party started to wind down around 12:30, they looked around for Jillian and left when they couldn't find her, assuming she caught a ride back into town with somebody else.

"When the deceased failed to return home last night, her parents went out looking for her," Agent Terry said. "When they arrived at the scene, the parents discovered a large fire burning in a fire pit. Upon closer examination they saw what appeared to be a body in the fire and immediately called 9-1-1."

There were plenty of other questions about the Dayton family, which were deflected each time. Terry grew visibly frustrated with each one, sticking to the company line before finally calling an end to the press conference.

As Matt gathered up his things and shoveled them into his bag, Bill stood up and exchanged a brief few words with Sheriff Schwab as he walked out.

Matt stood and looped his bag around his neck as Bill turned back to him.

"I'll meet you at the car," he said before walking over towards the doorway Ed Schwab had just disappeared through.

MATT SAT IN THE PASSENGER SEAT of Bill's car, anxiously watching the reporter from Channel 6 do his live spot. He couldn't imagine trying to condense all they'd heard into a 60 second sound bite.

"Girl killed... No suspects... Call if you saw it... Back to you, Ted."

It would be like trying to write his story on a telegraph.

The driver's side door popped open and Bill dropped in behind the wheel.

"Anything new?" Matt asked. He assumed Bill had hung back to talk to the Sheriff privately.

Bill shook his head.

"Ed wouldn't say much with the DCI hanging about, but he is plenty mad about them taking over the investigation."

"Great," Matt said, butting the back of his head against his seat.

"He also gave me an earful about your performance back there."

"My *performance*?" Matt shot. It was louder than he would have liked, but there was apparently more frustration built up than he'd realized. "I asked the questions that everyone else in there wanted to ask. Questions everyone else in there *should* have asked. Come on, Bill, you know that."

"You still don't get it," Bill said in the measured tone of a parent explaining something for the 12th time.

"I'm just doing the job you hired me to do."

"No you're not," Bill said. "This isn't the *Times*, and we have a certain way of doing things. We are part of a community, and we have an obligation to that community. Throwing the term 'serial killer' around certainly isn't it."

"But that's what this *is*," Matt said, trying to keep his voice level. "I'm not trying to sensationalize anything, I'm dealing with reality. How does sugar-coating this help the community?"

"If the authorities aren't using the term 'serial killer', than we are not."

"So Ed Schwab decides what's in our paper now?"

"No, I do," Bill snapped. It was the first time Matt had heard him truly raise his voice. "And if you plan on writing anything for *my* paper, you'd best remember that."

Matt turned and looked out the window, his professional pride taking a backseat to the guilt of disappointing his boss.

The sound of the ignition snapped the heavy silence as Bill put the car in gear.

"We'll go back to the office and write something for the web," Bill said. Matt thought it sounded like a peace offering, although it also meant that Bill would be looking over his shoulder as he wrote his story.

The silence returned as they pulled out of the parking lot.

Probably not the best time to tell him about Scott.

BACK IN THE OFFICE, Matt banged out his story in 20 minutes, going long on facts and short on speculation. The only mention of the Mackenzie Stamp murder was towards the end, when Matt used the "not ruling anything out" quote from Special Agent Terry.

The words 'serial killer' were never used.

After a quick approval from Bill, Matt posted the story to the *Graphic-Glimpse* website, then put a link on their Facebook and Twitter feeds. When he looked up from the computer, Bill had gone into his office. Matt pushed back from his desk and rolled across the floor, leaning back towards the office door.

"It's up," he called.

Bill stepped out of his office and turned off the light behind him.

"I need to get home," Bill said. "Ellie's probably waiting up for me."

"No problem. I'll shut this all down."

Bill remained in the doorway that separated the front office from the newsroom as Matt turned back towards the computer.

"You're a good reporter," he said. "Probably too good to be working at a small town rag like this. But right now, this is where you are, and we're going to do things the small town way. I need to know you can do that."

"I get that, but this isn't a small town story," Matt replied.

"Maybe not," Bill said, letting the sentence hang in the air. Matt waited for some folksy rationale that would both frustrate and chasten him, but it never came. Instead, Bill just gave a slight nod and walked out.

Matt sat in front of his computer, staring at the empty doorway. Eventually he stood up and started gathering his stuff. A manila folder poked out from under his black messenger bag.

The folder full of his theory.

His moment of glory.

His ticket out.

Matt reached out and grabbed it, but something fell out and fluttered to the floor.

Mackenzie Stamp smiled up from her senior portrait. She was a cute girl, Matt thought as he stooped down to pick up the photo, as if that made what happened to her worse.

He lifted the top off the scanner and grabbed the photo of Jillian he'd used with his story. She actually looked a lot like Mackenzie. Same sandy blonde hair, same dark eyes — the kind of cute small towns seemed to produce year after year.

The thought projected an image in Matt's brain from years ago that sent him running across the room to the archives, where every edition from the past 50 years was stored. But he wasn't looking that far back. Fifteen years would be plenty.

It didn't take much flipping to find what he was looking for. The captain of the 1996 Lake Mills Varsity Football Cheerleaders beamed off the page, her sandy blonde hair framing her pretty face and brown eyes sparkling. Matt had almost forgotten what Amy Martin looked like when she wasn't being choked out across a dark alley.

He dropped the pictures of Mackenzie and Jillian on either side of her. They weren't identical, but definitely came from the same mold.

Matt knew it didn't prove anything, but it chased away the doubts that had been creeping in. It wouldn't be enough for Bill, and Ed Schwab would probably rather arrest himself for the murders than listen to Matt at this point, but there was one person who would be receptive.

Matt fished his phone out of his pocket as he grabbed his stuff. By the time he was out the door he had found David's number and hit 'call'.

37

THE NIGHT AIR GAVE MATT a chill as he stepped out of the *Graphic-Glimpse* office, phone pressed to his ear. Fall was threatening to make just a cursory appearance before stepping back and ushering winter into the area. He was halfway to his car before he realized the phone must have rung 7-8 times. Did David not have voice mail?

"Hello?"

The voice surprised Matt.

"Oh, hey, David… it's Matt,"

There was a bit of a pause, during which Matt realized he'd made a phone call at 10:20 on a Sunday night.

"Sorry for calling so late. I didn't wake you up, did I?"

"No, it's fine. What do you need?"

Matt realized he'd called before actually contemplating what he was going to say. *I was just wondering if you could re-hash some painful memories for me so I could prop up a half-baked theory I've got about a serial killer who's killed and burned a pair of teenagers in town.*

"Well… I've actually got a few things I wanted to ask you about. It's nothing bad, I mean, I'm working on a story and wanted to ask you some stuff. Nothing on the record… just background stuff."

Matt was babbling. He should have gotten his thoughts together before calling. Or waited until the morning. The urgency he had felt earlier had melted away. He was about to apologize and hang up when David spoke again.

"Sure, want to stop by?"

Matt was legitimately surprised at the offer. He glanced at his watch again.

"Tonight? Are you sure it isn't too late? We could do something tomorrow or something."

"Nah, just come over now. I'll be up for a while anyway. You know where I am?"

Matt realized he had no idea where David lived. The only place he'd seen him since he'd moved back to Lake Mills was up at Frank's Place.

"No, actually. What's your address?"

David described how to get to his place, using the small-town address system of "two blocks past the railroad tracks, the white house across from where the Hill's used to live" instead of actual numbers. That was probably easier. Matt didn't know if he'd know where 1102 North Harrison Street was anyway.

By the time David was done with the directions, Matt was standing by his car. He popped the lock and slid behind the wheel, phone still glued to his ear.

"I'll see you in a minute."

DAVID LIVED ON THE NORTH EDGE of town, in a small house about two blocks from the giant grain elevator where area farmers brought their corn every fall after harvest. As Matt pulled into the driveway behind an old Ford Ranger, he noticed the white paint was peeling off the siding and one of the windows in the door of the detached garage was cracked. The lawn was shaggy, and the bushes in the beds along the front of his house hadn't been trimmed in a long time. Their tangled branches poofed up like an unkempt afro, covering the bottom half of David's front windows. Lilac bushes maybe? It was hard to tell. The blooms were long gone at this time of year. It was the exact opposite of his father's house, which was kept with precision of a drill sergeant with time on his hands.

He stepped out of his car and walked around towards the side of the house. The white metal storm door gave off a sharp knock under his knuckles, and David answered it almost immediately. He ushered Matt into the kitchen without a word, and the door quickly swung shut behind him with a bang.

The level of upkeep in the interior matched what was outside. At least three days of dishes were piled in the sink, while the diamond pattern on the linoleum floor looked like it hadn't been scrubbed in years. Swept, maybe, but the only liquid it had come in contact with was spills.

David cleared away a spot at the small kitchen table and offered Matt a seat. They exchanged pleasantries as he grabbed two cans of Miller Lite from the fridge and sat down across from Matt. David was wearing a dark, long sleeved t-shirt. It looked charcoal but may have been black many washes ago. Bags of the same color were under his eyes.

"So what can I do for you?" David asked, popping the top of his beer with a *pfffsh*. It was to his lips before the foam that had jumped out the top could make its way down the side of the can.

Matt left his beer on the table.

"You hear about what happened today? Well, last night?"

Beer still on his lips, David looked down the can towards Matt. He finished a long pull and set it down on the table in front of him.

"You mean…"

"They found another body out at North Shore," Matt said, suddenly too anxious to wait for the pace David seemed to be setting. "High school girl, burned just like Mackenzie Stamp."

David nodded slightly, his eyebrows raised in curiosity.

"Yeah, I caught that on the news."

Matt didn't wait to consider his approach, nor did he plan out what he was going to say. He plowed forward.

"So that's two girls in a month, in the same area, killed in the same way. At this point, you aren't dealing with something random. And while the cops won't come out and say it, that means there must be some kind of serial killer here."

Matt stopped for a second, allowing the absurdity of what he just said to wash over him. David was offering no reaction. He just stared across the table, waiting for him to continue. Watching David listen made Matt realize, for the first time, that he was quite possibly speaking out of turn. David didn't seem like the gossipy type, but if word got out that Matt was running his own little investigation, Sheriff Schwab would blow a rod. Not only that, but he'd burn Bill too. Matt could see the look his boss would give him after sitting through the Sheriff's red-faced tantrum and immediately changed gears.

"I can trust you to keep this between us, right?" Matt said. "It's just... I've got some things I want to ask you about, but if it gets back to the Sheriff..."

David cut him off with a wave of his hand.

"Don't worry about it."

Matt studied him from across the table, contemplating his next sentence. The silence hung, and he could hear the kitchen clock ticking. It reminded him of the giant clocks on the walls back in high school. During the quiet of a test, the seconds would echo across the room, reminding you that you better hurry up and finish, Jack. Time's a wastin'.

David nodded slightly, giving as much reassurance as he could in such a small gesture.

"You remember what you showed me our junior year?"

David's expression didn't change. For a minute, Matt thought he wasn't sure what he was talking about. But he had to remember. How could anyone forget that? Matt remembered it vividly, an early fall day, sitting in the park, watching his friend re-live the most terrifying day of his life before showing him something he'd found in a magazine.

The silence hung. Did David seriously not remember? Had he repressed it somehow? Erased it from his memories?

"You're finally ready to listen."

Apparently he did remember. David looked across the table with an odd mix of satisfaction and condescension. He looked like a schoolteacher who finally got through to his student, but only after some long, drawn-out battles. Matt hadn't known how David would react to him bringing this up, but that look threw him off a bit.

"Yeah, I guess," Matt said, trying to re-gain his footing. "You've... I guess you've already thought about this? About what's going on now?"

David's half smile was washed away as he took another drink from his beer and leaned back in his chair. His eyes followed the can as he set it down in front of him, twirling the half-empty can on the Formica tabletop with his fingertips. The liquid inside shifted as he slowly spun the can, but it never tipped.

"Yeah, you can say I've thought about it," David said, eyes remaining on the can.

"Well, what do you think?" Matt asked. Even as the question traveled across the table, Matt knew it was a stupid one. David let go of his beer can, and it completed one last semi-circle before settling upright on the table. His eyes rose up and met Matt's.

"Same as before."

This little dance Matt was doing was getting him nowhere. Time to jump in the pool.

"You think it could be him?"

"It doesn't matter what I think, does it?" David said. "Nobody listens to me anyway. Jesus, it took two dead girls just to get YOU here, right? Is that enough? Sure you don't want to wait for a few more?"

Matt was taken aback by the aggression in David's tone. Apparently this was something he'd been thinking about for a long time. Probably since high school.

"David, I..."

"No, seriously, what's it going to take to get somebody to listen to me? Because it's gonna keep happening until somebody does something about him."

Matt looked across the table in silence. David closed his eyes and exhaled, seemingly trying to blow the hostility out of him. When he looked back, his tone was more measured.

"I get it. You didn't see him as a kid… the things he did. But you DID see him in high school. That night, behind the Wreck. You saw it. Saw what he was capable of, even then, but you still didn't want to do anything about it."

Matt was on the defensive. Didn't want to do anything about it? What could they have done about it back then?

"Well I'm here now," Matt finally said. "I'm not saying he did it, but right now the police have no suspects, and between what we saw and everything you told me back then, I'd say he's a good place to start."

David sat forward in his chair and put his elbows on the table. He reached down and scooped up his beer, putting it to his lips and downing the rest. He stood up to get another.

"That's fine, but don't mention me. I want my name left out of it." David grabbed another Miller Lite from the fridge and stood behind his chair. "And don't tell the sheriff about me, either. I'm not testifying or anything."

"No problem," Matt said, wearing his most trusted reporter's 'assurance' face. "This isn't anything for court or anything. Anything you say to me is off the record."

David nodded, placed his unopened beer on the table then turned to his left and walked out of the kitchen. Completely confused, Matt leaned forward in his chair and tried to see through the doorway where David had disappeared. He heard footsteps trailing away from the other room, then what sounded like the squeak of a door hinge.

What the hell?

"David?"

No answer. Matt considered getting up to follow, but he found himself unable to rise from the hard kitchen chair. Just as he was about to call out again, David emerged from the doorway. He extended an old file stuffed with papers across the table. It was a well-worn manila folder, the edges soft and the tab on top blank. The spine had been creased multiple times from years of opening and closing. There was no doubt that it would lay flat on the table whenever you opened it up.

Matt stared at it, unsure of what to do. When he didn't reach for it right away, David dropped it on the table. The 'plop' echoed around the tiny kitchen.

"What's this?" Matt asked. He tentatively reached towards the corner, as if he was grabbing the tail of a snake. He grabbed the corner—with two fingers, just in case it bites—flipped it open and saw a stack of articles, some printed off the internet, some photocopies of magazines and journals. Each had some version of "Serial Killer" in the title.

On the inside cover of the folder, a small, faded red square of text had been secured with tape.

What Makes a Serial Killer?

"Jesus," Matt gasped. "What is all this?"

Now seated again across the table, David popped his beer and took a long pull.

"Just some things I've found over the years."

Matt leafed through the papers, both amazed and disconcerted that David had all this stuff in his house. By the condition of the papers and the dates on the articles, it was obvious that he'd been collecting these for quite a while.

Serial Killers: Nature vs. Nurture

The Psychology of Violent Serial Crimes

Animal Cruelty – A Window to Serial Killing?

"OK then," Matt said.

They spent the next hour going over what they knew about Scott Alston. Matt mostly listened and jotted the occasional note as David more or less went down his list, just like he did that day in the park.

When they started talking about Scott's early family life, David spun the folder around towards him and started leafing through the papers, eventually pulling out a photocopy of a newspaper article.

"Here's his biological father," he said, laying the copy in front of Matt as if he was dealing blackjack.

Calling what he saw an article was generous. In reality, it was a three-paragraph blurb, probably cut out of the third page of the 'State' section of whatever paper it came from.

Third Inmate Dies From Overdose

"He was abusive, heavy into drugs and was a violent psychotic," David said as Matt read. The article didn't quite put it that way, although the fact that he was in prison for domestic assault and distribution of methamphetamines certainly helped David's case. It also mentioned a previous history of arrests for everything from drug possession to breaking and entering.

David continued, talking about Scott's home life as a kid, although Matt was finding most of that speculative. Assuming somebody was knocked around as a kid wasn't going to convince anybody. Eventually, David got into the stuff he'd actually witnessed. The way Scott had talked to and about his mother (7. They hate their fathers and mothers), the incidents at school (9. Many serial killers spend time in institutions as children and have records of early psychiatric problems) and finding the kid diapers in his bedroom (12. More than 60 percent of serial killers wet their beds beyond the age of 12).

"Ok," Matt said, scribbling notes in the notepad David had gotten out for him. "What about the animal stuff?" He glanced up and made eye contact across the table.

"You know... the cat?"

While David returned his stare, Matt picked up on the clock again.

Tick-Tick-Tick

"Yeah... he did it," David said. "I told you about that."

"Right, I just..." Matt didn't know how to finish that sentence. Maybe David was right. What else did he need to know? "OK."

"There's all kinds of that shit," David said.

All kinds? Matt didn't know what David meant by that, but something about his tone prevented him from following up.

Matt looked down at the list, then over to his notes. Nothing concrete, but a hell of a lot of similarities.

"What about now?" Matt asked. They'd focused exclusively on Scott's past, trying to prove their theory that he could do this without ever looking into if he actually did. "What do we know about him since he got back?"

"He lives with his mom out by Rice Lake," David said. "Same place he grew up. He works second shift out at Larson's."

"Second shift... that's, what, three to eleven?""

"Yup."

"So he wasn't working when the girls got killed."

"Nope, it's one of the first things I checked," David said. "And with his mom asleep when he gets off, he's pretty much got the whole night to himself."

It wasn't proof of anything, but it did take away a potential alibi. Matt was surprised at how much David knew about Scott's life since he'd been released from prison, although considering the folder sitting on the table in front of him shouldn't have been.

"Have you ever talked to him?" Matt asked.

"You mean since he got back? No."

"I did. After Mackenzie's funeral."

"He was at Mackenzie's funeral?" David spat.

"Yeah, it's where I first saw him. To be honest, I hadn't thought about him for years." Matt looked down at the mess of papers spread across the table and realized he'd been alone in forgetting about Scott Alston.

"So here's the thing," Matt continued. "He didn't remember me at all."

David let out a disgusted sounding chuckle. "Yeah."

"I started asking around about him, and pretty much got the same story," Matt said. "Everybody says he's different now."

"You can't possibly believe that," David said, casting a doubtful look across the table.

Matt was immediately defensive.

"I didn't know what to believe, so I started researching it." he said, pulling his own manila folder out and plopping it on the pile of printouts that spanned the gulf between the two. "There's no real agreement, but most of the stuff I found said long-term retrograde amnesia — losing all your memories — is at best extremely rare."

"I looked into it. It's not even possible," David said. He opened the folder and leafed through the papers.

201

"Most say that personality changes from head injuries are possible, but temporary," Matt said. "As the person slowly re-gains his memories, he should revert to the person he was. Obviously, there can be some changes in behavior due to the accident that caused the injury—you know, someone could be less reckless or something—but the core personality would still be there."

He looked at David, who was poring over the articles Matt had printed off earlier. He had calmed considerably, and now seemed increasingly interested in what Matt had found.

"He's been putting on that act for years," David said, more to himself than Matt. "He hasn't changed a bit."

"Well, it would make life easier for him," Matt said. "But let's say he did have amnesia like the doctors said. Eventually his memories would come back, right, and he'd revert to who he was. So, if he was a psycho back in school, wouldn't that come back too? Amnesia would make the perfect cover if he didn't want anybody to suspect him."

The more they talked, the more convinced Matt became that there was indeed something here. There *had* to be. It all fit.

But it was still all speculative. If Matt wanted anyone to take a serious look at Scott, they were going to have to come up with something concrete.

"What we need is something that connects the victims to Scott," David said.

Matt reached into the folder and pulled out the photos.

"I just noticed this tonight," Matt said. He put them on the table and spun them around to face David. "Similar, right?"

Matt gave him a second to study before continuing. "If you put them next to a shot of Amy Martin, you'd be amazed. Same hair, same eyes—they could all be sisters."

David stared at the pictures on the table. "I can't believe I never saw that, but yeah. It's there."

"It's not proof, but, again, it would be an awfully big coincidence," Matt said.

David picked up both pictures and held them side-by-side in front of him. He spoke without taking his eyes off them.

"He watched them, you know."

"What are you talking about?" Matt asked.

"I'd see him at the school, parked across the street. Just sitting in his car when class let out. When all the kids were gone he'd drive away," Matt's gaze wandered as he spoke. "It's probably where he found them, at school. Maybe he picked them because they looked like Amy. It was his way to finish the job he started back in high school."

Matt was flabbergasted at the thought of Scott staking out the high school. If true, it was a huge mark against Scott. He couldn't understand how David had waited all this time to drop that on him.

"You saw him at the school? Watching kids? How have you not reported this?"

David's attention snapped back across the table. "I told you, nobody *listens* to me. That's why I'm telling you. You're the respected journalist. Like that story about the guys ripping off the flood money you told me about at Frank's that time. Didn't that get a bunch of politicians fired? If *you* write something about him, people will listen."

Matt wasn't sure how to proceed, as David didn't look like he was in the mood to hear an explanation of how libel laws work.

"I can't just write a story about how I think Scott Alston killed those two girls," Matt saw David's reaction coming before he finished his sentence, so he just kept talking. "What I can do is take all this to Sheriff Schwab — or Bill, and he can take it to the sheriff."

David did not look enthusiastic.

"If we can present a legitimate case, they will have to look into him," Matt continued.

David put his elbows on the table and cradled his face in his hands. Matt was about to speak again when David looked back up.

"When will you talk to him?"

"Tomorrow," Matt said. "I should go over there anyway to see if they have any new information. I'll lay out everything we know. He'll listen."

Matt looked up at the clock and was stunned to see it was almost 12:30.

"Wow, I better get going."

Matt stood up from his chair and reached down for the notebook he'd been using. It wasn't until they'd finished that Matt realized he had filled at least half of it with notes. He'd also taken down quotes from David. He certainly wouldn't need those when talking to the Sheriff tomorrow. And as he'd said, he wasn't writing any of this for the paper. They were the kind you would need for a book.

What's wrong with that? Better to have it and not need it, right?

He wouldn't be able to tear that many pages out.

"Mind if I take this?" He asked, holding the notebook up.

"Go ahead."

"Thanks," Matt stuffed it into his front jacket pocket, where it hung out awkwardly.

David remained seated, eyes down at the table but looking somewhere else entirely. Somewhere Matt couldn't see.

"This has to stop," he said. "This time, it HAS to stop."

Matt looked down at him as he zipped his coat. The end of the notepad caught on his arm and bent forward, threatening to pop out and tumble to the floor. He awkwardly swung his arm back around to pull his sleeve off the metal coil.

"Thanks again," Matt said, crossing over towards the door. "Sorry I kept you up so late."

David just stared at whatever he was seeing through the table.

"See ya," Matt said, waiting for a reply. Eventually, he pushed the door open and stepped out into the night.

DAVID SAT AT HIS KITCHEN TABLE. Matt had left five minutes ago, or maybe it was 20. His head was swimming with so many thoughts it was hard to tell. The one thing he did know was that this might just be ending. Somebody was *finally* listening to him.

It was good to know he wasn't crazy. There were times over the years that even David began to wonder.

He pried his eyes open and looked down at the table. The beat-up folder was lying there. Matt had gathered up all the papers, piled them inside and shut it before he left. Now it just sat there, looking up at him.

He never imagined how much that cheap little folder would cost him when he pulled it out of the back of a drawer all those years ago.

Hours digging through books at the library (*down in Mason City, up in Albert Lea – never here*). Afternoons (*when he should have been working*) clicking through web pages. Nights keeping a safe distance as Scott Alston drove (*not a Mustang anymore*) out to his mother's house after work.

Had he been obsessed? Yeah, he probably had been.

But who wouldn't be?

All time that could have been spent with Carrie, who wasn't a big fan of secrets. He could have told her, but David tried that with Matt and saw how that went and didn't want her to bail on him too.

In the end, she just assumed he was cheating on her.

When this all ends, maybe she would understand. Not that David expected her to come back, but at least she could see why.

If this ends.

No, it would. It had to. He always knew the hardest part was getting someone to listen to him, and Matt was listening. Just the thought caused the pressure behind his eyes to ease.

Unfortunately, it was too late for Mackenzie and Jillian.

The thought hit David hard. He hadn't known them, but saw them in the hallways at school. Both seemed like good kids. Way too good for what happened to them. He'd been worried for years that it would get to this point, that nobody

205

would listen until Scott actually did something. In that regard, he felt like a failure, but what else could he do?

David had immediately called the Tip-line after the news broke about Mackenzie, but they obviously did nothing, and Jillian paid the price.

Hopefully now they would listen. Hearing it from Matt Carlton, respected journalist, should help.

Assuming he would actually help this time.

David scooped up the folder and went to put it away.

38

WHEN HE GOT TO THE OFFICE Monday morning, Matt penned a recap for the print edition, similar to the one he did for Mackenzie Stamp, then worked on getting the rest of the paper in shape for Wednesday. Bake sales and wedding anniversaries didn't stop just because two girls were killed.

Bill stopped into the office just before noon to lend a set of eyes to Matt's story. Like the Mackenzie Stamp story, Matt placed the text under a banner headline with the dominant photo Jillian's school portrait. He also used a picture of the sheriff's blockade of the road into the north side boat access as secondary art below the fold. After a bit of internal debate, Matt ran Mackenzie Stamp's photo alongside his secondary story.

God they look like Amy.

He didn't come right out and write specifically about the potential connections between the two cases, but it was obvious to anyone who read the story. Bill gave it his approval and headed out. Matt considered telling him about what he and David had talked about the night before, but decided against it. Bill wouldn't be keen on Matt running his own little investigation and would just tell him to let the authorities handle it. Might as well go straight to the sheriff's department. That way, they'd at least hear what he had to say. Even if they didn't believe him right away, they might take it more seriously as time wore on without any other suspects.

Or if another girl gets killed.

Matt grabbed his cell and called the Sheriff's Department to set up a meeting with Ed Schwab. Unsurprisingly, his receptionist said he was busy all day and would have no time to meet with Matt. He asked about tomorrow and got another polite, but firm, answer.

No dice.

"He's pretty busy this week sweetheart." She sounded like a grandmother explaining why he couldn't have a cookie right before dinner.

Matt thanked her politely and assured her he understood. If there was one thing he had learned in his time as a reporter, it was always treat the secretaries well. They were the gatekeepers. Most were nice, but every one of them relished the chance to make life hard for a jerk. But if they like you...

"I can imagine it's crazy in there for all of you," he said. "People calling non-stop, asking a million questions. I don't mean to be a bother myself."

"Between mine and the Sheriff's phone, it's ringing almost non-stop," she said. "Lots of reporters like yourself. Couldn't have come to the press conference we had, though, they're special and gotta call me. Then we get the whacko-birds. Got nothing better to do than call the sheriff."

"I believe it," Matt said in his friendliest tone. "We're getting the same here. Everybody thinks they know something, don't they?"

"Amen. I can't wait 'til they get the bastard that did this."

Matt almost laughed at hearing the grandmotherly voice from the other end of the line break out the sailor talk.

"Actually, that's what I wanted to talk to the Sheriff about," Matt hoped their small bit of conversation had bought him enough good will for what he was about to ask. "As you know, Bill Harris and I have been looking into this from the beginning, and we've both talked with Sheriff Schwab about a lot of stuff. I've got some information he's going to want to hear, but I know he's super busy. I guess I could talk with the DCI, but I would really rather give it to the sheriff myself, you know? What do you think I should do?"

Matt waited anxiously on the line, listening to the elderly secretary think. He knew she was still on the line because he could still hear the sounds coming from her desk. Flipping through an appointment book maybe? Or just looking for the crossword? He hoped he hadn't laid it on *too* thick.

"Ed should be in the office all afternoon," She came back. "Why don't you stop by later and I can get you in."

"Perfect," Matt said, mentally high-fiving himself. "How about around four?"

AT 3:40, MATT CLOSED UP the pages he'd been working on, powered his computer down and headed out for Forest City. He'd grabbed the notebook he'd taken from David's house, although he didn't think he would need it. If what he had to say wouldn't convince the sheriff, documentation probably wouldn't make the difference. He mentally went over what he would say during the drive over, concentrating more on his case against Scott Alston than the road.

By the time Matt walked through the glass door at the Sheriff's Office, it was four o'clock and Sheriff Schwab was the only person in the office aside from Theresa, who handled both dispatch and secretarial duties. She looked exactly how she'd sounded on the phone. Her grey hair was pulled back into a tight bun and she wore a thin, yellow cardigan over her white blouse. Matt wasn't about to guess her age, but there was no doubt she'd been answering the phones here at least as long as the Sheriff had been around.

Theresa informed Matt that the sheriff was on the phone but she'd squeeze him in when he was done if he just wanted to have a seat. She offered Matt a cup of coffee, which he politely declined.

After ten minutes, Matt began to get antsy and regretted passing on the coffee. He pulled out his notebook and looked over his notes yet again, more to give him something to do than anything else. A while later, Theresa apologized for the wait. Matt made a joke about the non-stop phone calls, making Theresa smile, which only accentuated the wrinkles in her face.

"It's the DCI," she said, giving him a look that showed what this small-town secretary thought about those 'big-city' detectives. Matt rolled his eyes in return, making sure she knew he was on the right team.

A few minutes later, the Sheriff's door opened and he came out. He went to speak to Theresa when his eyes caught Matt sitting in one of the chairs across from his secretary's desk. The look on his face left no doubt whether Theresa had told him Matt was coming.

"What the hell are you doing here?"

Matt quickly tabbed through his file cabinet full of trusty reporter responses, but before he could put his finger on the right one Theresa spoke up.

"I told him to come," she said with the authority only a 70-year-old woman enjoyed. Sheriff Schwab looked down at her, and Matt was surprised to see a look that was just south of shocked deference on his face.

"He needs to talk to you about those girls." Theresa truly was the gatekeeper.

Matt braced himself for the angry rejection he'd been expecting since he left the *Graphic-Glimpse* office an hour ago, but it never came so he plowed forward. "I've got some information you'll want to hear."

"Well, why don't you step into my office and tell me."

The invitation threw Matt off-kilter. It was like descending a staircase in the dark and taking that final step when you expected to find the floor. The resistance he'd expected to encounter wasn't there, and it blew his equilibrium.

"Uh... sure." Matt pushed himself up from the metal armrests, dropping his notebook into his bag and looping it around his shoulder. As he crossed in front of Theresa's desk, she gave him a small nod that acknowledged they both knew who was really in charge of this department.

The Sheriff's office was small and devoid of almost any personal items. Procedural binders and books lined a pair of shelves on one wall, ending against three beige file cabinets. The other wall housed a coat tree in the corner and a folded American flag in a triangular box.

"OK, what do you have for me?" Sheriff Schwab asked as he closed the door behind Matt and motioned towards a chair in front of his desk. The sunlight streaming in from the window behind the desk was just starting to fade. Winter was coming, however slowly. Matt took a seat as the Sheriff dropped his 6-4 frame into the creaking leather chair behind his desk, which filled most of the back wall.

Matt mentally ripped through his entire theory as he sat down, stamping down any doubt that tried to second-guess his decision to come.

"How's the investigation going?"

"You'll have to ask the DCI, it's their investigation," Matt thought he picked up a note of bitterness in his voice, and it was obvious Theresa wasn't the only one who resented the presence of Iowa's Division of Criminal Investigation. Maybe that's why the sheriff was so willing to hear him out. His resentment could be useful. The thought reinforced his resolve.

"I think I know who might be doing this."

Sheriff Schwab smiled slightly. "You and everybody else in town. We've got calls about every jackass that ever looked crossways at somebody in the last few weeks."

Matt thought about all the false tips that could be generated in and environment like this. Small towns were friendly, but they were also insular and suspicious. Every unfamiliar face on Main Street could prompt somebody to call in, probably by old ladies who usually spent their time reporting kids who were 'driving too loud' on their street. Every divorced woman whose ex didn't pick up their kids that weekend was probably convinced he was the guy, even though he hadn't shown up for his kids three other times that month. Guys who had hated each other for years each thought 'there'd always been something off about him'.

"But nothing helpful?"

Sheriff Schwab leaned back in his chair.

"I'm not saying that, but it makes for an awful lot of work because you have to check them all out. That's what the DCI uses us for, so my deputies and I have spent all our time having conversations just like this one."

"So who do *you* have?" Sheriff Schwab asked.

"Scott Alston," Matt said, with as much conviction as he could put behind it. He didn't want to be lumped in with the crazies.

The sheriff leaned forward onto his desk again. The look on his face was hard to read, but the one thing it didn't seem was dismissive.

"OK, I'm game. Why him?"

"I went to school with Scott," Matt started. "And, honestly, I think there is a lot in his past to suggest he could be a killer. Not just a killer, but the kind of sick person that could do something like what happened to those two girls."

The Sheriff's expression didn't change, and Matt didn't know if that was good or bad. Either way, he pressed on.

"If you look at the signs that psychologists look for in serial killers, he displayed them all." Matt talked about the bed-wetting and animal torture, but could tell halfway through the sheriff wasn't going to be convinced by criminal psychology. He'd need to get to the concrete stuff.

"Then one night I saw Scott Alston choking his girlfriend out behind the Wreck. Saw it with my own two eyes."

He went into as much detail as he could remember, from the sound of Scott's voice to the way he'd stopped it by telling a group of kids the cops were coming.

Sheriff Schwab's expression changed from mildly amused to serious as Matt spoke.

"You saw him choke somebody?" The sheriff asked, although it sounded more like a statement. "How come you never reported it?"

Matt hadn't thought of that, but the answer came easy and honestly enough.

"I was a scared kid," Matt said. "What was I going to do? I figured nothing ever seemed to happen to him, and I didn't want to get involved."

The answer came out a little more defensive than Matt wanted, but what if the Sheriff was right. What if they had told somebody about what they had seen back then. Would it have made a difference? Would something have been done then?

Would these two girls still be alive?

The sheriff shook his head slightly as he spoke.

"That Alston kid was a shit in high school. A real shit. We picked him up plenty of times, but his Daddy was the pastor... self-righteous bastard in his own right. Always got him off, you're right about that.

"But then, as you probably remember, he got himself in a car wreck and killed two people — one a little girl with cancer. Daddy didn't have enough strings to pull on that one, and he got sent away. Old Pastor Alston never forgave me for that, either. Didn't say a kind word to me from the moment I arrested his son to the day he dropped in the back of his church."

"I remember," Matt said.

"Ten years for vehicular homicide," the Sheriff said. "But he only served six. Good behavior. It's amazing how good they can be after they get sent to jail, huh? Everybody's a changed man when they're in front of the parole board."

"But the doctors said he had amnesia and didn't remember anything from before. I thought it was bullshit at first, just some way to get him off. But I talked to him myself, and heck if they weren't right. Not that it matters, though. I kept an eye on him when he got back, but I'll be goddamned if he hasn't been quiet as a mouse. I talked with his parole officer a few times down in Mason City, and he says he's doing just fine. Hasn't bothered anybody. Actually, he seems to do a pretty good job of taking care of his mama. Ever since her accident, he drives her everywhere."

"Her accident?" Matt never heard anything about Karen Alston getting in an accident.

Sheriff Schwab raised his eyebrows and gave Matt a bit of a sideways look.

"Well, 'accident' is a pretty strong word," he said with a snort. "The old biddy's brakes went out when she was pulling out of her drive and she rolled into the ditch. Couldn't have been going more than 10 miles per hour. Hell, her airbags didn't even go off, but we had to send the ambulance out and everything. She hasn't gotten behind the wheel since."

Matt felt the conversation getting away from him.

"I'll be honest, you've got an entertaining theory," the sheriff said, "Even if I don't buy all that psychobabble bullshit…"

"It's *not* bullshit," he said, cutting the sheriff off. He knew it was a bad idea, but for the first time he felt the dismissal coming and wasn't going to give up without a fight. He hadn't even gotten to what they knew of Scott now.

"It is if I say it is," the sheriff said, his look hardening. "And right now, I say it doesn't mean anything—not only because it is bullshit, but because while you were sitting out in my lobby my deputies nabbed the sonofabitch that did this."

39

"WHAT?!?"

The sheriff's revelation shook Matt's mind like an Etch-a-Sketch, erasing everything he'd come in with.

"Us small town guys as incompetent as you think we are," Sheriff Schwab said. He wore a self-satisfied smirk as he spoke.

Matt sat staring across the table, shaken. Being dismissed out of hand was something he'd prepared for, but he never expected to be proven wrong. Last he'd heard there were no suspects.

"Who was it?"

The Sheriff squinted down at his watch, leaving the question unanswered for a moment.

"The guy's name is Chad Hickman."

"Hicksy? No, that… that can't be right." Matt said, still stunned. The name was a familiar one to anyone who graduated from Lake Mills in the past 25 years. Every small town had one of those guys who never grew out of his high school years, but Chad Hickman had turned glomming on to younger kids into an art form. He'd been out of school for almost ten years back when Matt was in high school, yet was a fixture at every party. Nobody ever invited him, but if you needed somebody to buy alcohol, Hicksy was always ready and willing to be of service. He was weird, but never in a dangerous way. They'd always just seen him as a pathetic guy who couldn't let go of his glory days.

"Of course, because Mr. Big City Reporter couldn't be wrong," Sheriff Schwab said.

"It's not that, it's just that Scott... he's been sitting outside the school, watching," Matt hated the desperation in his voice, but he'd become so wrapped up in his own investigation he couldn't fathom it turning out another way. "You can't just ignore this."

"I don't give a good goddamn where Scott Alston parks his car," The sarcasm was gone from the sheriff's voice, replaced with open hostility. "I've got a dozen witnesses that saw Hickman out at at North Shore Saturday night, and half of them say they saw him talking to Jillian Dayton before she disappeared. You can have all the stories you want from when you were a kid, but when all this happened he was the first one I thought of. Damn near 50 years old and still trying to hang around with high schoolers. Not only was he seen with Jillian Dayton right before she was killed, last week I find out this guy actually asked the Stamp girl out on a date. What kind of pervert asks out a girl less than half his age?"

Matt took everything the sheriff said in, trying to process it all. He still wasn't ready to give up on his notion.

"OK, but that doesn't prove he's guilty," Matt said, albeit with far less conviction than he'd hoped for.

"No it doesn't, but Agent Terry went out with a couple of my deputies to talk to him this afternoon. As soon as he saw them, the guy bolts out his back door. My boys chased him for half a mile before they brought him down and slapped on the cuffs. When they got back to go though the house they find his bedroom covered with pictures of high school girls, and I'll give you one guess as to what was front and center?"

It was obvious the question wasn't meant to be answered. At this point Matt wasn't sure if he could anyway.

"A big picture of Mackenzie Stamp, cut right out of the *Graphic-Glimpse*."

The tone of the sheriff's voice made Matt's stomach queasy, almost as if he'd he thought his story had something to do with what happened to the girls.

"They're bringing him in for questioning, and he'll probably be here any minute now, which is why I'm going ask you to leave."

The dismissal reminded Matt of his responsibilities as a reporter. He'd been so invested in proving his own theory correct, he was neglecting what the story actually was. Whether he believed Chad Hickman did this or not was irrelevant, he still had a job to do. The authorities had a suspect they were bringing here.

"Can I talk to him? To Agent Terry?"

Sheriff Schwab held open the door to his office. Matt could see Theresa looking in from her desk in the reception area, trying to figure out what her boss was saying.

"You can't, actually," The sheriff had no fake courtesy left. "Between this and the little performance you put on at our last press conference, I expect that this will be the last time we'll talk."

Matt felt air rush out of his lungs as if the words were an actual punch to the gut.

"What?"

"You heard me. We're done, you understand? I don't want you calling my office, I don't want you sitting in my lobby, and when we arrest this sonofabitch I don't want to see you at the press conference."

"Hold on, you can't just keep me out," Matt rose from his chair, which the Sheriff apparently took as a challenge. He let the door swing shut and brought his massive frame directly in Matt's path.

"I can do whatever the hell I want when it comes to you," Matt felt the temperature rise in the room as the Sheriff glared down at him. "And I say you are done here."

Ed Schwab reached past Matt and grabbed the bag hanging on the back of the metal chair and put it directly into Matt's chest.

He wasn't gentle.

217

"You tell Bill what I said. And let him know that if I see you again, HE'S done too."

MATT STARED AHEAD towards the reaches of his headlights as he barreled down the road towards Lake Mills. The sun was rapidly retreating to his left, and his mind was a mess of thoughts and theory fragments bouncing around like a fly in a light fixture.

The rational caucus had been re-energized by what Sheriff Schwab had said, insisting the measure of Scott Alston's guilt be dropped, or at the very least tabled until the next meeting. But no matter how loud they got, Matt could not let go of his suspicions.

Why?

Well, how many other people in this town showed signs of being a serial killer as a kid?

But that was then. He's not showing signs now, is he? Isn't that more important than how he acted 20 years ago?

Maybe not, but that would mean that the accident truly changed his personality, and almost everything he'd read said that wasn't a possibility. Besides, don't they say it's always the quiet ones? How many interviews have you seen where a neighbor says they never saw anything suspicious, he was always nice to them, kept to himself, after they found 15 nurses buried in the backyard.

Do you believe the story, or do you want *the story?*

There it was. Lurking in the background, sticking to the shadows. Him breaking the story. His face on the cable news show. Maybe promoting his book. It was his ticket back into the game. His ticket out of Lake Mills.

But *was* that why he was pushing it? It was definitely possible—a guy's subconscious could definitely affect how he saw things—but Matt didn't think so. Golden ticket or not, Scott made sense. Hicksy didn't.

Matt thought back to what he remembered about him. He'd been a nice guy, never had an edge. The only thing odd about him was the fact that he still hung around high schoolers. As for whatever happened tonight, there could be a million reasons he'd run from the police. It didn't prove anything.

Until there was an actual arrest in the case, Matt was going to keep looking into it.

Decision made, his eyes drifted out his side window where the streetlights blurred by in a lighted Morse code. He'd sped past the greenhouse, blew past the fire station and was halfway up Main Street before realizing he was still clipping along at highway speeds. He jerked out of his thoughts and slammed on the brakes. Matt shook his head, quickly looking to make sure nobody was around to witness, or worse.

Back in the moment, he hung a left on Washington Street and headed towards the office. There were plenty of cars on the street, but it was the red Ford Explorer parked in front of the *Graphic-Glimpse* that caught his eye. Bill had a spot around the corner that he had been parking in since before SUVs were a thing, but tonight his vehicle was on the street. Nothing that makes an 80-year-old newspaperman change his routine is good.

Ever.

He pulled up in the spot behind it and put his Camry in park. He remained behind the wheel and looked at the glowing rectangle of glass where Bill's office was.

The sheriff called him.

He'd been yelled at plenty during his career. He closed his eyes and saw a montage of red-faced editors 'motivating' their troops. That never bothered him. Newsrooms were high-tension environments, but that electricity is what powers the business.

But with Bill it was different.

Matt could picture his boss sitting at his desk, fatherly disappointment oozing across the polished wood.

He grabbed his bag off the passenger seat and pulled it out the door behind him.

Might as well get it over with.

40

"THAT YOU MATT?"

He hadn't even gotten to the reception desk before the words jumped out of Bill's office.

"Yeah."

"Step in here for a second, will you."

Any delusion that maybe Bill had driven into the office because he'd forgotten his favorite whatever died right then. Matt stepped into the doorway of the office and leaned against the frame. If he remained standing in the doorway, he not only had the high ground over his seated boss, but it would be easy to slip back out of the office. Make the meeting inherently temporary.

Bill motioned for him to sit down.

Matt's bag slid down off his shoulder and thumped to the ground as he lowered himself into the single chair across from the immaculate desk. Every other boss's desk Matt had seen was strewn with papers, notebooks, past editions— Bill's was the only one in the business where you could actually see the surface.

"Ed Schwab called me a little bit ago."

A battalion of responses rushed to the front of his brain, all anxious to engage in a vigorous defense, but Matt held them back. No reason to turn this confrontational. Sometimes the smart play was to take your beating and move on.

"I kinda figured he would," Matt said.

The hinges on the old leatherback chair creaked as Bill leaned back.

"I told you Ed was difficult didn't I? You've got to know how do deal with him."

"I know, I know," Matt pushed the defensiveness down once again as he spoke. "I'm just trying to do my job."

"That's just it," Bill said. "I think you have a problem with what your job is."

"I thought my job is to report the news." The valve was failing, and Matt's frustration was beginning to seep out.

"Unfortunately you can't understand how that is done here," Bill said. For the first time Matt realized he wasn't the only one holding back a wave of exasperation. "The people of this community don't want hard-hitting, front-line journalism from us. There's a million places they can get that, and the *Graphic-Glimpse* isn't one of them."

"But it doesn't have to be that way," Matt said.

"As long as I'm here, it does," Bill said. He stared out the blank blackness of the window for a moment before continuing. "Maybe it was my fault for bringing you here."

Matt suddenly felt the conversation shift. He was no longer solely concerned with taking a tongue-lashing and moving on.

"Hold on, Bill," Matt said. "I don't know what Schwab said, but…"

"It's not that," Bill interrupted. "I know you won't believe this, but just like the sheriff, I'm not one to let somebody tell me how to do my job either.

"That said, I do think it's time to put the brakes on all this. You just aren't made for it. You're too good of a reporter, to be honest. It's not fair to keep you locked up in this small-town cage. I was hoping that I could bring you back here and you would sit behind this desk for the next 30 years just like I did. But I think we both know that's not going to happen."

Just like a dying man—which in a sense he was—Matt saw his journalistic life flash before his eyes as Bill spoke. He saw flickers of high school sports from his teenage eyes, fighting with the outdated computer system in his collegiate newsroom, his first caucus night all the way though the halls of the state capitol.

He didn't actually hear how Bill phrased it, but the message made its way through the mental montage playing in his brain.

He'd been fired.

41

MATT SAT AT THE WORKSTATION he'd created for himself over the past six months, trying to process what had just happened.

Hey, you wanted out of Lake Mills, right?

Bill had stuck his head back and said something at some point, but Matt had no idea what. He'd left after that, so he couldn't ask him.

Matt moved the mouse to bring the computer to life and pulled the paper up once again. A row of smiling girls in brown vests beamed out at him. He couldn't remember what they'd done, but it must have been really important to get into the paper. Matt gave it one last look before hitting save and closing it up. He did it even though it wasn't his job anymore.

As Matt was powering down the newsroom for the last time, he thought he heard the door open. He craned his neck towards the front and stuck his ear out as far as he could, as if those two inches would allow him to gather sounds that would have otherwise disappeared into the ether. His acoustic gymnastics did little initially, and he was turning back towards the flatbed scanner when he heard somebody knocking on the reception desk.

"Hello?"

Matt maneuvered around the old layout station and headed towards the doorway that opened into the front lobby. David was standing in front of the grey receptionist station. He was leaning an elbow on the raised countertop that their secretary Audrey hid behind, playing solitaire all day. David wore his beat up Lake Mills Lumber ballcap and once again had a good couple days of stubble on his chin.

"Hey," Matt said, surprising himself with the causality of his voice. "What's up?"

"Not much," he said. David still had dark circles under his eyes, but they seemed brighter than Matt had seen in him since he'd moved back to Lake Mills. He looked anxious, but not in a nervous way. More like a school kid waiting to get on the bus for a field trip.

"Saw your car out front and thought I would stop in and say 'Hey'."

"Well, I could use a beer, so I was going to head down to Frank's if you wanna come. Just let me finish shutting things down." Matt turned back towards the newsroom. "It'll just be a second. You can come back if you want."

Matt glanced back as he went from the lobby to the newsroom. David was making his way around the reception desk, and he didn't wait for the bar to ask about what he came for.

"You get a chance to talk to the sheriff yet?"

It took Matt a second to remember why David would stop by that night, but of course that's what he wanted to know. Getting canned sure can cloud one's memory.

Matt continued across the newsroom to power down the last of the electronics that allowed a single person to put out a weekly newspaper. He looked up at David, who was leaning in the doorway, looking as casual as can be. Or at least trying to appear so.

"Yeah, he wasn't really buying it," Matt said. "In fact, they have somebody else they are looking at. Probably have him locked up right now from what the sheriff was saying."

David pushed himself off the doorjamb and snatched the hat off his head. His arm flew down to his side and slapped the old cap against the wall he'd been holding up just a second ago. It made a sound like a wet towel snapping in a locker room bully's hand.

"Are you fucking kidding me?" He said.

Matt stood up from the computer. The final "OK" button remaining unclicked so he could turn back towards his friend. He had been taken aback by the abrupt reaction.

"Yeah, you remember Hicksy? They brought him in tonight." Matt said, feeling oddly defensive, almost as if David blamed *him* for not convincing the sheriff.

"Chad Hickman did not do this," The tone (and volume) of David's voice made Matt nervous. The guy looked like he was about to punch a hole in the wall.

"Schwab says they've got witnesses that say he was talking to Jillian Dayton the night she disappeared. And apparently he asked Mackenzie out a while back."

"That doesn't mean jack shit," David spat. The situation in the newsroom was getting a little hot, and Matt wanted to pacify it as soon as possible. David's eyes bored into him, waiting to hear a rationale that he would never accept anyway.

"I know, but apparently he had pictures of both girls in his room, too," Matt said. "When they went out to talk to him tonight he took off. Deputies had to chase him down to haul him in."

David was unmoved.

"He took off because he's got a fucking meth lab out back," he said.

"What?"

"Hicksy's been cooking that shit for the last five years."

Matt hadn't ever known Hicksy to be involved with drugs, but with the way methamphetamines had spread across the Midwest in recent years, it wasn't much of a stretch to imagine him dipping his toes in it. One more service he could provide the kids.

"Look, Hicksy didn't do this, you *know* that," David's voice had calmed down, but was still bristling with the religious intensity of a man who had no doubt he was right. "You're the reporter. You've got to keep digging. Find the truth and people will listen to you."

"Well that's the thing, I'm not a reporter anymore," It sounded weird saying it out loud, as if it hadn't been real until then. Matt looked over at David, who wore the confused look of a dog after you changed his food. "The sheriff didn't take the talk we had too kindly and had one of his own with Bill, who decided I was 'too good a reporter' for the *Graphic-Glimpse*."

"Well then this is it," David said. "You prove Scott did this and get your job back."

"Maybe I don't want it back," Matt said. He stepped over to his bag, which was lying on the counter next to the printer.

"Come on, Matt," David said. The aggression was replaced with a pleading note that was utterly foreign to him. "He can't keep getting away with this. I need your help."

Matt stood, looking down at his bag. His reporter's bag, full of pencils, pens and paper. Notebooks. The one he'd taken from David's house was in there too. The one full of notes about Scott Alston. Notes never intended for a newspaper article, but subconsciously tabbed for a true-crime book. The bestseller that only a fearless reporter who defied everyone from his boss to the authorities could write.

The one he would write when he got Scott Alston arrested for the murder of two young girls.

"We're going to need more evidence," Matt said. "Even when this thing with Hicksy falls apart, the Sheriff is probably stubborn enough to ignore Scott out of spite. We have to give him something he can't ignore."

The thought of bringing Sheriff Schwab irrefutable evidence lit a fire in Matt's belly. He could almost taste the look he'd get after they arrested Scott.

Matt looked back at David, who'd sat down in one of the chairs near the layout desk. He was studying something on the bulletin board that hung on the wall in front of him. Or he had just spaced off, lost in thought. He sat for a while, not saying anything. With the wide swings of emotion David had shown since showing up at the office, Matt had expected more of a reaction to his offer. At least some sort of reaction. In the fluorescent light of the newsroom, the bags under David's eyes were much more pronounced, like kisses from a bar fight. Matt was beginning to wonder if he was nodding off when David blinked his eyes a few times and was back.

"I've got an idea, but I don't think you will like it," he said. "Hell, I don't know if *I* like it."

"OK, what?"

David leaned back in his chair. The metallic squeak gained a few decibels bouncing off the metal filing cabinets and ping-ponging between the linoleum floor and the drop ceiling. It sounded like a pterodactyl, or at least what the movies would have you believe a flying dinosaur sounded like. He rubbed his eyes with his palms, then sent his hands up through his hair and settled them on the back of his neck, where he kneaded the base of his skull.

"I've been researching this stuff for a long time. Since high school. You might say I was obsessed. Carrie sure thought so."

David trailed off briefly, and Matt wondered again if he was going to lose him.

"Anyway, one thing that kept coming up was guys like this usually keep something from their victims. Some sort of trophy or something. It's a way to re-live the experience. Why anyone would want to re-live something like that is beyond me, but we're dealing with sick fucks, right? Psychos."

Matt was unsure how to respond, or if he was even supposed to, so he just sort of nodded.

"I bet I know where he keeps that stuff."

It took Matt a moment to realize what David had just said, and once he did, he wasn't sure how to process it. All the questions he needed to ask were immediately jockeying for position at the front of his brain, only succeeding in creating a logjam from which none were able to emerge. As is often the case in such a situation, the smallest, least consequential one is able to slip through as the others are fighting, crawling through the legs and sneaking around the edges.

"Huh?"

David leaned forward and placed his elbows on the table, burying his face in his hands. He remained silent, allowing Matt to try and squeeze another question through the door.

"What are you talking about?"

Not much better than the first, but at least it consisted of words. Before any more competent contenders could break through the mad rush, David looked up at him and said just two words.

"The fort."

All the questions stopped pushing and shoving. If there was to be any understanding of this at all, there was going to have to be a triage. That's what being a reporter was all about. Find out the most important information first, and right now Matt's brain was sending a research assistant to the archives to pull any information about a fort.

He came back quickly, probably because there wasn't that much in the file. That day in the park, David had told him about the fort he'd helped Scott build in the woods behind his house. He'd talked about it a lot, actually, describing their building process and everything. Supposedly it was pretty impressive. For something a couple of kids built, anyway.

But that was a long time ago. It couldn't still be there, right? Even if it was, what made David think anything was back there now? Both important questions that would get their time on stage, but now that the chaos inside his head had subsided, he needed to establish some more basic facts and get a foothold in this conversation.

"You mean the fort you guys built when you were kids?"

"Yeah."

"It can't still be there, can it?"

David shrugged his shoulders a bit, but the look of doubt that would normally accompany that motion was absent from his face.

"Probably," he said. His eyes drifted towards the ceiling as he talked, probably accessing his own archive. "We built it pretty good, and that tarp would make it waterproof…

more or less. Besides, if he's been keeping it up there's no reason to think it wouldn't last forever. It was in pretty good shape the last time I was out there."

"Yeah, but that was 25 years ago," Matt said.

David didn't take his gaze off the ceiling, his eyes tracing the black dots in the tiles, maybe connecting them like some sort of weird newsroom constellations.

"No, it was more recent than that," he said. His voice sounded like a resigned confession. "I was back there in high school, you know, before…"

He trailed off again, eyes still upward. The silence in the back of the Lake Mills *Graphic-Glimpse* offices was thick, and Matt didn't know how to break through. The questions that had been trying to push through in his brain had all stopped, now listening to David themselves.

He continued without prompting. Matt wasn't even sure if he was talking to him anymore.

"It was a lot different than when we built it, but I guess it was the same too. More lived in? I don't know, but you could tell he was out there a lot. He had magazines… a couple of pornos. And *National Geographics* full of dead bodies. War photos. Bodies burned, stacked… But that back wall, Jesus. Just bones. I have no idea how many… 100? 500? How can you tell, it's not like you could count them. Lots of skulls. He must have been doing it for years. Get 'em in the trap, put 'em in the bucket.

"Then, right in the middle. 'MINE'."

Matt was hesitant to speak, scared to interrupt whatever this was, but if he remained silent he risked getting completely lost on whatever path David was trying to lead him down.

"Mine? What do you mean?"

"He made it out of bones. Spelled it out right on the wall. MINE."

The two of them resumed their silence, Matt trying to process what David was telling him, and David assumedly trying to process what he wanted to tell Matt next. David was the first to break through. He looked over at Matt for the first time since he started speaking.

"I guess those were his trophies then. The bones... skulls. If he's got any more, that's where they'd be."

The eye contact snapped Matt's brain out of its fugue, and the questions started scrumming up again. But this time, a clear winner emerged.

"You were out there in high school?"

The distant look that had been camping on David's face gave way to a more uncertain one.

"I had to go check things out beforehand," he said, a beat slower. "I couldn't just go out there and wing it. Had to have a plan. To be sure."

A siren went off in Matt's brain, and it cleared out the mass of questions that had been clogging up the place. His line of inquiry was completely clear.

"A plan for what?" Matt asked slowly. He knew he needed to know, but wasn't sure if he wanted to.

"Don't give me that shit," David said, his voice raising. He looked at Matt like a parent talking to a lying child. More disappointed than angry. "You know goddamn well *what*. If you wanted to pretend back then that you had no idea, that's fine, but please... we're fucking adults now. At least give me that courtesy, eh? Don't pretend you don't know what I did. What I had to do. *Alone*, mind you. You knew what I knew. Saw what I saw. But when it was time to do something, you bailed. Left me alone."

David's eyes drifted back towards the ceiling, voice drifting back to high school.

"And when it went bad, you couldn't get away from me fast enough."

Matt wanted to say something, defend himself somehow. But he didn't know how, or what he was even defending himself from. His brain was silent when his research assistant came running in from the back, holding another folder he had pulled from the archives. It was the transcript from a conversation they'd had on the golf course in high school. It was a deep pull, something he hadn't thought of in years. Something he had probably figured he wouldn't ever need again, so he'd filed it WAAAY back in the archives. Or maybe it was something his subconscious hadn't wanted to see again.

Do you think it's OK to kill someone to save somebody else's life?

Not long after that conversation, Scott Alston had his accident.

What if you could completely get away with it?

As the realizations started lining up in his brain, his expression must have changed, because he didn't even need to ask any questions. David just answered them.

"It was supposed to be the trees, you know. How would I know he was going to jump into the other lane?"

Matt still had no response. How could he? It was really too much to process. Had David somehow caused Scott's accident? The accident that had killed a little girl and her mom? Had he been sitting on this guilt for all these years? Watching an entire town grieve, blaming and hating somebody else for it? Jesus, there was still a scholarship named after the girl given away every year to a senior volleyball player. *Had* he known, deep down? David certainly thought so. If he didn't, *should* he have?

Before Matt could fully put all this information together, a massive snap echoed through the newsroom as David slapped the desk in front of him. It sounded like the crack of a sniper's rifle.

"IT WAS SUPPOSED TO BE THE FUCKING TREES!!!" he screamed, composure flying out the window. David pounded the table with his right hand, fist flying around in a giant windmill and slamming against the desk with every pass. The chair he'd been sitting in had been shoved back by his knees, and he stood in an awkward crouch as he rained blows down. The few papers that had been on the desk fluttered to the floor as David's fist pulled more off with each strike.

Matt rolled back a few feet from the mayhem and watched with this mouth agape. The rage abated as quickly as it had arrived, and David collapsed back towards his chair. His backside just caught the edge of it and the seat shot back, dumping him onto the linoleum. David made no attempt to get up and sat with his face hanging towards the floor, shaking in time with the tears now streaming down his face.

Matt wanted to help him up. Set him back in his chair and comfort him. Say something that would be reassuring, to pull his friend from this tailspin. But he didn't. He just sat there, looking down at a grown man having what looked like a full-fledged breakdown on the floor in front of him.

Again, David didn't wait for the questions. For the first time in 15 years, he talked, and once it started it gushed out like water from a broken dam.

He talked about seeing Scott slide through the intersection.

He talked about seeing Scott choke Amy.

He talked about his dreams, his plans.

He recounted, in almost cinematic detail, the night he woke up, biked out to Scott Alston's house, put holes in his brake lines and returned home.

He talked about waking up the next morning, walking around school before anybody knew what had happened.

He talked about sitting in that assembly, hearing that not only had he failed in his plan, but that he had caused the death of two innocent people.

He talked about the guilt that had filled him since that day. Watching the town grieve for a little girl with cancer, knowing he was the one responsible.

"And now, here we are," David said, his voice suddenly calm. All traces of the breakdown he'd just had were gone. Maybe the confession had been cathartic for him. It was probably the first time he had talked about it, probably ever.

"After all that, he's doing it again."

Matt went to say something, but after 20 minutes of sitting in rapt attention, his voice didn't work on first attempt. His lame attempt at comfort came out as a half word-half cough. He cleared his throat as he stepped forward to offer a hand to David, who Matt just realized had remained on the floor throughout his entire confession.

"It's all right," he finally said. It wasn't much, but it was all he could offer.

232

David looked at him as he stood. The tears were gone from his eyes, but they still had the crimson tint of someone who'd been in the backyard burning a huge pile of leaves.

"Not yet, but it will be," David said, still holding Matt's hand. "When he's gone for good, then it will be all right."

Matt's face was washed over with a look of horror.

David read it, and quickly responded. "Not that," he said defensively. "Jesus, you think I'd go through that again? *He's* the killer."

Matt was ashamed at what he'd thought, although after what he had just heard you could hardly blame him.

"So what do we do?" he asked.

David bent down to pick up the papers that had fallen to the floor during his initial outburst. He stood and squared the papers together, setting them down in a neat pile in the middle of the desk blotter. Anybody who came by would never know the desk had been viciously attacked just 10 minutes before.

"Like you said, we get evidence. Something real. No matter how much Schwab hates you, he can't ignore hard evidence." David stopped tidying up the desk and looked back at Matt. His face was serious. It was amazing how normal he looked so soon after a complete emotional breakdown. It was as if it never happened. "And I'm willing to bet anything there's something in the fort."

The motivation to shove this in the sheriff's face had subsided, but Matt had been convinced they needed to do something. David was right that Schwab wouldn't ignore something tangible. And even if the sheriff was that hard-headed, Bill wouldn't be. He wouldn't write a story about it, but he'd take it to the authorities. They'd have to do something about it.

"Yeah," Matt said. "If we bring him something he'll have to listen."

A look of relief washed over David's face, as if after years he'd finally gotten the answer he needed.

"Then let's go get it."

42

WITH DAVID'S BREAKDOWN in the past, they spent the next half hour going over what they were going to do.

David's plan was simple. The layout at the Alston's was the same as it had been back in high school, so there was no reason to think it should be any different getting back to the fort. He went over the route with Matt, walking down the middle of the treeline to the backyard, shooting across to the shed, then back to the path. Fall was in full swing, but there should still be enough leaves on the trees to provide plenty of cover for them.

Once they get back to the fort, they look for anything they can find that could connect Scott to Mackenzie and Jillian. If they find anything, Matt will take pictures and bring them to the sheriff. They couldn't take anything and risk tipping Scott off or tampering with the chain of evidence. Pictures should be enough to convince Schwab to investigate.

"How do you want to get out there?" Matt asked. David had ridden his bike when he was out there in high school, but that wasn't going to happen now, and it wasn't like they could just pull into the Alston's driveway or leave their car on the Quarter Mile. Even in the middle of the night, they couldn't risk somebody driving by and seeing it. An abandoned car along the road wouldn't necessarily arouse suspicion, but it wasn't a chance Matt was willing to take.

"I'd say we drive out to the golf course and walk from there," David said. "Tonight is poker night at the clubhouse, so if anyone does happen to see the car in the middle of the night, they'll just assume somebody had one too many and caught a lift back into town."

"Tonight?" Matt asked.

"Yeah," David said. "It's got to be tonight. Too much could happen if we wait."

Matt was on board for going out there, but he hadn't thought it would be this quickly. They needed at least a day or two to plan, think it over. Maybe run through the whole thing in the light of day, just to make sure he wasn't crazy for considering it.

"Well... don't we need to think this over? Make sure we have the plan down?"

"The plan is solid. I've done it before, nothing's going to change in a day. Except maybe Scott gets nervous and moves all the stuff. Or maybe he finds another girl. This needs to happen now. We can't wait."

Matt felt like a high school girl being pressured in the back seat of her boyfriend's car. He could tell David was adamant about getting this taken care of tonight. Who could blame him, really? If Matt had been living with the kind of guilt David had just displayed, he'd probably be anxious to make things right too.

Although, even if they found everything they needed to put Scott away for life, that wouldn't change what David had done, and it certainly wouldn't bring those two people back to life. For the first time, Matt realized what kind of information he had been given. His friend, his *best* friend from high school, had caused the death of two innocent people. No matter what his intentions were, they were dead due to his actions. And no matter how prophetic he may have been about Scott Alston, it probably wouldn't matter if he were in front of a jury.

Would he ever be there? Was there a statute of limitations on whatever crimes he had committed? Could he even be charged if Scott had already served time for it?

Wait, could I get mixed up in this too?

David had seemed convinced that Matt had known what he had done in high school. Would he testify that Matt had known, yet said nothing? Would that make him an accomplice? Matt had no idea, but he knew there was a lot of thinking to be done on this.

Unfortunately, it didn't look like he was going to be given the time.

"OK," Matt said.

David looked up at the clock. It was just short of 9 o'clock.

"It's nine now," he said. "The clubhouse closes down at 10, and Scott gets home around 11:15. If we head out there around two, we should be fine. He goes to bed shortly after getting home and his mom is always asleep well before that."

Matt briefly wondered how David knew when Scott and his mom went to bed, but this time he figured it was better not to ask. He'd already met his quota for information he didn't really want to know tonight. He looked at the clock himself. Five hours until two. Matt had wanted extra time to think, but he needed days, not hours. The nerves had already settled into a gymnastics routine in his stomach, and at this point every minute until they left would be torture.

"OK," Matt said. "What do we do until then?"

As anxious as Matt was, David's face was the epitome of calm.

"Let's go over to Frank's and get that beer."

KNOWING THEY WERE JUST KILLING TIME before heading out to Alston's made pulling up to the bar at Frank's Place surreal. It was like everything Matt's senses brought in came through a filter of nerves. Trying to act natural was a sure bet you weren't going to look natural, but look like you were trying to *act* natural. In reality, Matt pulled it off better than he ever thought he would. He and David each downed a pair of drinks, which may have played a part. They made easy conversation between themselves and the bartender, who by now Matt knew as Marty. There were few competing conversations late on a Monday, and their voices seemed to resonate around the bar.

Thankfully, there was no mention of Mackenzie Stamp or Jillian Dayton. It was all the weather, high school football and what was going to happen with the service station now that Little Willie was going to retire.

The 10 o'clock news brought some video of the Governor, which prompted Marty to ask Matt about him. He'd probably told the same stories at some point during the last six months, but it gave Matt something to talk about. His nerves probably added plenty of superfluous detail to his stories, but Marty didn't seem to mind.

Eventually, both hands on the Coors Light clock behind the bar pointed at the 12. Marty was out from behind the bar wiping down the tables when David leaned over.

"Well, I'm gonna head out," He said for Marty's benefit, then lowered his voice and leaned in. "Head over to my place in a bit and we'll leave from there."

He motioned towards Matt's shirt, which was light blue with an orange plaid pattern.

"Might want to change that. Grab something darker."

David dropped some cash on the bar, stood up and headed for the door. Matt watched him nod to Marty on the way by, then fished for his own wallet.

After settling up, Matt considered going home to change before remembering he had a black pullover in his backseat that would work well to darken him up. It wasn't until he was out the door that he realized he hadn't eaten dinner, so he drove down to the Qwik Stop to grab a candy bar and Mountain Dew. The butterflies in his stomach had eaten away his hunger, but he felt obligated to eat something nonetheless. Besides, it was a way to kill a bit more time before picking up David.

It was almost 12:30 by the time he arrived at David's house, where he let himself in the kitchen door. He wasn't sure why, but he figured they were beyond knocking at this point.

The two sat at the same table as the night before. Matt's can of beer remained where he'd left it, holding a leftover half-swallow of warm backwash.

Once again, they went over their plans for the night. It was probably unnecessary, as it was a simple and tested route, but it made Matt feel better to talk it out so David indulged him.

They had time to kill anyway.

43

THE ONLY SOUND during the ride out to Rice Lake was the tires on the road. Matt didn't know what to say, and probably wouldn't have been able to get it out if he did. He looked over at David, who remained eerily calm. Matt hoped he would remain so. He was realizing more and more that this could potentially be a highly emotional moment for his friend. The breakdown back at the *Graphic-Glimpse* had been frightening, and now he was returning him to the scene of a horrific childhood trauma. This was something that had obviously scarred David deeply, shaping the course of his entire life.

Not just his *life.*

No, it wasn't just David. How many lives had been destroyed by what started back in that fort?

But then again, maybe this would be cathartic. If he was right and they found something, it wouldn't change what David had done, but maybe it would somehow alleviate some of the guilt that had built up over the years. And if they were wrong, maybe he'd finally be able to move on.

No, that wouldn't happen. If they didn't find anything, David would just look elsewhere. He'd been holding onto this since he was a child, there was probably no amount of evidence that would get him to let it go.

So let's hope he's right.

Matt looked down at the dashboard clock.

1:17

It was a little earlier than they had originally planned, but that was fine. Matt couldn't sit around anymore, and David probably realized if they waited any longer his friend was in danger of losing his nerve.

He turned the Camry onto the Quarter Mile, driving past the same spot where they had seen Scott go flying through the stoplight back in high school. The spot that, according to David, gave him the idea for Scott's accident in the first place. The place it would have ended, had it not gone so tragically wrong.

It didn't even register with Matt as he accelerated past.

As they approached the Alston house, David shifted forward in his seat and peered out the window.

"Slow down a bit," he said.

Matt checked his rearview mirror, looking for any headlights approaching from behind. There were none. He hadn't seen another car since they left town.

Matt dropped down to about 35 mph and eased past the Alston driveway.

The house was dark.

"Looks quiet," David said.

"Yeah."

"There's a motion light above the garage," David said. "But we'll be behind the trees, so it won't be a problem."

He looked back at Matt as they sped up towards the golf course.

"You OK?" he asked.

Matt nodded as he turned his head back towards the road. They had already come up on the course. Hole #6 stretched along to their left. Matt pressed down on the brake as the entrance to the course rapidly approached. He took a left by the carved wooden sign that proclaimed 'Rice Lake Golf and Country Club'.

They headed down the drive and Matt pulled into a spot about a dozen spaces from the clubhouse door, just out of reach of the one light post that illuminated the lot. He shut the car off and looked over at David.

"Well?"

"Let's do it," David said, opening the passenger door and stepping out into the night.

Before he opened the door, Matt scanned the parking lot for any sign of activity. It was barren. A thick strip of trees created a wall on the far side of the parking lot, leading all the way towards the back of the clubhouse, which was as dark as the Alston house had been. The cart sheds, all closed up for the season, stretched back towards the trees. There probably hadn't been anyone out here for at least an hour, after the last of the clubhouse staff locked up and left.

Matt eased the driver's side door open, a squeak he'd never noticed blasted through his ears and ricocheted around the parking lot.

David apparently didn't hear it, and motioned his head towards the course as Matt stepped onto the asphalt. He turned and walked towards the path that led to the first tee box, and Matt walked around the car and jogged a few steps to catch up.

"Where are you going?" he asked in a low voice, bordering on a whisper, but again it seemed to reverberate off every surface of the deserted parking lot.

"Better to walk through the course," he said. "That way no passing cars will see us. Besides, it's quicker."

Matt's head kept jerking around, looking for any sign of activity as they entered the golf course. They quickly left the light of the lamppost behind, and Matt's eyes did what they could to adjust to the little light coming from the night sky. The cement path they followed glowed faintly against the shadowy background of the grass. It continued past the first tee and towards the 10th hole, where they stepped into the dark grass. The two cut across the teebox and crossed into the 12th fairway. The four-inch rough grasped at Matt's shoes as he pressed on while a huge row of oak trees on his left cast shadows in the dark.

The trees and their shadows were left behind as they approached the middle of the course. As his eyes eagerly drank in the moonlight, Matt began to feel incredibly exposed. He could now see the road up ahead, and had to repeatedly remind himself that there was no way a driver could see them approaching. Even if someone looked right at them as they drove past, the course would be nothing but a black blur from inside a moving car.

"Pretty, isn't it?" David said. The sound of his voice broke the protection of silence and sent a fresh wave of anxiety though Matt.

"What?" Matt whispered. As hyper-vigilant as he was, he couldn't comprehend what David could be talking about.

"The pond," David said, pointing towards the water hazard that surrounded a nearby green. The moon's light slowly waved across the surface, which contained barely a ripple.

"There's nothing better than a night like this," he continued. "So peaceful."

Matt glanced over towards the pond, but kept walking. He wasn't ready to enjoy the scenery. When he looked back he noticed a tranquil look on David's face, which was tilted towards the night sky.

As they approached the Quarter Mile, David veered left towards the far corner of the course. Eventually, the pair made their way past the sixth hole alongside the road. David stopped at the edge of the course, just before a line of knee-high grass that stretched about 15 feet before ramping up a short incline to the road.

"OK, let's head up," he said. "The house is about 100 yards down. We'll go in on the other side of the driveway, then just stick to the trees."

David raised up on his tip-toes and looked down the road.

"If you see headlights, just hit the ditch," he said.

Matt's nerves ramped up to a level he'd never experienced, and it felt as if he'd swallowed a sparrow. Before he could say anything, David stepped into the grass and made his way up towards the Quarter Mile. Matt quickly followed, stepping in the spots where David's footsteps trampled the grass.

Matt's foot slipped as he crested the ditch, and he fell forward onto his hands. His right palm landed in some gravel from the side of the road, sending a jolt of pain up his arm.

"You OK?" David asked.

"Yeah, yeah," Matt said, jumping up and brushing his hands off on his pants. His head whipped back and forth, searching for oncoming headlights and seeing none.

David turned and started jogging east along the side of the road. Matt immediately followed. The crunch of the gravel under his feet echoed in his brain, so he quickly shifted onto the blacktop.

The Alston's mailbox marked the entrance to the driveway on the other side of the road. As they neared, David remained on the north side. It wasn't until they had jogged past it that David suddenly cut left and crossed the asphalt. He was already halfway down the ditch when Matt reached the far side. He instinctively took another look back along the road before following David down. The trees David had planned on using for cover separated the Alston property from the cornfield that ran along the south side of the Quarter Mile, and he waited for Matt alongside the first row.

"See what I mean, nobody's going to see us," David's voice finally the whisper Matt's nerves needed him to use. He motioned down the treeline as he continued. "Just past the garage."

David turned into the trees and disappeared. Matt leaped over a patch of tall grass and followed. Dispersed amongst the trunks were small bushes and evergreens that provided even more cover. The canopy of trees grew together and formed a roof over the corridor that robbed Matt's vision of the light it had grown accustomed to, but the protection of the shadows still couldn't expel the tension that had taken root in his gut.

He caught up with David as they passed the garage without any sign of activity from the house. Ten yards farther down, the orderly windbreak of trees blended into the woods that bordered the backyard.

David slipped between a pair of trees and crouched next to a large bush. Matt crept up beside him and saw the back of the Alston house for the first time. There were no trees in the yard, just a small vegetable garden in the far corner. A few windows lined the back of the house, but they were the smaller kind that probably looked out from bedrooms. That made sense, since Matt remembered seeing a large picture window in the front of the house, which was probably the living room.

A flowerbed that contained a few shrubs and what looked like a good load of hostas surrounded the back of the house.

David motioned to their right, towards the back of the yard where the woods started. A small red shed with classic white trim sat directly back from the garage.

"The path starts behind there," he whispered. Before Matt could respond, David stepped out from behind the shrub and quickly made his way along the trees towards the shed. Matt watched him for a second, then bolted after one last glance back at the house. If he felt exposed on the golf course, leaving the sanctuary of the trees for the expanse of the backyard made him feel like an agoraphobic.

Matt ran, keeping as close to the trees as he could. He broke into a sprint when he had to cross the open grass to get to the shed. When he finally rounded the corner to the backside of the shed, he barreled into David, almost sending them both to the ground. David put his right arm against Matt's chest in a backhanded grip, preventing him from going forward.

"Hold it," he said. David motioned toward the ground in front of the path, which did in fact start right behind the shed. "Follow me."

Instead of walking right onto the path and heading back from there, David ducked through some trees and made his way through the undergrowth. He remained alongside the path for about 15 feet before stepping out on the thin ribbon weaving back amongst the trees. Matt did his best to keep up. He met up with David on the path, where he was looking back towards the back of the shed.

"What," whispered Matt, unable to keep a small amount of panic form creeping into his voice.

David shook his head.

"There was a lot of soft dirt up there," he said. "Didn't want to leave any footprints."

Footprints? Matt hadn't thought about that. He immediately looked down at the ground he was standing on. The path was covered with at least a few years worth of leaves. That should prevent them from leaving a trail, but still. He spun around, looking all about the ground.

"We'll be fine back here," David said. "It was just..."

Matt looked up towards his friend.

"What?"

"I don't know," he said. "There was just a large bare spot where the path started. Almost... I don't know. Like it had been raked up or something."

Matt looked at David with concern.

"Don't worry," David said. "We'll be fine. Just be careful, I guess. Come on."

He set out down the path. "It's fine."

Matt followed David down, keeping one eye on the darkened path. No more bare spots popped up as the leaves carpeted the forest floor. He saw David take a large step ahead of him, then noticed the small log that had crossed the path. Probably fell in the years since David had been back here, Matt figured as he hopped over it. Who knew what they would find back here?

Lots of things change in the woods over the course of 15 years.

Eventually, David came to a stop ahead of him. Matt stepped up beside him and looked into the darkness of the small clearing they had reached.

"It's still fucking here," David muttered.

44

MATT WAS AMAZED by the small structure that stood before him. Enough moonlight squeezed through the sparse roof the clearing provided that he was able to make out the little hut made of scrap wood and branches. The elements had worn the outside, but it looked amazingly solid for something built by a pair of kids more than 20 years ago.

They approached it slowly, allowing Matt to see more of the details of construction. The front wall looked to be a large piece of plywood, while a tree seemed to supply the support in the back. As he got closer, he saw a branch from the tree that sat about six feet high served as a ceiling beam. The pale blue glow of a tattered plastic tarp poked out at the corner. It was draped over more plywood to form the roof, then covered with various branches. The roof was the perfect height for a kid, but most adults would have to stoop to stand inside.

As Matt took it in, he realized that part of him hadn't expected to find anything along this path. Maybe just a long crumbled childhood fort, or nothing but a figment of a damaged man's imagination. The fact that it was still standing after so many years was testament to the care that had been taken to build it.

"Wow," he said, the word slipping out of his mouth like air from a balloon. Matt looked over at David, who stood motionless, staring at the fort. Even in the scant light, he could see something happening behind those eyes.

"You OK?"

David blinked a few times before responding, pushing back whatever was rattling around inside.

"Yeah."

The silence hung for a moment as Matt waited for David to take the lead. He looked back towards the fort and tried to imagine what he could expect on the inside. For the first time, Matt's anxiety shifted from somehow getting caught to thinking of what they may actually find and he started to get excited. If David was somehow right, this could be the biggest thing Matt had ever experienced. He could find evidence that would break a serial killing case wide open. The dreams of a bestseller danced in front of him.

On that note...

Matt pulled out his phone and started taking pictures of the fort. He knew shots of the fort wouldn't do anything for Sheriff Schwab, but once this became a crime scene, who knew if he'd get another chance at them.

Pictures sold books.

David took a step back as Matt snapped a shot of the front of the structure. He was amazed at how much the tiny flash lit up the clearing. He looked around, briefly paranoid the flash would serve as some sort of beacon to anyone in the area, but quickly realized the woods were thick enough to keep any artificial light from reaching the house. Matt stepped closer and took a few more shots of the fort. He looked back at David, who was standing back in the clearing. His eyes had drifted towards the sky again. The moon had crept across the sky to the point it was just peeking through a tiny window in the trees above the fort.

"So, what do you think?"

While Matt's trepidation had waned, David looked hesitant for the first time that night. He kept his eyes on the sky for a beat, before slowly looking back towards Matt.

"I guess we better get it over with," he said quietly, hands stuffed in the pockets of his black sweatshirt.

Matt nodded and turned towards the entrance of the fort, which was basically an opening left in the near corner.

"I'll go in," David said.

Matt stopped short and looked back over his shoulder. David had crossed the clearing and moved past him towards the doorway.

"You stay out here, just in case," David said, tilting his head towards the path.

"Um... OK," Matt said. He was anxious to get inside and see what there was, but a lookout wasn't a bad idea. Besides, David might need a minute alone. Matt could tell this was becoming a bit more emotional than he had let on.

The point of the blue tarp that covered the roof hung down about a foot into the doorway. David pushed it aside with as he ducked into the fort.

A thought struck Matt as he stood just outside the fort. He pushed the corner of the tarp aside and stuck his head in.

"You need a..."

His question was cut off when a blinding white light filled his face.

"Jeez," Matt exclaimed, immediately jerking the back of his head into the plywood above. Between the sudden light in his eyes and the blow to the crown, Matt's vision filled with pinwheels and stars. He crouched down and retreated from the door, rubbing the back of his head. David emerged from the door.

"What?" he asked sharply. "You OK?"

Matt's vision began to clear as stood up. David stood just outside the fort looking at him intently.

"I was gonna see if you wanted my phone," Matt said. "For the light."

David held up a small, but powerful, flashlight he'd produced from somewhere. He flashed it a couple times in Matt's face.

"I'm good," He said as Matt tried to blink the light away. "Just give me a minute, OK? Keep an ear out."

Matt tried to rub his eyes back to working order as David disappeared into the fort again. He turned and scanned the clearing while he waited for his vision to adjust

248

once again. The night was quiet, the only sound being David's shuffled footsteps filtered through the scrap wood walls of the fort.

Matt took a few steps up the path when he heard David's whispered shout from inside the fort.

"*Get in here,*" he said.

Matt immediately whirled around and ducked into the fort. This time in he noticed the musty forest smell, suggesting 15 years of mildew. David was standing in front of the far wall, the top of his head scraping the roof. His flashlight beam danced off the walls and ceiling before settling under his chin. He looked like a teenage boy telling a ghost story.

"Over here," David said.

His back stooped slightly, Matt made his way across the fort. It seemed empty as his eyes adjusted, but the edges of David's flashlight beam were just catching the back wall. The bones he had talked about were still there, casting a manic tapestry of shadows like demented wallpaper. Matt pulled his phone out, switching on the application that turned its camera's flash into a flashlight. He swept it across the wall, chasing the shadows away from the bones and skulls before settling the beam in the center.

"Jesus," Matt whispered.

The bones that had formed the *I* and part of the *N* had fallen off, but there was no doubt what it had once said.

MINE.

It was just as David had described it. He stared at the twisted mural on the wall, mind whirring at the implications. He hadn't doubted David when he had told him of it, but standing in front of it—seeing it for yourself— was different. That made it real, and much more terrifying.

"Look at the skull," David said, pointing just to the right of Scott's one-word declaration of ownership.

Matt aimed his phone in the direction David indicated and settled on an off-white piece of bone hanging on the wall. It was not much bigger than a baseball, but had massive eyeholes that made it look it look alien. The skull tapered down towards the floor to a nasal cavity, which sat just above a pair of fangs. Without fur and skin to cover them, their true size was terrifyingly apparent. It took Matt a good few seconds to realize he was probably seeing the remains of a common cat.

The initial shock of the skull kept Matt from noticing what David was pointing out, and it wasn't until the gold chain dangling from the right canine threw back a glint of the flashlight that he realized what he was supposed to see.

Necklaces.

"Holy shit," Matt said, watching the light of the flashlight dance off one of the small charms.

There were two, each hanging from the mouth of that cat's skull. The longer of the two had a pendant from Lake Mills High School, while the other was a Black Hills Gold charm.

"Yeah," David said. "I fucking told you."

Matt instinctively reached out to touch one, then stopped. He didn't know how fingerprints would work on something so small, but he figured it was better to be safe than sorry. His mind went back to the pair of leather gloves he'd left in the car, doing him no good sitting on the backseat. He pulled his hand inside the sleeve of his windbreaker before putting it behind the small cluster of leaves forged in three different colors of gold. He lifted it into the light and a small diamond chip in the center spat out a few sparkles. He looked over at David, who had crept up beside him.

"You think these are…"

"Of course they are," David shot back. He lifted up the other pendant and Matt noticed he had a pair of work gloves on. He didn't remember him wearing them out. Must have had them in his pocket and pulled them on when he got in here. Good thinking. "That is Mackenzie's Senior Key. The whole class got them at the beginning of the year."

"OK…" Matt said.

David let Mackenzie's necklace slide down and cocked his head towards the door.

Matt's heart suddenly filled with panic.

"What?!" he whispered.

250

David kept his head towards the door for a beat, then shook it and turned back towards him.

"Nothing," he said. "OK, get some pictures of these and we'll get out of here."

"All right," Matt said, letting the small charm fall back towards the wall. "Should we look around something more? Find out if there is anything else?"

David looked back towards the door again and swept his flashlight around the fort. It looked empty, although you never knew what could be hiding in a dark corner.

"What else could we need?" He said. "You wanted something to tie him to the girls, and you got it. Get some pictures on your phone and let's be done."

David was right. Matt couldn't imagine what more the Sheriff could need. Hell, this was big enough they shouldn't wait until morning. He would call tonight. By tomorrow morning, Schwab and his crew could be out here with a search warrant. Scott would be arrested by noon.

"I'm going out," David said.

Matt watched as he quickly made his way towards the door, then turned back and snapped a picture of the necklaces. With David's flashlight gone and Matt's phone in camera mode, the only light left in the fort was the soft glow of the touchscreen. He took a few close-ups of the pendants, then a wide shot of the entire wall, the flash briefly lighting things up each time.

That should be enough, he thought, and turned towards the door.

But then again, tomorrow this would be a crime scene.

Pictures sell books.

Matt turned back and pulled his phone up again. He took pictures of the inside of the fort from every angle he could. The flash lit up the far corner, exposing a dark bucket with an old piece of plywood on top. Matt crossed towards it, turning his phone around to use the small bit of light from the screen to cast an eerie gray light on his path. The intermittent flash from the camera never allowed his eyes to fully adjust.

He flipped it around and took a picture of the bucket, then paused as he considered lifting the lid.

"You coming?" David's voice drifted in from outside.

"Yeah, gimmie a sec," Matt said. He weighed knowing what was in the bucket against David's growing impatience, but realized he had to know. Or at least his book did.

Hand in his sleeve again, he lifted the plywood off and stuck his phone in the bucket.

Nothing.

Oh well. He took a picture anyway—*pictures sell books*—and placed the lid back down. Matt scrolled through the shots on his phone, making sure he had enough. He scanned the screen of his phone back around the inside of the fort and it didn't pick up anything of interest.

That was probably good. For the inside at least. He stood back up and headed over towards the entrance. Maybe he'd snap a few more of the outside, just in case.

"All right," Matt said quietly as he pushed the tarp aside and emerged from the fort. "Let's..."

A massive flash of light filled his vision as something crashed into the back of his skull. His eyes were unable to process the sight of the clearing floor rushing up towards him as he fell.

45

A SMALL BIT OF LIGHT penetrated the black fog that filled his head. Not much, but just enough to stir Matt back into consciousness. It was hard to tell the dark of night from the black of unconsciousness, especially with the pain radiating from the back of his skull clouding any attempt at rational thought.

Why were his feet cold?

His socks were damp from the ground, collecting the cold air from the woods around him and holding it against his toes. He tried to move his feet, but they were stuck. It was so hard to think with that fog swirling around the periphery of his brain, waiting to rush back in, but yeah, his feet were stuck together somehow. Matt wanted to at least rub them together, but his legs didn't want to cooperate.

Trying to get the fog out of his head, he rolled over and his face slid down into something wet. When he eventually lifted it up, some of it stuck to his face. It was cold, too. Like his feet. That was no good. He didn't want his face to feel like his feet. His feet were cold.

Wipe it off.

Good idea. But his arms didn't want to cooperate. They were stuck... somewhere.

Just like my feet.

Where were his hands? They could be really useful now. They could make his face feel better. Then maybe even rub his toes. Make them warm.

Wait… why are my feet cold?

It didn't make any sense, really.

Unable to move much, Matt laid. He was still really tired. Maybe he'd sleep some more. This would all probably make more sense when he woke up.

Why don't you sleep on it?

Isn't that what all those smarties said? Matt thought they did. And they were smart, so it must be a good idea.

That small bit of light retreated, allowing the black fog to roll back in.

46

THE NEXT TIME LIGHT CAME, it was brighter. Well, bright wasn't really the right word, because it was still pretty dim. But there was more of it.

Enough to chase away the black fog. Enough for Matt to see stars. Real stars this time, not the sprites of light that had been dancing on the back of his eyelids.

Matt blinked his eyes as the fog slowly seeped from his head. As it drifted away, it uncovered a walnut-sized lump of pain at the back of his head.

Bigger than a walnut, actually. It felt like someone had dropped a train on him.

Matt tried to move and immediately realized his hands were bound behind him. His ankles were lashed together as well.

Still woozy from the blow to the head, it took a second for the next thought to hit.

What the hell happened?

Matt rolled onto his back and pulled his legs up like an inchworm. Pushing his arms against the ground, he tried to sit up but was unable to get his center of gravity under him and crashed back to the ground.

The sudden rush of blood made the pounding radiate from the back of his skull. He closed his eyes until the sloshing inside his head had died down to its original level.

Matt gradually rolled to his side and peered out to take in his surroundings. His head lay on the ground, which was a bed of mud and trampled wild grass. Ahead of him, the grass had been allowed to grow and was at least four feet high. It looked like someone had made a small clearing amongst the grasses, maybe 12 feet wide.

He knew he was out of the woods, as he could see the brilliant silver disc of the moon glowing in the blackness. He raised his head as much as he could and saw the trees stretching towards the sky only 50 feet or so away from where he was, so he hadn't been brought far.

The movement brought the throbbing back, but curiosity was now taking priority over pain.

The black fog had burned off for good, allowing Matt access to his memories once again.

The fort. They'd been in the fort, looking for... something. Evidence. Something to prove Scott Alston had killed those two girls.

And they'd found it.

Necklaces that belonged to Mackenzie and Jillian. They'd found them hanging from the mouth of a skull.

Good God, the bones.

They covered the wall, a twisted tapestry assembled by a teenaged — and apparently very damaged — Scott.

He remembered taking pictures. Pictures they needed to show Sheriff Schwab so he could arrest Scott. Pictures for his book.

Pictures sold books.

He was walking out of the fort to show the pictures to David when something happened.

A bright light. Then the black fog rolled in.

David. Where was David?

Matt looked around the clearing, then rolled over to his other side.

There was no sign of him.

He was alone.

For the first time since he regained consciousness, Matt thought to test the bonds that held his hands and feet. There wasn't much give in either of them. Whoever tied him up had done a good job. His wrists were flat together with little wiggle room. The rough feel against his skin made Matt think it was some kind of rope holding them together. Maybe twine.

He tested the rope around his legs, and found his ankles had a little give. His shoes were off, so given some time he might be able to wiggle a foot out.

Wait, where were his shoes? Why would somebody tie him up and take his shoes off? Matt had no idea, but it seemed like a low priority at this point. Not wearing shoes could only help him slip out, so he wasn't about to look a gift horse in the mouth. He straightened his left leg while pulling his right leg towards him, but it only moved up an inch or so before the rope pulled taut. He switched up and tried the left leg, but it was the same story.

Matt kept alternating between his legs, and when that didn't work he tried scissoring them forward and back. That yielded the same results. The rope felt like sandpaper against his skin, but he continued. If he would be able to get his legs under him, he'd be able to get out. He assumed the trees he saw were the woods behind the Alston house. The woods with the fort. David had said if something went wrong they could head out this way. There was supposed to be a cornfield out back. Just disappear into it. Make your way back to the Quarter Mile. Or find the creek and follow it all the way to Highway 9.

But what about David? Where was he? Had he gotten away, or was he tied up somewhere too?

Or worse?

Even if he could get his feet out, if his hands were still behind his back, he wouldn't be able to help David. But if he could get out he could find somebody. Send help.

Matt blocked out the pain in his ankles and pulled harder. He had to get out.

He was on his back, face towards the sky and legs pumping like he was riding a tiny bicycle when a crunch of trampled grass made its way into the clearing. Matt's head craned to his left and he saw a figure emerge through the grass. Between the low light and the blow to the head, it was

257

blurry at first, but eventually it got close enough to make out.

"David?"

47

"YOU'RE AWAKE," David said, stepping across the trampled grass towards him. "Wow. I must say, I'm impressed. You took a pretty good pop. I figured you were out for the count."

Matt looked at David with a mask of confusion. The knot on the back of his head and his rope-burned ankles were forgotten as Matt tried to process how his friend could be so casual about finding him.

"What happened?" Matt asked as David walked towards him. He casually sat down on the ground next to Matt and reached down to unlace his shoes. Matt saw David had on a pair of brown, low top Keen trail hikers just like his.

Exactly like his. The wet cold surrounding his toes leapt back into Matt's mind.

"What are you doing with my shoes?" Matt asked.

David stopped unlacing and sat up. He looked down at Matt with a neutral expression.

"I got the idea when we came down the trail," he said. "All that dirt behind the shed, remember? I figured a bunch of your tracks around the house would help."

David slowly turned his head back towards the woods.

"Maybe that's how it happened," he continued. His voice was slow, that of an old man trying to remember a sad day from his youth and coming up short. "You were snooping around late at night, trying to dig up some clues or something. He sees you out the window…"

David's voice trailed off as his eyes drifted towards the sky.

"Maybe that kitchen one. I put a bunch under there."

Matt's blood went cold. Captain Panic was mobilizing his troops in the back of Matt's brain, just waiting for the word to start a full-scale invasion.

"Jesus, David. What are you talking about?"

His head jerked away from the dark expanse above and locked on Matt.

"*HEY,*" he snapped. The laces of Matt's Keens flopped around as David surged to his feet. He loomed over Matt as he spoke. "You said you wanted to help, just like you always do. But I know what help from Matt Carlton is worth, so I figured you don't get a choice this time. No chance to bail on me. To abandon me. *TO STAB ME IN THE FUCKING BACK!*"

The last words bounced off the woods and echoed over the cornfield that started just a few feet beyond the grass their clearing had been carved from.

Matt looked up at David and saw nothing but hatred in his eyes.

"David, I don't know…"

"*BULLSHIT!!!*" he screamed. "I told you *everything.* I trusted you, and you still bailed on me. Left me to do all this shit on my own."

Tears were welling up in David's eyes as he spoke. His voiced dropped considerably.

"And the worst part is, you knew I was right. You fucking knew it, and you still left me to fend for myself. Why? Even this time. You were doing it *again!*"

Matt looked up with a mix of terror and confusion. His brain was spinning like mad, trying to figure out how he'd gotten to the point that his friend would lead him into the woods, knock him cold and tie him up.

"David," Matt said, keeping his voice in the most calming range he was able. "I want to help you. I always did. But I can't help you if I'm tied up here. Let me out, huh?"

David wiped the back of his hand across his eyes and looked down. The rage had left, but his look was nothing close to friendly.

"The *only* way you will help me is being tied up there," he said.

David reached into the pocket of his jacket and pulled something out. At first, Matt thought it was a flask. When David popped the top off, Matt's nose caught a telltale whiff.

Lighter fluid.

Matt's eyes grew wide at the sight of the bottle, the image of Mackenzie Stamp's charred body hanging in front of him. "What are you doing, David?"

"Showing everybody that I was right," he responded and sent an arc of fluid down on Matt's legs.

Panic hit as the lighter fluid soaked into Matt's jeans, and his legs activated on their own. He did his best to squirm away, but David stepped forward and buried the toe of Matt's own shoe into his midsection. Matt felt every breath in his body go whipping out his mouth on contact, leaving him gasping on the bed of trampled grass. Over the sound of his lungs rattling, doing everything they could to fill again, Matt heard the spitting of the bottle as the last of the lighter fluid drained out. David swore and Matt felt the empty bottle strike his hip and bound off into the dark.

When he began to get his breathing under control, Matt coughed and rolled over onto his back again, looking up at David.

"Why?" he rasped.

David kneeled down next to him, knees sounding like gunshots as they popped in the quiet night.

"Because somebody has to," David said. His voice was flat and emotionless, which made it much scarier than when he was ranting. If somebody is freaking out, there's always a chance you can settle them down. Not if they are already calm. "I fucked it up once, and that little girl got killed. I admit that."

David paused, his gaze going to the sky again. Unable to move, Matt just stared at David.

"You know what that was like? Seeing that little girl's face everywhere? It was hard," David said, looking back down at Matt. "But they sent him away, and it was better. He was gone, and that was the whole point, right? To get rid of him. Get him away from here. He can't hurt anybody then, right?

"But he fucking came back. Not even ten years and here he was, back again and a changed man. Bullshit. Changed my ass. I don't care what he says about his memories, psychos like that don't change. But everybody in town fucking forgets. They get sucked in by his bullshit amnesia crap."

Matt tries to blend into the grass—anything to keep the attention off him—as David continues ranting. His eyes keep drifting away as he talks, and then Matt does whatever he can to wiggle his wrists loose. There is almost no give to the knot, but he pulls anyway.

"No fucking way I'm buying that act. So I keep an eye on him. I sit out here every night and watch him act. Carrie says I'm paranoid. Wants me to see a therapist. Fuck. She didn't see what I saw. I fucking KNOW. But he just keeps up his act and everybody buys it."

"You knew," David says, Matt again freezing under his gaze. "You saw it too, but you left. So I've gotta do something, right? I can't let him get away with it. That guy is a ticking bomb and it's just a matter of time, no matter how well he is acting. *Somebody* has to do something.

"I tried the car again, but that was stupid. I wasn't thinking straight. Ends up it wasn't even his car."

David shook his head in embarrassment.

"I talked to him once," David said. "I know I said I hadn't, but I lied. Sorry about that."

The apology sounded sincere enough that Matt answered before he realized the absurdity of the situation. "It's OK."

"Ran into him at the gas station. Filling up his mom's car. You know what he did? Said 'Hi'. That's when I knew for sure. He just said 'Hi', like it was nothing. But he didn't give me that fucking smile of his. He *always* gave me that smile. Every fucking time he saw me, it was that smile. Now, no smile. *That's* how I knew it was an act. He knew if he gave me that fucking smile, I would know it was still him in there. So he didn't. He hid it from me."

Matt watched as David unraveled in front of him. His legs cooled as the lighter fluid seeped through his jeans. He continued to covertly pull at his bonds, but it was no use. There was just no give. He wasn't going to get out by himself, so he quit trying.

"Hey man, I know exactly what you are talking about," Matt said.

David glared down at him.

"Yeah, I know you do," he said. "That's what burns me the most. You were the only other person who knew, but you still abandoned me. Not this time."

He stood back up and reached into his other jacket pocket. Matt was instantly terrified he was going to pull out a book of matches.

"I know, and I'm sorry," Matt pleaded.

Keep him talking and he can't kill me.

"But I'm here now. I'm here with you now, and I want to help."

David's hand came out of his pocket, but it wasn't matches. He held Matt's phone.

"You are helping," he said, tossing it into the grass back towards where the path emptied out. "In fact, this whole thing was pretty much your idea."

"What?" Matt asked.

"That first night you were back, you were telling me about that story you did. The one that got all those politicians thrown in jail down in Des Moines. Something about flood money, right?"

"Yeah," Matt was more confused now than ever. He tried to pull up the conversation that night at Frank's. He'd probably done some resume bragging, sure. What that had to do with this, he had no idea. "I guess."

David bent down and started taking Matt's shoes off again.

"It made me realize going after him directly was stupid," David sat on the ground and yanked a shoe off. "But if I could get him sent away again, then it would be OK, right? Only this time, it had to be for good—none of this vehicular homicide bullshit. I figured serial killers don't get out in six years no matter how good their behavior is. They stay away forever."

David reached over to Matt's feet and tried to put his shoe back on, but with his ankles lashed together so tight it proved impossible. David reached into his pocket and produced a wicked looking hunting knife. The blade threw a flash of moonlight as it unfolded and locked in place. He slipped it between Matt's feet and sawed the rope free, then proceeded to shove the shoes back on and lace them up.

"I was hoping you'd be able to figure things out for yourself," David said. The knife balanced on his knee as he crouched by Matt's feet. "I mean, serial killings in a town where a known serial killer lives? Who else could it be?"

Something was fluttering around Matt's brain, but watching the knife wobble just in front of his face took priority. He didn't care if it had liberated his feet or not, it was currently the part of the equation he was most terrified of.

"But I really didn't want to take it this far, so I gave you one more chance," David continued, still squatted down next to Matt, knife sitting on his knee. "Tried pushing you in the right direction, and to your credit you actually went to the sheriff with it. Part of me didn't think you would even do that."

David stood up and tucked the knife into his belt, right in front of his hip. Matt was very concerned that he hadn't folded it up and put it back in his pocket.

"Unfortunately, you bailed again, and here we are."

Matt used the newfound freedom in his legs to sit up, and David immediately stepped forward to return him to the ground.

"You think I wanted to do all this?" He shouted. "If you could have figured things out for yourself I could have stopped a week ago."

Matt had assumed he'd maxed out on terror that night, but hearing that clicked the final pieces together and opened a whole new door. He'd assumed getting away was just a matter of convincing his broken friend there were better ways to call attention to Scott's crimes.

But now Matt knew they were well past that.

"David, think about this for a second," he said.

"I *HAVE* thought about it," David yelled. "For 15 goddamn years I've been thinking about it. Now it's going to end, and I won't have to think about it anymore. *HE* killed those girls. *YOU* figured it out. *YOU* talked to the sheriff about him, but the sheriff didn't listen. *YOU* came out here and found evidence, but while you were snooping around he saw you, so *HE* killed you."

"But he didn't do any of this David. *You* did."

David stopped and a hurt look crossed his face, like a child who couldn't believe his Mom didn't like the beautiful mural drawn on the kitchen wall.

"To prevent him from killing," David said. "I'm stopping a *killer*."

"But he's not a killer, David. Scott has never killed anybody."

"*BECAUSE I'M STOPPING HIM!!!*" David screamed. "Why can't you understand that? He's *never* going to kill anybody because I am stopping him before he does. If he's rotting away in jail, he can't act out his sick, psychotic fantasies. Who cares how he gets there? You're worried about two girls? Think of how many people I'm saving by doing this. I'm stopping him before he ever starts."

David dug into his pants pocket and came out with a book of paper matches. Matt's eyes widened at the sight of it. The panic welled up in his throat, followed by the only voice he could find.

"But you already stopped him," Matt said.

David paused, eying Matt suspiciously.

"Back in school, you were right," Matt continued, trying to get his words out before he couldn't. "Scott was a psychopath, and you were the only one that saw it. You told me about it, and you were right, but I was too afraid to do anything. I'm sorry. I'm sorry I left you. There's no excuse, except I was afraid. I was afraid—but you weren't."

David's hand dropped to his side, the matches wrapped in his palm.

"You did what you could to stop him, alone, but just because it didn't work out the way you planned, it doesn't mean it didn't work. The crash... *that* stopped him. It scrambled his brain. He forgot everything, including who he was. Everyone said he was changed. Even the doctors said he changed. I didn't believe it until now, but now I see it. You changed him. You *stopped* him. Back then. If you hadn't done anything, he would have become the killer you knew he would be. But because of you, he didn't."

Matt watched as David's face softened. A glint of silver shone off the tears welling at the bottom of his eyes. For the first time since David stepped into the clearing, Matt thought he'd be able to get out of this after all.

"You don't have to do this."

The silence in the clearing was all encompassing. It was as if every owl, raccoon and cricket has ceased their nocturnal routine to see how this would play out. Their own little forest soap opera. David's gaze had drifted upward yet again as he began to pace around the clearing. Matt stared at him in the hope this would all come to an end.

David reached down and picked something out of the grass. His voice came so quiet, it was barely audible.

"Yes I do."

He turned and stepped back towards Matt. Dangling from his right hand was what looked like a white tube sock filled with a baseball-sized mass of sand. David's arm cocked back and brought the sock flying towards Matt's skull. Matt dropped his head back and rolled with the blow, allowing the homemade blackjack just a glancing shot off his temple. Even without taking the full force, it was enough to send him to the ground. His eyes tried to fight their way through the stars and pinwheels that danced in his vision as he rolled to his back and looked up towards David. He'd secured the sock under his arm left arm and was lighting a match when they both heard a shout emerge from the darkness behind.

"*HEY*"

David's head snapped around just as the match caught. A figure was standing just into the grass about 20 feet away. David's hands came together as he looked, with the lit match setting off the entire book in a burst of flame.

David shrieked, dropping the burning matchbook to the ground. It landed just shy of Matt's feet in a patch of grass that had received a good dousing of lighter fluid and immediately set it ablaze.

The fire ripped Matt's mind back into focus as he jerked his highly flammable legs away. He kicked his way across the clearing as the fire quickly grew, then turned just in time to see David fly into the figure with a shout of rage. The two tumbled into the grass, rolling around in a primal embrace.

Matt split his attention between the rapidly expanding fire and fight going on just out of sight. The tall grass hid them from view, but Matt could see the movement of the grass and hear the grunts and cries. Hands still securely locked behind his back, Matt worked his way onto his knees as the movement from the grass slowed. One of the men stood with his back to Matt, looking down at where the other presumably still lay. When he turned towards the clearing, the fire had grown bright enough to illuminate his face.

Scott Alston.

48

MATT GAPED AS SCOTT APPROACHED him through the clearing. An already insane situation had just been flipped on its head.

Again.

"Are you OK," he asked, kneeling down next to Matt, who had fallen back onto his backside.

He wanted to say something, but with everything that had happened in the last hour, coherent speech was probably more of a goal than an expectation.

"Here, let me help," Scott said, circling back around him and beginning to work on the ropes. Matt peered over towards where Scott and David had fought, but saw no movement in the grass.

"What happened?" Matt asked when he finally found his voice.

"I was hoping you could tell me," Scott said, releasing Matt's hands from the rope. "I was up getting a drink when I thought I saw some guy sneaking around the backyard. By the time I went out to look, he was gone. I was headed back inside when I heard shouting back here, so I came to check it out and found you guys."

Matt saw Scott's eyes pulled across the clearing towards the fire. The lighter fluid had given it a good start, and it was finding more than enough grass to feed itself. The flames danced off Scott's pupils. Remembering the lighter fluid on his pants, Matt stood and put some more distance between himself and the blaze.

There was something dark smeared across Scott's shirt. In the flickering light it looked black, but Matt could see the dark red where it had smeared on Scott's hands.

"Is that blood?" he asked.

Scott spoke without taking his gaze from the fire.

"I don't think it's mine."

David.

As he ran back to the spot where David and Scott had been wrestling, Matt marveled at how quickly he'd forgotten that David—his best friend—had tried to kill him. Just out of the clearing, David lay on his back. His eyes were fluttering and his breath was clipped. Matt crouched down next to him, scanning his body for some sort of wound. He put his hand down into something warm and sticky, then saw a dark shimmer on David's jeans. He followed the expanse of blood up his friend's thigh to a deep rip in his jeans just south of his groin. He instinctively pushed his palm down on the wound, eliciting a wince from David, who briefly tried to sit up but didn't have the strength.

Matt looked up at David's face, which showed little pain. He could feel the blood leaching out between his fingers. David's ragged breath was slowing, and a bubble of saliva stretched between his lips. Matt knelt in the grass, hands now covered in blood, watching as his friend's breath became more labored. The rasp in and out was barely audible over the crackle of the fire. Eventually it slowed to the point he wasn't sure if it was still there. He leaned in to check and was jolted when David's body racked with a series of wet coughs.

When it passed, he was gone.

"I'm sorry," Matt said. It was all he could think of. "I should have been there."

Somehow it didn't feel odd that he was apologizing to a person who just a few minutes before had planned on killing him. He even felt partly guilty for what happened with David.

But only partly.

He stayed there for a minute, hands still on David's leg, holding back blood that had stopped pumping.

Eventually, Matt stood and walked back to the clearing. Scott hadn't moved from where he had left him, still staring at the fire as it slowly died back. The orange light lit up his face and skipped shadows across the grass. Maybe he was in shock. Poor guy walked right into the middle of an insane situation that had followed him since he was 12 years old, and didn't even know it. Who knew what he made of all this?

It would be enough to scramble anyone's brain for a bit.

"Who is that?" Scott asked, looking down at the blood on his hands. He had an odd look on his face, which looked even stranger in the dancing light of the fire.

Matt paused for a second before answering. For some reason, he felt a brief need to protect his friend.

"David Rowe,"

"David Rowe?" Scott said slowly, eyes focused ahead of him. He shook his head as if to clear it, raising his hands to rub his temples. He blinked a few times, finally taking his eyes off the fire and looking around the clearing.

"God, I haven't been back here for... years," Scott said, his eyes focused again. "What the hell were you guys doing in my woods?"

Matt could think of no way to explain it, so he punted.

"It's a really long story."

Matt turned back towards the long grass and searched the ground for his phone, finally catching a reflection of light off the touchscreen. He scooped it up and paused. After a second's deliberation he dialed 911.

He'd call Bill next.

49

DEPUTY JACOBS WAS ON DUTY that night, so he was the first one there. Matt met him in the Alston's driveway and led the way back through the woods. He was able to relay most of the story by the time they reached the clearing where David's body lay. Scott was nowhere to be found, maybe he'd gone in to wake his mother.

Deputy Jacobs immediately set about securing the scene and called in the cavalry.

By the time the sun cracked the horizon, the Alston house was a zoo of law enforcement and emergency response. Sheriff and DCI personnel had swarmed in and buzzed everywhere from the front yard to the field beyond the clearing where this whole thing ended. Photos were taken and every conceivable piece of evidence was tagged and bagged. Matt even had to surrender his clothes to the lab technicians. Luckily, Mrs. Alston had produced an old track suit of Scott's for him to wear.

For a woman who had been awakened at 3 a.m. and told a murderer was killed in her backyard, she was surprisingly in her element. The coffee was immediately brewed and a box of cookies produced from the back of the pantry.

"Sorry they aren't fresh, but it's all we have."

Matt was summoned to talk with Sheriff Schwab as soon as he arrived. For the third time, he recounted exactly how he ended up in back of the Alston property that night. He sat at Karen Alston's kitchen table and told him everything David had told him, from 11th grade until tonight. The sheriff's jaw almost hit the floor when Matt told him about David's role in Scott's accident.

"That sick sonofabitch," Sheriff Schwab said.

"The guilt," Matt said. "It must have pushed him completely over the edge."

The sheriff shook his head.

"Don't give me that bullshit," he said. "It's no excuse."

"I'm not saying it's an excuse," Matt said. "It's just... a reason I guess."

The Sheriff huffed as he pushed his chair back.

"Tell that to the Daytons and the Stamps."

Matt watched him walk over to a pair of officers, then head with them out the door. He wanted to call Bill again, to see if he was on the scene yet, but his phone had already been taken into evidence. Matt rose from the table and headed towards the front door. It opened just as his hand was about to the handle and Scott almost bumped into him.

"Sorry," Matt said.

Scott nodded and slid past him.

"Hey Scott," Matt called after him. "Sorry about all this. I mean... I don't know... I guess... sorry."

"Don't worry about it," Scott replied. "It's Matt, right?"

Matt nodded and Scott managed a half-cocked smile. He turned back to look for whoever it was that wanted to talk to him next.

Matt watched him leave, then turned through the door and out.

He wanted to find Bill.

EPILOGUE

ERICA DUNN RIPPED AROUND HER HOUSE in a desperate search. She tore the cushions from the couch, sending crumbs and coins raining down on the living room floor.

But no keys.

She looked at her watch.

8:16

Shit. Even if she were in the car right now she'd probably be late.

She stood upright and closed her eyes.

Came home, coat off, changed clothes, dinner…

Wait… she'd stopped in Lilly's room on her way downstairs.

"Lil," Erica called out to her youngest daughter. "*LIL!!* Have you seen my keys?"

She heard a faint response from outside. Erica cut back through the kitchen towards the door. As she reached for the door handle, her eyes caught something sitting on top of the refrigerator.

Her keys.

Erica stepped over and snatched them before heading back out the door.

Lilly was out by the garage of their country home. The Dunn's had moved out to this house when Erica got a job in Mason City. It cut a good 10 minutes off her commute, and

Phil loved being so close to the Rice Lake Country Club that he didn't mind having to drive into Lake Mills for work everyday. Even after that awful business that took place less than a mile down the road, she couldn't imagine living anywhere else.

But she had found it harder to leave her kids out here all alone since school got out.

Erica mentally scolded herself.

That monster is dead and gone, and it's not like something like that could happen in a town this small again.

Lilly turned around at the sound of the door opening.

"Mom, I can't find Biscuit."

Erica hopped down the steps and cut over to give her youngest a quick kiss goodbye.

"What's that sweetie?"

"I can't find Biscuit anywhere," she said. "He wasn't at the door this morning and I can't find him anywhere."

The family cat loved to stalk the woods and fields in the area, often bringing home the trophies he acquired during the night. Just two weeks back, Erica stepped out of the kitchen and came down on a dead rabbit. She had to kick it into the bushes before Lilly, who was following right behind her, came out and saw it.

"I'm sure he's around here somewhere," Erica said.

Lilly looked up at her mom with a worried look.

"But he's not," she said, the panic of youth filling her voice. "He's *always* here in the morning. Can you help me look for him?"

Erica knelt down by her 6-year old and put her hand on her shoulder.

"I can't right now, honey, because I'm already going to be late for work," she said. "I'm sure Biscuit is fine. He'll be around in a minute, OK? He's probably just out playing in the back."

Erica stood up and hoisted her purse back up over her shoulder.

"Jack's still sleeping upstairs, so don't wander too far. Tell him you guys can have the leftover pizza for lunch, OK?"

"But mom…"

"I gotta go, sweetie. I'm sure Biscuit is fine, but I tell you what. If he doesn't show up by this afternoon, maybe Daddy can take you over to Mrs. Alston's house when he gets home from work and you can see if she has seen him over there, OK?

"Love you."

Acknowledgments

As I said in the dedication, there is no way this book happens without my wife Erin. Her support allowed me to chase this silly little dream. My two girls also inspire me every day.

No book gets done without help, and I needed tons of it. Huge thanks go out to Shana Drehs, Gail Hansen and Cristin Bock. You liked enough early on that I didn't get discouraged, but made sure I saw what wasn't working so I could (hopefully) fix it. I'd also like to thank Chris Todd Miller, Heidi Brockbank and Angela Eschler at Eschler Editing for their excellent work. They showed me that I was trying to edit with a Band-Aid when surgery was needed. The Rochester Writer's Group gave me a place to bounce chapters off of and kept my creative pump primed by reading their work.

I'd like to recognize every barista from The Java House in Iowa City to Dunn Bros., Caribou Coffee and Steam in Rochester for keeping me fueled and not kicking me out when my cup was long empty. Thanks to Jack and Meg White, the whole Doomtree crew, Rodrigo y Gabriella, John Roderick, R.E.M., The Replacements, Lizzo, LCD Soundsystem and every other musician I cranked up while writing this.

Finally, thanks to my friends and family for putting up with my weird, vague answers whenever you asked me about my book. You can read it now!

Thank You!

Did you like the book you just read? The best way to support authors is to leave a review on websites like Amazon.com and Goodreads.com.

If you'd like more information on what I'm up to, visit my website at www.tonywirt.com. There, you can join my e-mail list to keep up to date on everything from author appearances to new book releases. You can also find me on facebook at www.facebook.com/tonywirtfiction or on twitter @wirter.

Made in the USA
Lexington, KY
02 April 2017